THE PERFECT LIE

Also by Dinah McCall in Large Print:

White Mountain

THE PERFECT LIE

DINAH McCALL

Published in 2003 by arrangement with Harlequin Books S.A.

Wheeler Large Print Softcover.

The text of this Large Print edition is unabridged.
Other aspects of the book may vary from the original edition.

Set in 16 pt. Plantin.

Printed in the United States on permanent paper.

Library of Congress Cataloging-in-Publication Data

McCall, Dinah.
The perfect lie / Dinah McCall.
p. cm.
ISBN 1-58724-499-3 (lg. print : sc : alk. paper)
1. Intelligence officers — Fiction. 2. Drug traffic — Fiction. 3. Birthfathers — Fiction. 4. Kidnapping — Fiction. 5. Large type books. I. Title.
PS3569.A4565P47 2003
813′.54—dc21 2003053817

THE PERFECT LIE

National Association for Visually Handicapped
serving the partially seeing

As the Founder/CEO of NAVH, the only national health agency solely devoted to those who, although not totally blind, have an eye disease which could lead to serious visual impairment, I am pleased to recognize Thorndike Press* as one of the leading publishers in the large print field.

Founded in 1954 in San Francisco to prepare large print textbooks for partially seeing children, NAVH became the pioneer and standard setting agency in the preparation of large type.

Today, those publishers who meet our standards carry the prestigious "Seal of Approval" indicating high quality large print. We are delighted that Thorndike Press is one of the publishers whose titles meet these standards. We are also pleased to recognize the significant contribution Thorndike Press is making in this important and growing field.

Lorraine H. Marchi, L.H.D.
Founder/CEO
NAVH

* Thorndike Press encompasses the following imprints: Thorndike, Wheeler, Walker and Large Print Press.

Oh, what a tangled web we weave,
when first we practice to deceive.
— Sir Walter Scott
1771–1832

When I was small, my mother seemed to always know when I was embellishing the truth. At the same time, I could never figure out how she knew it.

Now I understand that it comes from the same motherly instinct that warns a woman when her child is in peril.

A lie is the beginning of danger. Caught early, it becomes nothing more than a shame to overcome. But let go, it can grow into something dark — even evil. Then only God can make it right.

So I'm dedicating this book to my mother, Iris Smith, who taught me the value of truth.

To the truth in all of us.

Prologue

Bel Air, California

The words Felicity Blaine had yet to speak already left a bitter taste on her tongue, although God knew she'd practiced them long enough that they should have spilled out without a qualm. She'd chosen the opulence of her father's library to give Jonah the news because it represented everything she didn't want to lose. Granted, Jonah Slade was more man than she'd ever had before, and she loved him as much as she was capable of loving someone other than herself. But when her father, Declyn Blaine, had confronted her with her choices, she'd been more than a little appalled at how easily she'd been swayed.

She shrugged, reminding herself not of what she was losing but of what she would gain. Then she heard the sound of an arriving vehicle and turned toward the library window just in time to see Jonah getting out of his car. There was a moment of regret as she watched him striding toward the door. In the sunlight, his hair was as dark and shiny as a raven's wing, and she knew all too well how beautiful his body was beneath his sport coat and slacks. When she was being brutally honest with herself, she could admit he was the best thing that had ever happened to her. It didn't matter. She drew a deep, shuddering breath. It was over, and there was no easy way to say what had to be said.

Moments later, she heard the sound of his footsteps coming down the hall toward the library. She turned toward the doorway, bracing herself for the confrontation as the man who loved her came into the room.

Jonah patted his pocket as he strode down the hall toward the library, making sure the engagement ring he'd purchased yesterday was still there. No matter how many times he'd been with Felicity — and God knew there had been plenty — the sight of her still made the breath catch in the back of his throat. And now, knowing she was carrying his child . . . words failed him. He'd thought all night about what it would be like to be a husband as well as a father. The responsibilities were great, but he was more than ready for them.

Moments later, he entered the library, smiling as he saw Felicity standing at the window. He hurried toward her, his voice lowering huskily as he took her into his arms.

"Hey, baby . . . you look beautiful," he said, then laid his hand on her belly. "Feeling okay?"

Felicity stiffened, then pushed herself out of his arms. She needed distance between them to say what had to be said. When she pulled away, Jonah frowned.

"Felicity . . . honey . . . is something wrong?"

She lifted her chin and tossed her hair, giving Jonah a brief, brittle smile.

"Not anymore," she said briefly. "As of nine o'clock this morning, there is no baby."

If she'd pulled out a gun and shot him point-blank, Jonah wouldn't have been any more shocked.

"You miscarried? My God . . . why didn't you call me? Are you all right?"

Felicity's stomach turned. The hurt on his face was actually making her nauseous.

"No, I didn't miscarry, and of course I'm all right. I wasn't ready for motherhood, that's all. And before you say anything else, this thing between us just isn't going to work." She frowned, then pouted when Jonah's expression went flat. "Don't fuss. You know how I hate it when you fuss."

"Fuss?" Jonah's voice was just above a whisper. "You think I'm going to fuss?"

Suddenly the look on his face was frightening, and Felicity wished that she'd let her father stay with her, as he'd wanted to do. Subconsciously she put her hands to her throat, as if protecting her most vulnerable spot, and then took a step back.

"I wasn't sure how you would —"

"You had an abortion. Without a word to me first?"

Felicity was getting nervous. It was time to cry.

"You don't understand," she said softly, knowing full well how luminous her blue eyes looked filled with tears. "I'm too young to settle —"

"Jesus Christ," Jonah muttered, more to himself than to her, then shuddered as he turned away. He had to get out. Now. Before he put his hands around her throat and choked the life out of her — just as she'd killed their child.

When Felicity realized he was leaving, she knew she would never see him again. There was a part of her that regretted that more than anything else she had done. Before she could stop herself, she called out.

"Jonah, wait!"

He paused, then turned, and as he did, she wished she'd never called him back, because she would forever remember that the last look on his face had been one of pure hate.

"We were good together . . . weren't we?" she asked, and then was ashamed.

Jonah shook his head, as if trying to clear his thoughts, then stared at Felicity as if seeing her for the first time.

"You were nothing but a fuck," he said, and then he was gone.

Felicity gasped. The ugliness of what he'd said was not as painful as the truth of it. And it was truth that sent her to her knees. She heard the car door slam as he got inside, heard the sound of his engine rev as he sped out of the driveway, and then he was gone. Hot tears spilled out from beneath her eyelids as she covered her face with her hands.

"Sissy . . . what's wrong? Why were you and Jonah fighting?"

Felicity looked up. Her little sister, Macie, was kneeling at her side.

"Get out," Felicity sobbed. "Leave me alone."

So she did. Moments later, Felicity was left with nothing but dreams of what might have been and the echoes of the perfect lie.

1

Sixteen Years Later

"Agent Slade, please have a seat."

Jonah Slade sat. When the director of the CIA ordered, his men were trained to obey.

"We have some intelligence from the DEA that is causing some concern on the Hill," the director said.

Jonah sat up a little straighter. From time to time, different branches of the Federal government got information that was out of their jurisdiction. He wasn't surprised that the Drug Enforcement Agency had come up with information. Quite often the people they arrested were willing to make a deal to lessen their own sentences. Obviously something like that had occurred.

"Yes, sir?"

"You're familiar with Miguel Calderone?"

"The Colombian drug lord of the moment . . . yes, I am."

"There's a rumor that he's going to back an assassination attempt on the president. If this is true, at the least we need to know how, when and where. If you can find out how many are involved, so much the better.

You know the drill."

Jonah nodded.

"You speak Spanish fluently. All your previous undercover work has been in the Middle East, so your face is not known in South America."

"That's correct."

The director looked up from the file on his desk. "Start working on a look. Don't shave. Don't cut your hair. Immerse yourself in the language so you won't miss a nuance of the conversations. In two weeks, your papers will be ready. You'll show up at the Calderone *hacienda* as a mercenary looking for work."

"What guarantee do I have that they won't shoot me on sight?"

"None."

Jonah grinned. "Thank you, sir. Just what I wanted to hear."

The director sighed. "It's not an ideal situation, but it's vital that we learn what we can. Be prepared to stay under for several months, if need be. Your contact will find you, so don't worry about passing on any information that you learn."

"Yes, sir," Jonah said. "Is there anything else?"

"Yes. I would appreciate it if you did not get yourself killed."

"I wouldn't dream of it, sir."

"Good. Then that's all for now. We'll be in touch."

* * *

Six months later

"Juanito! The *padrone* wishes to speak with you."

Jonah laid down the rifle he'd been cleaning and brushed off his hands as he stood and followed a woman named Elena into the house. She was Calderone's woman of the moment, although, to be fair, she'd lasted longer than the others had. If gossip was to be believed, she'd been living in the Calderone stronghold for almost two years and had even borne Calderone a daughter. A child who had stolen his heart.

And, like every other man here who wanted to see the next sunrise, he ignored her sexual teasing and the sway of her hips as she led the way into the *hacienda*.

Jonah took off his hat as he entered the home, welcoming the cooler temperatures inside the vast, high-ceiling rooms. His footsteps echoed on the red Spanish tiles as he followed Elena into the main room.

Calderone was dandling a baby girl on his knee as Jonah walked in. Calderone laughed as he looked up, then stood abruptly. He kissed the baby soundly on her cheek, ruffled her thick, black curls, then handed her to her mother.

"*Chica,* it is time for her *siesta.*"

Elena took the baby but gave Calderone a

sultry look as she ambled out of the room with the baby on her hip.

"Juanito . . . you have children?" Calderone asked.

Jonah shook his head. "No, *Padrone,* I have none."

Calderone shrugged. "Myself, I have four. My sons, Alejandro and Miguelito, an older daughter Juanita, who is studying in a convent, and my little *chica,* Raphaella, who is the child of my heart."

"She's very beautiful, *Padrone.*"

"Of course she is, but that's not why I asked to speak to you," Calderone said.

"How can I serve you?" Jonah asked.

Calderone beamed. If he had more men like Juanito, his organization would be perfect. As it was, there were too many lazy Indians on his payroll, but he needed the hands to process the cocaine.

"There are some very important men who will be coming here tomorrow. I want you to make sure that security is tight before their arrival."

Jonah nodded. "Will they be staying in the *hacienda?*" he asked.

Calderone frowned, then realized that Juanito would need to know their locations to assure their safety.

"*Sí.* All four will be here with me."

"*Bueno.* It will make security much easier."

Calderone nodded, reminding himself that

he was going to have to get over this constant feeling of danger. At least here, in the depths of the jungle and beneath his own roof, he was safe.

"Do what you have to do. When it's time, I will ask you to accompany them back to the airstrip. The time is drawing near when our plans for the future will need to be put in place."

Jonah nodded, but his heart began to race. Months ago he'd learned that Calderone was indeed harboring dreams of killing the U.S. president, whose policies and their stringent enforcement were hurting the drug trade. In Calderone's mind, getting rid of the man would get rid of the rules. Jonah would have liked to explain the way democracy and justice worked in his country, but he didn't think Calderone was ready to hear it. Now this meeting led him to believe that the plan to take the President's life was about to be put into motion. He had to find a way to alert his contact without getting himself killed.

"*Padrone* . . . if I might be so bold as to ask."

"What is it?" Calderone asked.

"We are running low on ammunition. If I could take a truck to Bogotá, pick up the necessary supplies and whatever special foodstuffs you might want to serve your guests, I think it would be a good idea."

Calderone hesitated only briefly, then waved his hand.

"Take Alejandro with you."

The last person he wanted along was Calderone's eldest son, but he nodded agreeably.

Jonah nodded. "Is there anything special you wish us to bring back?"

"I will have the cook make a list, but I know for certain that we will want some of the finest Russian Vodka, as well as the most expensive Saki to be found in Bogotá."

Saki? Vodka?

Lots of people drank both, but he would bet a year of his life that the men who would be coming to see Calderone were connected to the Japanese Yakuza and the Russian Mafia. If that were true, the president was in a world of trouble.

Eighteen hours later, the four men arrived and Jonah knew he'd been right. Now all he could do was hope that his contact in Bogotá got word to the right people before it was too late.

It was *siesta,* the hottest time of the day, when it all came apart. One minute Calderone's men were lolling lazily on the veranda and beneath the huge trees — anywhere there was silence and shade — and the next all hell erupted.

Calderone came running out of the *hacienda*

only moments before the first of the helicopters came into sight. It was a bloody battle that was over almost before it began. The DEA was all over the place, taking people into custody, confiscating computers and log books.

Ostensibly, Jonah was still one of the bad guys, and he was in the act of being handcuffed by a fellow agent when a shot rang out. Suddenly Danny Cordell's brains were all over the legs of his pants. That was when he lost it. He grabbed Cordell's rifle as he spun. Alejandro Calderone was standing on the roof with an assault rifle in his hands, grinning at Jonah for what he'd just done.

Jonah swung the gun upward and fired. Blood sprayed out from behind Alejandro's head, and then he dropped out of sight onto the roof. And Miguel Calderone saw it happen.

It was unfortunate, but not earth-shattering. Calderone had no idea of Jonah's true identity or what he really looked like beneath all his hair and beard, and he had no family of his own for Calderone to hurt. Even as Calderone was calling down every curse he knew on Juanito's head, Jonah was walking away.

A week later: Bel Air, California

A black van with heavily tinted windows

pulled up to the iron gates of Declyn Blaine's estate. A hooded man jumped out and aimed a can of spray paint at the lens of the security camera, while another man short-circuited the gate controls. Seconds later the gate began to open. The men jumped back into the van as it started up the driveway.

The thick growth of trees and shrubs provided much desired privacy: a high selling point for the owners of the exclusive estates in the area. But now the privacy had become an accomplice, hiding the van and its occupants.

There were five hooded men inside the van. They sat quietly without talking, awaiting the moment when they would reach the main house. Each knew his role in the event that was about to take place, and failing was not an option. Not if they wanted to live to see another day.

Thanks to the skill of a famous Hollywood surgeon, Felicity Blaine's forty years had yet to show on her finely toned body. As the eldest daughter of multibillionaire Declyn Blaine, she had never turned her hand to a day's work or wondered where her next meal was coming from. She was a perfect hostess, a better than average tennis player, and although she'd never been married, was the mother of a fifteen-year-old boy. She'd named him Evan for no other reason than it did nothing to remind her of the man who'd fathered him.

A series of nannies had fed and diapered Evan, and when he was older, Declyn had stepped into the role of surrogate father, grooming the young man for the day when he would take over the reins of the massive fortune and all that entailed.

Felicity glanced at the clock, blew herself a kiss in the mirror, then turned to pick up her tennis racket and bag as she left her bedroom and started down the stairs. She had just enough time to drop Evan off at school before her court time at the country club, and she was halfway down the stairs when the doorbell rang. Although she was closer by yards than the family maid, Felicity had not been raised to answer her own door. She paused on the stairs, waiting for Rosa to appear.

Rosa Guitiero had worked for the Blaines for many years, and when she heard the doorbell, she quickly moved from the library, where she'd been dusting, into the foyer to answer the door. Her hand was on the doorknob as Evan Blaine came out of the breakfast room with his backpack slung over one shoulder. His thick black hair was short and spiky. His jeans rode low on his hips, and the T-shirt he was wearing bore a Make Love — Not War slogan on the front that Declyn abhorred. It was mostly why he wore it. Still chewing the last bite of the croissant he'd had for breakfast, he was looking up the staircase at his mother as Rosa opened the door. After that, it seemed that everything happened in slow motion.

Hooded men in black knit thrusting guns in Rosa's face.

Rosa screaming in Spanish and then being shoved aside, where she fell into a corner.

Then an abrupt burst of gunfire.

Felicity staring in disbelief at the red blossom of blood spreading across the front of her white designer tennis shirt when the first bullet hit.

Evan shouting his mother's name and then turning to run.

The anger on Declyn Blaine's face turning to a look of utter disbelief as he dashed out of his office.

The echo of rapid gunshots, then running footsteps on fine Italian marble.

The violent impact of bullets ripping through cloth and then flesh as the shots lifted Declyn off his feet.

Evan's fear giving way to a scream for help as the men gave chase.

They caught Evan at the doorway to the kitchen, rendering him unconscious with one blow.

The silence, after the sudden butchery, was startling. With one man carrying the unconscious teenager over his shoulder, they headed for the door. Another paused at the foot of the stairs and dropped a note beside Felicity's body. They paused in front of Rosa, who was on her knees in prayer. One of them aimed a gun, but another spoke sharply and shoved his hand aside. Moments later, they were gone.

For a few disbelieving seconds Rosa crouched where she'd fallen, unable to believe what had just happened. And then her gaze focused on Felicity and the blood pooling beneath her body, spilling down the stairs. She staggered to her feet and stumbled into the hall, where she saw Declyn lying in the doorway of his office. It was then that she began to scream. She screamed until her head felt as if it was going to shatter as Felicity's had done, and she might never have stopped had it not been for the grandfather clock in the hall. When it began to chime, the sound shattered her hysteria. Clasping both hands to her mouth, then stifling a moan, she ran for the phone.

The same day — New York City

Mercedes Blaine set aside her jeweler's loupe, then straightened abruptly as she turned to face the two men on the other side of her desk.

"I like them," she said briefly. "Consider the deal a go. When can I expect the first shipment?"

It was all the two South Africans could do not to clap their hands in glee. Landing a contract for their exclusive line of jewelry with Blaine Imports was a coup for their company.

"Thank you, Miss Blaine. We are so delighted! I will send the e-mail to our shipping office today. You can expect thc first shipment before the end of the month, if that's all right?"

She nodded and shook their hands while deftly escorting them to the door.

"Gentlemen . . . it's been a pleasure doing business with you. If you'll stop back this afternoon, my secretary will have the contracts ready for you to sign."

The two men were so happy about closing the deal that they didn't realize they were being hustled out of the office. Mercedes' mind was already on her next appointment when Julia, her secretary, caught her eye. Mercedes looked past her to the two men in dark blue suits in the doorway. She frowned, wondering if there was a meeting she'd forgotten.

"Miss Blaine . . . these gentlemen are here to see you," Julia said, then added, "they're from the FBI."

Hoping there hadn't been some kind of irregularity or illegality with one of her foreign shipments, she smiled cordially as they both flashed their badges. The older one spoke for them both.

"Miss Blaine, I'm Agent Sugarman. This is my partner, Agent Clark. If we could have just a moment of your time?"

She smiled again. "Certainly. Won't you please step inside?"

She stood back, waiting for them to enter her office, then followed them inside and closed the door.

She circled her desk. "Have a seat," she said, and then sat down without waiting for them to comply. "Now, to what do I owe the honor?"

The look that passed between Sugarman and Carter made the hair rise on the back of her neck. Sensing that this was news she didn't want to hear sitting down, she stood abruptly and leaned forward, flattening the palms of her hands on her desk.

"What's wrong?"

Her question took them by surprise.

"Miss Blaine, I'm sorry to inform you that your father's home was invaded this morning."

"Oh, my God," Mercedes gasped. "My family! Are they all right?"

Carter sighed, his expression filled with unspoken sympathy.

"No, ma'am, I'm sorry to say they are not. Your sister, Felicity, was shot and died on the scene. Your father has been hospitalized in critical condition, and your nephew, Evan, has been abducted, although as of this hour, no request for a ransom has been received."

Mercedes stood behind the desk without moving, watching the man's mouth as it continued to move, but for her, all sound had ceased. She tried to speak and instead felt her throat tightening with unshed tears. Felicity dead? Evan kidnapped? It couldn't be! It still took a virtual act of congress for her to get past the security at the front gate, and she knew the codes. It didn't occur to her that she'd all but ignored her father's fate. They'd parted company in anger years ago, and she still could not think of him and what he'd done without getting sick to her stomach. She leaned forward, then started to shake.

Carter motioned to Sugarman, who got up and strode quickly to a wet bar in the corner of the room and poured a double shot of whiskey into a glass, then thrust it into her hands.

"Here, Miss Blaine . . . drink this," Sugarman said.

Mercedes grasped the small glass with both hands and downed the amber liquid in one gulp, thankful that the quick burn gave her reason for the unshed tears scalding her eyes. She looked at Carter again, her voice shaking.

"Is there . . . are you sure there wasn't a mistake?"

He shook his head. "I'm sorry, Miss

Blaine, but there has been no mistake."

"Sweet Jesus," she whispered, and covered her face. "How did they get past Declyn's security?"

"It's a little unclear," he said. "But they left a note."

She looked up. "For ransom?"

"No. More of a warning . . . or, I guess I should say, a reason for the abduction."

"What did it say?"

Carter checked his notebook to make sure he didn't misquote. " 'An eye for an eye. A son for a son.' " He looked up. "Do you have any idea what it might mean?"

A son? But Evan wasn't Declyn's son, and everyone knew that. Her stomach tilted. She didn't know what it meant, but there was someone who might. The only problem was, she had no earthly idea how to find him.

"No. I don't," she muttered. "Who's in charge of the investigation?"

"Agent Arnold Ruger. He's expecting your call."

"Please tell him for me that I'll be there before the end of the day."

"But . . ."

"This was —" Mercedes took a deep breath "— is my family. I won't do this long distance."

"Since we don't yet know the full ramifications of the situation, there's the possibility that your life could also be in danger. We recommend that you —"

"I'll be fine," she said; then her voice broke, and for the first time, tears spilled down her face. "Just find my nephew. Please. Find Evan and bring him home."

"Yes, ma'am. We're doing all we can, and we're sorry for your loss. When you're ready to go to California, we'll be happy to escort you."

"No. I'll get there under my own steam, but thank you."

A few moments later they were gone. Mercedes couldn't let herself think about Felicity being dead. Not yet. For now, her focus had to be on the living. Grieving would come later, after she knew that Evan was safe and her father was going to survive.

There was a knock on her door; then her secretary peeked in.

"Miss Blaine . . . are you all right?"

Mercedes made no attempt to hide her tears. "No. Cancel all my appointments until further notice. I'm going to California. Oh . . . and get Senator Chaffee on the phone."

"Yes, ma'am." She hesitated, then couldn't help but ask, "Are we in trouble?"

Mercedes sighed. "No, Amelia . . . the company is fine. It's personal."

"Is there anything else I can do for you?"

"Yes. Charter a jet. I need to get to Los Angeles as soon as possible, but get Senator Chaffee for me first."

"Of course."

"Oh . . . Amelia . . ."

"Yes, ma'am?"

"Please close the door on your way out."

Wednesday morning: Arlington, Virginia

Sunlight came through the partially opened draperies, painting a warm stripe along the bare chest of the man asleep on the oversize sofa. One of his legs was slung over the arm, the other had slipped off sometime in the night and was resting, heel first, on the carpet below. His sleep was restless, his muscles jerking intermittently as he fought the demons of his life within his dreams.

His hair was long and black — as unkempt as the beard covering the lower half of his face. But even in sleep, it was the semiautomatic he cradled on his belly that attested to the condition of his mental state.

Outside, the sound of a distant siren pierced the serenity of sunrise. His eyebrows knitted across his forehead as the sound permeated the dream, mingling with his memories to add sound to the hell he was reliving.

A snow-white macaw swooped across Jonah Slade's line of vision as he stood on the veranda of the hacienda. *Heat permeated his body all the way to his bones, but after six months in the Colombian jungle, he'd become immune to all but the worst of it.*

"Juanito!"

Long ago attuned to his undercover identity, Jonah turned abruptly.

"Sí, padrone?"

Miguel Calderone exited through the French doors of his mansion, his usual swagger missing in his haste.

"Intruders come!" Calderone shouted, waving his arms and pointing toward the sky.

Jonah pivoted sharply, hiding his surge of emotion. If Calderone's high-tech radar setup was on the up-and-up, he knew who the intruders were. His own elation came in realizing his contact in Bogotá had received his last transmission after all. Soon enough his identity would be discovered, but for now, it behooved him to run with the pack. He grabbed his assault rifle, running for cover along with the other members of the Calderone organization.

Calderone himself was like a bulldog, running back and forth on his short, stocky legs, barking out orders in both English and Spanish. His two sons, Alejandro and Juan Carlos, were already on the roof, along with more than a dozen of his best marksmen and a half dozen rocket launchers. They lined the roof like Roman candles on an American Fourth of July, waiting to be lit.

Jonah slipped behind an ornate iron screen, situating himself so that he not only had a clear view of the air, but of the area in which Calderone's men were hiding. He squatted, resting the butt of his assault rifle against his belly, and silently cursed as a swarm of black gnats circled his head. Anticipation of what was coming made the muscles at the back of his neck crawl and his belly knot. There had been a time when he would have relished what was about to occur. But no more. He'd been under cover a long damned time. Maybe too long. Or maybe it was just that this lifestyle was getting old. Playing cops and robbers had been fun when he was a kid — it was what had gotten him into this business. But he wasn't a kid anymore, and it wasn't fun anymore. It was time to get out — to bring these men to justice and end the self-imposed isolation that he kept putting himself in.

The sound of approaching aircraft ended his musing. He tensed.

The shrill peal of a ringing telephone just above Jonah's head brought him up off the sofa, shouting in Spanish, with his gun aimed. He did a quick one-eighty as he scanned the room, thinking he was back in Colombia, believing the firefight was still ongoing, believing that Agent Danny Cordell's brains would still be splattered on the legs of his pants — feeling the kick of his assault rifle as he shot Alejandro Calderone between the eyes for what he'd done, unaware, until it was too late, that Miguel Calderone, who was already in DEA custody, had witnessed it all.

When it became apparent to Jonah that he

was in his apartment, he turned, staring at the phone as it continued to ring. He was in no mood to talk, no matter who might be calling, so he let the machine pick up the call and strode out of the room.

He hadn't been in his kitchen more than twice since his return, and his focus was on the coffeepot on the counter. But he stopped abruptly, wincing as he stepped on something sharp. Frowning, he bent down, feeling along the bottom of his foot until he came to the offending object, then pulled out a small, hard pellet from the bottom of his big toe.

"What the . . . ?"

A single grain of mummified rice had cut into the flesh of his foot. He'd been back in his apartment for less than twenty-four hours, so it had to be at least six months old. A thin layer of dust was still evident on the chairs and tables, and there was a huge pile of junk mail on the floor near the front door, dropped through the mail slot with useless irregularity. He'd long ago set up a means of having his basic bills paid by bank draft, so that when he was gone, nothing seemed out of place. But he'd never been comfortable with strangers coming into the apartment while he was gone, no matter how dusty it got. Now that he was back, he could always call a cleaning service, but for now, the need for coffee was uppermost in his mind.

He tossed the bit of rice into the sink, then

filled the coffeepot with water before opening the freezer. His groan was audible when he realized the coffee can was empty.

"Hellfire and brimstone," he muttered, as he slammed the freezer shut, then headed for the small pantry and began digging through the meager assortment of cans and boxes, relaxing only after he found a small jar of instant coffee with just enough granules for one good cup. Unwilling to wait for the water to boil, he dumped the coffee into the largest mug he owned, shoved the cup beneath the hot water faucet, gave the mixture a couple of quick stirs as the cup filled, then took that first desperate sip. It wasn't good. It wasn't even hot. But it had caffeine and just enough of the taste he craved to make the day bearable.

With a soft moan of satisfaction, he rolled his head, easing the tension in his shoulders, then headed for the bathroom, drinking as he went.

It wasn't until later, as he was climbing out of the shower, that he caught a glimpse of himself in the mirror. He stopped and stared, then unconsciously dropped his arms, the towel hanging limply in one hand as he stared at the man looking back. It wasn't the unkempt beard or long hair that was shocking. He'd almost always changed his appearance while undercover. But there was no way to disguise the lack of expression in his eyes.

Burnout.

He'd seen it before, but never in himself. Frowning, he turned away and reached for his coffee, downing the last of the tepid liquid in an angry gulp. When he was through, he opened the drawer below the vanity mirror, picked up a pair of scissors and started cutting at his beard. A short while later, he emerged clean-shaven from the bathroom, his hair pulled back in a ponytail and his belly grumbling for food. Shopping had been the last thing on his mind yesterday as he'd emerged from debriefing. He'd gone straight home, locked himself in his apartment, then, before he could even get to the bedroom, passed out on the sofa from exhaustion. He wasn't ready to admit, even to himself, that when he wasn't on the job, he had a tendency to withdraw from the human race.

But if he was to remain a functioning human, he needed food, which meant breakfast at the local Denny's and a trip to the supermarket down the street. He finished dressing in record time, then grabbed his car keys from a small table in the entryway. It was then that he remembered the phone call he'd ignored earlier. He stared at the blinking light on the machine, telling himself to ignore it, but too many years of following orders from the United States government prevented him from walking out without at least listening. Besides, it might be from Carl. His smiling face had been a welcome sight as he'd jumped out of the chopper to help put Calderone in irons, the first time Jonah had seen his friend in six months. He wondered what Carl was doing, then realized he didn't care enough to give him a call. Instead, he punched the play button, listening as an unidentified female began to speak.

"That which was taken from me, will be taken from you."

Jonah felt a moment of unease, then shrugged off his concern. Ignoring the vague, ambiguous message, he palmed his car keys and walked out the door. It wasn't enough that the unsuspecting public had to endure telemarketing, but now it sounded as if religion was following suit. If television evangelists were moving to the phone lines, as well, then communication as the world knew it was going to hell.

Three hours later, he pulled back into the apartment parking lot and got out with a sack of groceries in each arm. His ponytail had been replaced by a thick cap of black, spiky hair, barely three inches long. Changing his hairstyle had been a symbolic parting with the past six months, but already he felt pounds lighter as he strode toward the building.

It wasn't until he reached the doorway that he realized there was a woman standing in his path. He paused, expecting her to step aside. Instead she spoke his name, then came toward him.

Mercedes Blaine was scared — as scared as she'd ever been in her life. The last time she'd seen Jonah Slade, she'd been thirteen years old and running down the front steps of her father's home, begging him not to go. Her thick red hair had been an uncontrollable mop, and her teeth had been adorned with braces. She'd been awkward and leggy and madly in love with him, despite the fact that he'd had eyes for no one but her older sister, Felicity.

And she couldn't blame him. At twenty-three, Felicity had been stunning — a willowy blonde with perfect hair and perfect teeth, attributes to which thirteen-year-old Macie could only aspire.

But something had gone wrong that day. Something that was driving Jonah away. It had taken another couple of months before she'd learned the depths of her father and sister's deception, but by then it was too late. Too late to tell Jonah that the baby Felicity had been carrying — his baby — hadn't been aborted after all. Declyn Blaine had wanted Jonah Slade out of their lives, and he'd gotten his wish. Felicity was beautiful. That was a fact. But she was also weak, and the threat of being cut off without a cent had been enough to make her go along with the lie that Declyn had persuaded her to tell.

Now she feared that time and that lie had caught up with them all, and it was up to her to try to make things right.

"Jonah."

Jonah frowned. The woman seemed familiar, but he was certain that if he'd been with her, he wouldn't have forgotten. She was stunning — tall and slender, and she walked with an easy sway that said she was used to getting her way. Sunlight caught and burned in the flame color of her long, wavy hair, and even from where he was standing, he could tell her eyes were ice-green.

"You have me at a disadvantage," he said shortly. "I don't believe we've met."

Mercedes sighed. "Granted I'm fifteen years older and minus a lot of wire in my mouth, but have I really changed that much?"

Jonah's heart skipped a beat. Fifteen years ago? Where had he . . . ? *Oh hell.*

"Macie?"

Hearing her old nickname made her smile. She nodded. "It's been a while since anyone's called me that, but right now it feels right."

"Why are you here?" he asked.

"Can we talk?"

Instantly Jonah's defenses went on alert. Fifteen years ago she'd been nothing but a kid, but she was obviously a very grown-up woman now, and that meant, based on his experience, no more to be trusted than Felicity had been.

"I don't think we have anything to talk about," he said shortly, and walked past her into the building.

Macie frowned. She'd known this wouldn't be easy, but there was too much at stake for her to quit. She hurried after him, entering the elevator just before the doors shut.

Jonah sighed. His conscience was digging at him, reminding him that Macie wasn't responsible for her sister's actions.

"Look, kid . . ."

"I'm not a kid any longer."

Jonah looked at her then, letting his gaze linger rudely on her womanly shape before challenging her with a look.

"Yes, I can see that."

Macie flinched. She hadn't expected this, but she should have. What Declyn and Felicity had done to him had been unforgivable.

"Please, Jonah, you have to listen to me."

"No, I don't."

The elevator opened, and he got out, shifting the grocery sacks to a more comfortable position as he headed for his apartment. Macie was right behind him. When he set the sacks down to reach for his keys, she grabbed him by the arm and physically yanked him around.

"Yes, damn it, you do! Felicity is dead . . .

murdered. Declyn is in L.A. in intensive care, and Evan has been kidnapped."

The floor swayed beneath Jonah's feet — or at least he thought it did. He heard what she said, but he couldn't get his mind around the truth. Felicity — dead? He hadn't thought all that beauty and privilege would ever fade, let alone die. Finally he managed to mutter a response.

"I'm sorry, but none of that has anything to do with me."

Macie took a deep breath. There was no easy way to say what had to be said.

"Yes, it does," she said. "There's still Evan."

"Evan? Who the hell is Evan?" Jonah asked.

"Your son."

2

Blindsided by the pain, Jonah grabbed Macie by the shoulders and pinned her against the wall.

"I don't have a son, remember? Felicity took care of that fifteen years ago."

"You're wrong," she said. "They lied. Declyn told Felicity he would cut her out of his will if she married you." Then she held her breath, watching as shock spread across Jonah's face.

"She what?"

"She didn't abort the baby. I swear to God it's the truth! Think about it, Jonah. Declyn is too vain for that. He wouldn't dispose of anyone who carried his blood. But he wanted you gone. That was the deal. Lie to you. Keep the boy for his own."

Jonah's belly lurched. A son. He had a son. And he'd missed the first fifteen years of his life — and all of the firsts.

Oh God, the firsts.

First smiles.

First steps.

Every damned first that a child has — and he'd missed them all.

"Son of a bitch," Jonah said, then turned

away, unwilling for her to see how the news had affected him.

He jammed his key into the lock, picked up his groceries and kicked at the door, intending to shut Macie out, but she was ready for him. She pushed her way inside, still talking, desperate to make her case.

"The men who took Evan left a note by Felicity's body. It said something about an eye for an eye — a son for a son."

The hair rose on the back of Jonah's neck. He turned slowly, staring at the red light on his answering machine and remembering the odd message. His hands were shaking as he pushed the Play button again and heard the words again.

"Oh, my God," Macie gasped.

Jonah's face was expressionless.

"This makes no sense," he muttered. "I didn't know I had a son. How could anyone else?"

"Evan knows your name. Two years ago, when Declyn enrolled him at Exeter Academy, Evan put down your name as one of his parents. Declyn was livid, but by that time, Evan didn't care. He and his grandfather do not see eye to eye on much of anything." Macie smiled slightly, more to herself than to Jonah. "I don't think Declyn counted on genetics playing such a strong role in Evan's personality."

"What do you mean?"

Macie put her hand on Jonah's arm, tugging gently at the fabric of his jacket as she continued to plead her case.

"He's you, Jonah. A younger version, but you just the same, right down to the dark hair and brown eyes . . . even the stubborn streak. He doesn't like pâté, but he loves barbecued ribs. He hates soccer and continues to root for the Dallas Cowboys despite every snobby, upper-crust behavior Declyn has tried to instill in him. He's only fifteen, and he's already over six feet tall."

Jonah kept picturing a boy verging on manhood who refused to give up on the father who seemed to have given up on him. The images hurt — more than he could have imagined. Suddenly he turned around, popped the tape out of the machine and dropped it in his pocket as he headed for his bedroom.

"Where are you going?" Macie asked.

"To find my son."

Macie went weak with relief. She so needed Jonah Slade on her side, but she had been terrified he would turn her away. She followed him into the bedroom.

"Thank you, Jonah. Thank you more than words can say."

"I'm not doing it for you."

Macie flinched, but remained silent. Even though it hurt, she understood his distrust, but she didn't want to be lumped into her family's web of deceit.

"I was only thirteen. Don't blame me for what they did."

Jonah dropped a handful of socks into his suitcase and then looked up, remembering the skinny little redhead with a mouth full of braces who'd tagged his every step. She was right. He knew she was right, but it was difficult to remember the kid when the woman standing before him was anything but a child.

"I'm the one who told Evan about you," she said.

Jonah glared at her in disbelief.

Macie sighed. Making him believe her felt like a losing battle.

"You? Why?" Jonah asked.

"Because he asked me. When he was six, he asked me where his daddy was. I told him his daddy was a soldier, fighting in a war. It satisfied him for a while. Then, when he was twelve, he asked me why you never came to see him. I told him the truth. He wasn't too surprised at his mother's ability to be manipulated, but he was furious with Declyn. Felicity never forgave me, and Declyn forbade me to set foot in the house again." Macie's voice was shaking now, as she relived the emotional years that she'd spent with her nephew, remembering what a lonely little boy he'd been, despite the monetary wealth. "I haven't been back to Los Angeles since that day . . . until yesterday, of course, although I kept in touch with Evan through phone calls and e-mail."

Jonah was surprised by her admission. He knew all too well what it meant to defy Declyn Blaine. He was still watching her face when her composure broke.

"I had to identify Felicity's body at the morgue and sign consent forms to keep my father on life-support." Then her lips twisted bitterly. "That was the hardest thing of all, because my instincts were to let the bastard die."

Jonah flinched. As overwhelmed as he was by what he'd just learned, her own loss was greater, and her emotions were obviously in shreds.

"I'm sorry, kid. . . . I know you and Felicity were close." Then he took a deep breath, trying to untangle his good sense from the pain. "You told Evan about me, but . . . why didn't you tell me about him?"

"I couldn't find you. I tried three times, but it was as if you'd dropped off the face of the earth. All I knew was that you worked for the U.S. government. Once I heard Felicity talking about spies, but I thought she was making it up. Obviously she wasn't. Yesterday it took every favor owed to my father to find out where you were, and then I chartered a plane to get here. I've been waiting on your doorstep for over two hours, and I don't know if Evan is still alive. He's a good boy,

Jonah. You would be so proud of him. He's not like Declyn at all." Then her voice broke. "Evan is all the family I have left, and I don't want to lose him, too."

It was remorse that made Jonah take Macie in his arms. He pulled her tight against him, her heartbroken sobs wrenching through him like knives slicing his flesh. He told himself that he'd hugged her plenty of times before, and that this meant nothing other than two people consoling each other in a time of crisis. But fifteen years was a long time, and Macie Blaine had turned into one hell of a woman. Finally he pushed her away, needing to see her face when he said the words.

"I'll come with you . . . and I'll find my son. But be warned, I won't lose any more time with him. I'll be in his life, whether the Blaines like it or not."

Macie nodded, unashamed of her tears. "That's fair enough, although there aren't any Blaines left except me . . . and Declyn, of course, but he's in no shape to argue with anyone. Thank you, Jonah. Thank you more than words can say."

Then she cupped his face and kissed him. Jonah didn't respond, nor had she expected him to. She didn't know that it was shock that kept him motionless, or that by the time his libido kicked in, she had turned him loose. What she'd done had been an impulse borne of relief, but she'd liked the taste of him far too much to ignore.

Jonah kept his thoughts to himself as he continued to pack. Just as he was closing the lid of his suitcase, his phone rang. He answered abruptly.

"Yeah?"

There was a brief hesitation, then a chuckle on the other end of the line. "Well now. That just answered my first question before I could ask."

Jonah relaxed. It was his friend and partner, Carl French.

"Sorry, Carl. I'm a little preoccupied."

"Hope I didn't wake you. I know you had a rough trip home. Have you already been debriefed?"

"No, you didn't wake me, I've been up a while, and yes, I've been debriefed."

"Great. Want to go get something to eat later?"

The impulse to tell Carl what was happening was strong, but he'd learned years ago that the fewer people who knew, the safer the secret.

"Not today. I'm sort of tied up at the moment. I'll check in with you later, okay?"

"Sure. Take care," Carl said, and hung up.

"Who was that?" Macie asked.

Jonah picked up his suitcase. "A friend." Then he looked at Macie. "Are you ready to go?"

"Yes."

"Then we're out of here."

Nausea rose at the back of Evan Blaine's throat as the van in which he'd been riding began to roll to a stop. He thought he'd been transferred into different vehicles twice, but since he was both blindfolded and gagged, he couldn't be sure. He had no memory of being put in the first vehicle or leaving his grandfather's estate. The last thing he did remember before his world came to an end were the sound of Rosa's screams and the gunshots and his grandfather crumpled on the floor.

Once, when he'd come to, he'd tried to cry, but his emotions seemed to be on hold. He knew he'd been kidnapped, but the reality had yet to sink in. He also knew that his mother was dead. He'd seen the bright red spill of her life force seeping out from underneath her ruined face. He'd tried to look away, but the shock of her platinum-blond hair turning a dark, strawberry-red had been both horrifying and mesmerizing.

Then he'd been running, running past his grandfather's body, running for his life — only to realize he wasn't going to get away. After that he remembered nothing except vague impressions of being dragged from one vehicle into another, then riding for hours before repeating the process all over again. This time, when they stopped, he tensed, bracing himself for another transfer.

It didn't happen. Instead he was pulled from the vehicle. When his feet hit a hard surface, he stumbled. Someone cursed at him in Spanish and yanked him up before he could fall. From the heat and the wind on his face, he knew it must still be daylight. He listened for the sounds of a city and heard nothing but waves crashing against cliffs and the sounds of seagulls overhead. He smelled the sea and dust, and his footsteps began to echo on some sort of wooden floor, and he knew they had entered a building. He hesitated, and as he did, one of his captors roughly yanked at his arm.

"You walk."

The man's voice echoed within the walls and Evan knew that wherever they'd taken him, it was big — and empty. Even as they were pulling him along, he was trying to focus on new clues that would help him figure out where he was. Because his thoughts were elsewhere, he was unprepared for the weight of a hand in the middle of his back. Before he could brace himself, he went flying. He fell forward, hard and fast, and with his hands still tied behind his back, he went down head and shoulder first, biting his tongue and scraping his forehead on impact. Immediately the copper taste of blood filled his mouth, as did a sharp pain. Still gagged, he had no option but to swallow, which only added to his nausea.

As he groaned, a kick to his ribs, accompanied by a rude burst of laughter, sent him rolling across the floor. Still reeling from the pain, he was only vaguely aware of receding footsteps and then a slamming door. It took a few moments for him to realize his wrists were no longer bound and then a bit longer before he could pull himself to a sitting position. Feeling was slow to return to his arms and hands, but as soon as he could, he ripped off the blindfold and the gag, then rolled onto his hands and knees. His head was throbbing, his ribs aching from the kick, but for the first time since he'd been snatched from his home, he was unfettered and alone. And with that knowledge came despair. As weak and flighty as she'd been, Felicity had still been his mother. As overbearing and dictatorial as Declyn had been, he'd still been his grandfather. And he'd watched them die. There was no one left of his family except for his aunt Macie. He wouldn't let himself think of, let alone depend upon, the man who'd fathered him. Struggling with pain and nausea, he managed to stand, and, for the first time, he got a good look at his surroundings.

The room was small and looked to have been partitioned off from a larger area. The ceiling was rounded, like the roof of a cave, but the construction was of some corrugated metal with a small, smelly bathroom off to one side. After relieving himself, he tried to wash his hands in the sink, only nothing came out of the taps but a beetle. Startled, he jumped backward in shock and disgust, then staggered out of the cubicle to a boarded-up window. Hoping to get a glimpse of something that would tell him where he was, he tried to peer through the slit between the boards, but all he could see was a faint glimmer of light. He thrust his fingers into the tiny crack, then clenched down with his fingernails, gritted his teeth, then pulled. Nothing budged. He tried again, thrusting his nails even farther into the minuscule space and pulling even harder. His fingers were still tingling from lack of circulation, and the muscles in his arms were stiff and aching, but if there was even a chance that he could get away from this hell, he had to try.

Muscles corded while sweat beaded across his forehead and rolled into his eyes. The salty sting was almost welcome — reminding him that he was still alive, and while there was life there was hope. His fingertips started to sting; then the pain moved from the flesh to the nails. He was straining so hard that the nails had begun to separate from the skin beneath. The pain was unexpected and excruciating. At that moment his fingers slipped and he staggered backward, his finger tips shredded and burning from small wooden splinters now embedded in his flesh.

"God," he moaned, then went to his knees.

He looked down at his hands, saw the bits of wood barely visible beneath the skin and the tiny droplets of blood seeping out from under the nails and started to shake. With that came long overdue tears — constant, burning, choking tears borne of hopelessness and fear.

"Help me," he whispered, and then slid to the floor and rolled onto his side. "Somebody help me."

Curling his knees up against his chest, he covered his head with his arms and gave in to the grief.

Afternoon: The Blaine estate in Bel Air

The hair crawled on the back of Jonah's neck as the cab pulled up to the Blaine estate. The massive iron gates were standing ajar, while a couple of blocks away, a phalanx of media crews hovered behind yellow crime scene tape, trying to get a bit of film footage that would be usable on the six o'clock news. He felt Macie shrink a little closer to him, as if trying to stay out of range of the lenses. A part of him wanted to play the hero, but she didn't seem like the helpless type, and he wasn't sure how far he wanted to go in making peace with a Blaine.

The cab moved forward, and Jonah realized

they'd gone through the gate and had started up the driveway. The last time he'd been here, he'd been dying inside. It did not please him to realize that the passing of fifteen years had done little to change the knot in his gut. He didn't want to be here, and but for the fate of a child he hadn't known existed, he never would have come back. He turned and looked out the back window toward the conglomerate of media and frowned.

"Why aren't there any guards at the gates . . . and why the hell are they still open?"

"When we get to the house, you'll see why," Macie said.

The cabdriver took the drive slowly, negotiating the winding twists and turns with ease. As the house came into view, it became apparent to Jonah that the feds had pulled out all the stops. A kidnapping was always a high-priority crime, and when it involved the grandson of a billionaire power broker like Declyn Blaine, everyone wanted a piece of the action. There were government-issue vehicles all over the place, along with several marked police cruisers. There was no need to have guards at the gate. The house itself was under virtual lock-down.

"Damn. Makes you wonder if there's anyone left to hold down the fort in D.C."

Macie handed the driver a handful of bills and then got out of the cab. Jonah took his suitcase from the trunk and followed her up the walk to the door. A pair of uniformed officers stopped Macie on the steps, but before she had time to identify herself, a tall, lanky man in a dark blue suit walked up behind them.

"That's Mercedes Blaine," he said briefly. "Let her pass."

Macie acknowledged the agent she'd met briefly yesterday.

"Agent Ruger, right?"

"Yes, ma'am," he said shortly. "For future reference, until this is over, when you leave town, let me know."

"I had my reasons," she answered.

"Is he one of them?" Ruger asked, eyeing Jonah.

"Ruger. It's been a while," Jonah said.

Macie's mouth dropped. "You know each other?"

Jonah shrugged.

Ruger nodded, then added, "What the hell are you doing here? This is out of your territory."

"Jonah is Evan's father," Macie said.

Now it was Ruger's turn to be surprised. "The hell you say," he muttered, staring at Jonah as if he'd never seen him before. "I didn't know you had a kid."

"Neither did I," Jonah said shortly. "What do you know about the abduction? Has there been a ransom demand?"

Ruger frowned, wanting to pursue Jonah's cryptic answer, but it was obvious by the look on Slade's face that he'd gotten all he was going to get.

"We don't know much of anything, and no, there's been no demand . . . not that we expected one. The note left by Miss Blaine's body leads us to believe the abduction is some sort of payback, but so far we haven't been able to link anything in Declyn Blaine's past to this."

"That's because it's directed at me," Jonah said, then took the tape from his answering machine out of his pocket and handed it to Ruger. "This message was left on my machine this morning."

Ruger was as stunned as he looked. "You? Why do you think this is about you?"

"Ever hear of Miguel Calderone?"

"The Colombian drug lord? Of course."

"Four days ago I killed his oldest son."

Ruger cursed beneath his breath and then turned sharply, yelling as he went.

A small Hispanic woman scurried into the foyer, passing Ruger as he stormed away.

"Miss Blaine! You are back!"

Macie nodded. It was obvious that Rosa had not welcomed being left on her own with the authorities. Even though she was now a legal citizen and no longer under the gun of the INS, anyone with a uniform and a badge made her nervous.

"Yes, of course I came back," she said softly, then impulsively hugged the little woman who'd been in her father's employment for twenty-two years. "Are you feeling better?"

Rosa started to cry. "My heart is so sad. Miss Felicity . . . Mr. Declyn . . . and the *niño . . . madre de Dios!*"

It was all Macie could do not to cry with her. "I know, I know. I can't bear to think of what Evan is enduring, but we have to believe he'll come back to us."

Rosa pulled a handkerchief from her pocket and blew her nose as she stepped back. As she did, she realized the man beside Macie had no intention of leaving as the other agents had.

"*Señor?* Is there something I can do for you?"

Jonah picked up his suitcase. "There's got to be a spare bedroom in this place. I'll be needing one for a while."

Startled, Rosa glanced at Macie, who nodded. "Put him in the room across the hall from mine," she said.

"Señora?"

"This is Jonah Slade. He's Evan's father," Macie said.

Rosa gasped and then crossed herself quickly before yanking the suitcase from Jonah's hands.

"Praise be to God," Rosa said softly,

casting a curious look Jonah's way.

"I can carry that," Jonah said, but Rosa shook her head. "No, *señor* . . . it is my honor. Please, follow me. We use the back stairs until the cleaning crew is gone," she added, and then crossed herself again as they passed the staircase where Felicity had died.

Macie wouldn't look at it again. She'd seen it before. But Jonah hesitated, eyeing the three men in coveralls who were down on their knees on the stairs. The scent of cleaning solution was strong enough to burn his eyes, but it was the faint blood stain embedded in the carpet that brought him to a halt.

Felicity of the easy smile and laughing eyes — the woman who'd betrayed him in a way he would never have believed — had died there. He stared, imagining the life spilling out of her, knowing that Evan must have seen that — and more. Anger came slowly, filling him with a sense of helplessness.

If they hadn't lied to him, none of this would have happened. He would have taken another path in his career. Every undercover agent knew that you took the chance of making deadly enemies, but you never gave them a chance to take it out on anyone but yourself. Now, without knowing it, he'd put an innocent teenager into harm's way. The kicker was that the boy was his.

"Jonah."

He blinked and then shuddered as he turned away. Macie was waiting for him near the back stairs. Rosa was already out of sight.

"This way," she said.

He looked up the long, winding staircase and felt a knot in the pit of his stomach. He half expected Felicity to be standing at the top with that taunting smile on her face.

"Yeah . . . I remember," he said, then started upward without waiting for her to follow.

Macie sighed, her heart too sore and heavy to worry about what Jonah must be feeling. She couldn't let herself care that coming back here must have brought back a lot of bad memories for him. Her entire focus was on doing whatever it took to get Evan back alive.

Jonah reached the second floor and saw Rosa waiting for him down the hall.

"This will be your room, *señor.* If you have need of anything, please let me know."

"Thank you," he said briefly, then glanced at her as he passed. "I remember you, don't I?"

She nodded. "You fix my car one day when it wouldn't start."

"Yeah . . . I remember now. It was a sixty-two Ford Falcon, right?"

She smiled. "*Sí, Señor.* You were most kind."

His expression froze. "It was a long time

ago," Jonah said, then took the bag from her hands and closed the door behind him.

Macie smiled at Rosa as they passed in the hall.

"You want dinner tonight?" Rosa asked.

Macie sighed. Food was the farthest thing from her mind, but they had to eat.

"Yes, please . . . but nothing fancy. Maybe some soup and cold cuts, okay?"

"Oh, no, Miss Macie . . . I will make dinner . . . just like always. You eat. You will feel better, okay?"

If letting Rosa cook would make *her* feel better, then it was the least she could do.

"Yes, thank you," she said. "It will be very okay."

Glad to have someone from the family back in the house, Rosa went back to her kitchen. At least there, her world had not changed.

Macie was not so fortunate. She'd grown up in this place and despite the often overdone opulence Declyn favored, it had been home. When Declyn had virtually disowned her for telling Evan about his father, she'd never expected to be here again — and certainly not under these circumstances.

The knowledge that her sister was lying in a morgue somewhere made her want to scream out with rage. The fact that her father was hovering near death in an ICU would normally have been a matter of great concern, but Evan's abduction had taken precedence over everything else. She could only imagine how frightened he must be. She wouldn't let herself think of anything else. Evan of the tender heart and gentle smile had to be all right.

3

It took Jonah less than ten minutes to unpack, and in that short span of time, the past had come at him from every angle. It had been fifteen years since he'd laid eyes on Felicity Blaine, and while he knew she was dead, her presence in this place was so strong, he kept expecting her to appear. He'd spent so many years hating her for what he'd thought she'd done, and now he was having to come to terms with a whole new set of betrayals. Even though she hadn't aborted the baby, what she and her father had done amounted to thievery of the worst kind. They'd stolen his child. Now Miguel Calderone had stolen him again. Jonah got sick to his stomach every time he thought about what Evan might be enduring — and on his behalf. He'd seen firsthand what insidious tortures Calderone was capable of perpetrating and if Calderone gave the word, a fifteen-year-old kid didn't have a chance in hell of surviving them. He still couldn't figure out how Calderone had learned of Evan, or how he'd figured out who Jonah really was. All he'd known was a man named Juan Diego Ramirez. Someone had talked.

He needed to know who, and he needed to know why. Having settled that in his mind, he got ready to leave the room.

Just then his cell phone rang. Startled, he looked at the caller ID and then frowned.

"This is Slade."

"Is there something you want to tell me?"

It was the director. Jonah's frown deepened. He was guessing that Ruger had already contacted his superiors, who had, in turn, contacted the director of the CIA.

"I've got a problem," Jonah said.

"So I understand. How can we help?"

"Find my son before Calderone butchers him."

There was a brief silence and then a sigh. "Unofficially . . . we've offered our help in any capacity Agent Ruger names."

"Thank you, sir."

"Of course."

"Sir . . . I have a favor to ask."

"Yes?"

"I think the fewer people who know where I am, the better off Evan will be."

"Why?"

"Calderone only knew me as Juan Diego Ramirez. He had no way of knowing my real identity or that I had a son. Hell, sir, and pardon me for saying that, but *I* didn't know until earlier today."

"I see. Yes, there could be a leak. I'll look into it personally."

"Yes, sir. Thank you, sir," Jonah said.

The director added, "You know that you can't participate actively in the investigation. This is FBI business. Besides, as you say, Calderone's people know you now."

"Yes, sir . . . I'm well aware of that, but I know Calderone. Even if he's in custody, he's still running the show. I believe he took my son to make me suffer. I'm guessing we have less than a forty-eight-hour window before he starts sending Evan back in pieces. Obviously they don't know that I didn't know Evan existed until today or they would have chosen another method of revenge. But that's moot now. They have him. Now they have to make sure I know where he is so I suffer as Calderone is suffering. But if they can't find me, it may buy us some time to find Evan."

"Yes, I see your point, and since you know Calderone better than anyone, we'll do it your way . . . but only up to a point. Ruger is in charge, Slade. Don't play hero."

"I'm not playing anything, sir, and there is no way in hell this is a game. Just know that I'll do what it takes to find the boy."

"Be realistic, Slade. It may already be too late."

"Then God help Calderone, because there won't be enough bars between him and me to keep him alive."

Jonah disconnected before his boss could issue orders he might have to disobey. He'd already said more than he meant to, but this was too close to the bone to mince words. Whatever happened to him was immaterial if it meant saving Evan.

As he took a deep breath, there was a knock on his door. Still angry, he spun abruptly, the tone of his voice echoing his emotions.

"Yes?"

Ruger walked in, ignoring Slade's behavior. "If you've got a few minutes, there are some things I want to run past you."

"Here?" Jonah asked.

"No, downstairs."

"Okay, but there's something we need to get straight. I don't want my whereabouts leaked to anyone beyond what's already been done. Also, as far as anyone else knows, I'm here strictly for Miss Blaine's benefit. Call me a bodyguard. Call me a boyfriend. Call me whatever the hell you choose. Just don't call me by name or refer to me as Evan's father in front of anyone else, got it?"

"There are a couple of agents who already know," Ruger said. "They're analyzing the tape you brought as we speak."

"Then ask them to keep it quiet."

"Sure, but why the secrecy?"

"Trust me . . . it might keep the kid alive a little longer. Now, what was it you wanted to talk to me about?"

"We have a video from the security system

here in the house. It isn't pretty, but it caught most of the abduction, and since I understand you've been vacationing in Colombia for the past few months, you might see something about the perps that we're missing. Something that might help us ID them."

Jonah grimaced. Vacationing? Right. In hell.

"Yeah, all right."

"Good. Follow me," Ruger said.

Jonah had never thought about what a condemned prisoner might feel like while making that last walk to his execution, but he knew it couldn't be much worse than what he was feeling right now. The guilt level was close to choking the life right out of him. Damn Miguel Calderone to hell and back, and damn Declyn Blaine, too.

To make matters worse, Ruger took him down the front staircase. The cleaning crew was gone, but the scent of professional strength disinfectant was still strong in the air. He paused at the head of the staircase, staring down at the damp places where they'd cleaned the blood from the carpet.

"Son of a bitch," he muttered.

Ruger stopped and turned. "What?"

Jonah swallowed, then shook his head. "Nothing."

"This way, then," Ruger said, and took the stairs two at a time.

Jonah followed, trying to ignore the fact

that the woman he'd once thought he'd loved more than life — the woman who'd born his only child — had died here.

"In here," Ruger said, waving Jonah into the first room to the right of the main staircase. It had once been Declyn's home office. Ruger had turned it into a conference room.

Other than a muscle jumping at the side of Jonah's jaw, there was no outward sign of what he was feeling. A half dozen agents were sitting in pairs around three different tables. One table was covered with high-tech tracing devices, in hopes that the kidnappers might call. Two other agents were hard at work at a second table, analyzing the tape from his answering machine. The fact that he couldn't actively pursue part of the investigation made him feel helpless. It was the first time he'd ever been on the victim's side of a case. One of the agents looked up and saw him, then gave him a nod before returning to his task.

Jonah knew the men were skilled at their jobs and that any interference from him would not be welcome. Besides these men, there was no way of telling how many were already on the streets, following up leads. The kidnapping, as well as the murder of Declyn Blaine's eldest daughter, was the lead story on every television channel. Jonah knew that fact alone would be generating all kinds of leads from the public, all of which would demand thousands of man hours from the local authorities, as well as at the federal level. What rankled most was that this was his son and he was relegated to the role of bystander.

"Have a seat," Ruger said.

Jonah sat down in an easy chair in front of a portable TV while Ruger shoved the security tape into the VCR, then glanced at Jonah.

"Are you going to be okay with this?" Ruger asked.

"Just play the damned tape," Jonah growled.

Ruger aimed the remote, pushed the play button and sat down. He'd seen it dozens of times before, but the brutality of it still grabbed him.

It started out so ordinary.

The doorbell ringing.

Rosa appearing within camera range and then opening the door before being shoved onto the floor.

Gunshots.

A thin, high-pitched scream, and then Felicity falling into camera range.

Jonah flinched. He could tell she was dead before she hit the stairs, but the spill of blood was horrifying.

Then more gunshots.

Rosa screaming and praying aloud in Spanish, begging for mercy. Begging them to stop.

Jonah knew that Declyn had been shot somewhere in there, but the camera hadn't caught that on film. What he did see next was his son being dragged into view — limp and unconscious.

He stood abruptly.

"Play it back," he said.

"But —"

"God damn it, Ruger, play it back. That's my son. I want to see his face."

Ruger hit the remote, rewound a bit of the tape and then replayed it.

Again Felicity screamed, then fell into view. Again the blood spilled out from under her head and onto the stairs.

"Oh God, oh God."

Jonah spun. Macie was standing in the doorway with her hands pressed to her mouth. Her eyes were wide and filled with shock. Before he could move, her eyes rolled back in her head.

"Catch her," he yelled, but it was too late. She fainted, hitting the floor with a thump.

"Damn it," Jonah muttered, as he scooped her up in his arms. "Why wasn't someone watching her? She didn't need to see this."

"Sorry," Ruger said. "I thought she was upstairs. Should I get a doctor? She hit her head pretty hard."

"Hell if I know," Jonah said. "I'm taking her back to her room. Someone go get the maid and send her up."

Ruger pointed at one of the agents, who got up from his chair and followed Jonah out of the room as he carried Macie up the stairs. This time he didn't even notice the damp patches on the carpet. His focus was entirely on the lack of color in Macie's face and how frighteningly limp she was in his arms.

Moments later, he gained the second floor, only to realize he didn't know which room was hers, so he carried her into his room, instead. He laid her gently on his bed and then hurried into the bathroom, dampening a washcloth before rushing back to her.

He slid onto the side of the bed and laid the damp cloth across her forehead while cupping the side of her face. Her eyelids fluttered, and then she moaned.

"Easy honey," Jonah said softly.

At that moment Rosa burst into the room, took one look at Macie lying unconscious on the bed and clasped her hands to her mouth.

"Madre de Dios . . . the niña . . . the niña."

"She's all right," Jonah said. "She just fainted." Then he grabbed Rosa's hand and laid it on Macie's head, where a small bump had arisen. "I need some ice. Do you have an ice bag?"

"Yes, yes, *Señor* Jonah. . . . I hurry."

Rosa bolted out of the room.

A phone rang somewhere downstairs, and Jonah flinched, praying to God that it was the kidnappers. They needed a break in this mess, and they needed it fast.

Macie moaned again, then reached toward the lump on her head. Jonah knew it must be hurting.

"You're okay," he said gently. "You bumped your head, but you're okay."

Her eyelids fluttered, then opened. Jonah found himself caught in her gaze.

"This is a nightmare," Macie whispered, and then she started to cry.

Jonah groaned softly, then lifted her off the bed and into his arms. "I'm sorry you saw that."

"Poor Felicity . . . poor Evan. Oh God . . . is he dead, Jonah? Is he already dead like Felicity? Am I just kidding myself?"

Jonah held her close, rocking her gently in his lap, and struggled to find an answer that wouldn't be a lie.

"I won't lie to you. There's no way of knowing for sure, but I don't think so. At least, not yet. I told Ruger not to tell any more people who I am. I think Calderone will come after me next. I think he will want me to see Evan die. But we can buy some time if they can't find me. Maybe even enough time to find Evan first."

Macie's chin quivered. "I can't believe this is happening."

Jonah saw his own reflection in her tears and shuddered.

"Me either," he said, then leaned forward, intent on kissing the side of her cheek.

Instead Macie turned her head. Their lips met.

There was a brief moment of shock, then a slight increase in pressure, as if both of them were testing the depth of the connection. Before they knew it, Macie's arms were around Jonah's neck and his hands were sliding up her back beneath her sweater.

Suddenly Jonah thrust her backward and stood, all but dumping her off his lap. Before Macie could object, Rosa hurried into the room carrying the ice bag. She hurried to Macie's side and pressed it against the lump beneath her hair.

"Poor little head," she said. "Poor *niña*."

"I'll be downstairs," Jonah said to Macie. "Send Rosa if you need me."

Macie was left with no option but to watch him walk away. It was all Jonah could do not to run. All the way down the stairs, he kept asking himself what the hell he was thinking. He'd come to save his son's life, not get mixed up with another woman named Blaine.

When he got back downstairs, he cornered Ruger.

"How is she?" Ruger asked.

"She's all right," Jonah said. "I, however, may never be all right again. You and I know that it may already be too late to save my son. I pray it's not . . . but in my world, facing reality is what's kept me alive. There is a chance that he's still alive, small though it may be, and I'm counting on it. I don't know Evan Blaine. I wouldn't know him if I passed him on the street, and that alone makes me sick to my stomach. I can't be publicly involved, but I need to do something."

Ruger sighed. "I have a seventeen-year-old and a fourteen-year-old. I can't imagine the hell you're going through, let alone that you never knew about the kid's existence. We're doing all we know how, but I'm not going to lie to you. This is the worst case I've ever worked. We have nothing. Not one lead has panned out. Frankly, Slade, I'm scared shitless."

"I want to see the video again," Jonah said. "Maybe there's something . . ."

"Be my guest," Ruger said. "I'll take all the help I can get. Tony's working on it now. Pull up a chair and make yourself at home."

Jonah dragged a chair up beside the man Ruger had referred to and then focused on the computer screen where the video was being analyzed. Another agent had the security tapes from the front gates on a different screen and was doing the same to them. Jonah didn't know which one to look at first.

Thirty minutes passed with nothing remarkable becoming apparent on the interior video. At that point Jonah turned his chair to the other monitor and then leaned back, letting his mind focus on the images and not on his fears.

"What are we looking at?" he asked.

Agent Bobby Joe Thomas momentarily stopped the tape, then checked his notes. "The security tape for the day before the abduction."

"How many have you gone through?"

Thomas looked up. "So far . . . a dozen, going back through the past twelve days."

Jonah frowned. "And nothing?"

"Nothing obvious," Thomas said. "If there's something to be seen, we aren't seeing it. Maybe you'll see it from a different perspective."

"That's why I'm here," Jonah said.

"What do you want to look at first?"

"Just finish running the one you've got, and then we'll go backward from there."

Thomas nodded and resumed his analysis.

For a while there was no activity on the tape other than the sound of traffic passing by on the street and the occasional bird flying by the camera lens. Then an old pickup truck pulled into view. Jonah leaned forward.

"Who's that?" he asked.

"The gardener," Thomas said. "According to the last twelve tapes I've viewed, he arrives at this time every day."

"Oh."

Thomas's explanation made sense, but still Jonah kept staring as the small Mexican leaned out the window of his truck and reached toward the keypad to punch in the code. As he did, Jonah caught a glimpse of the man's profile, but it wasn't his face that caught his attention. It was when the sleeve of his shirt caught on the window, revealing a good portion of his forearm, that Jonah bolted upright.

"Son-of-a-bitch!"

Everyone in the room froze, staring at Jonah as if he'd just lost his mind.

"What?" Ruger asked.

"The gardener. He's one of Calderone's men."

Ruger frowned as he shuffled through his notebook. "He can't be. He's been working for Declyn Blaine for . . . for five years. If Evan's kidnapping is retribution toward you, then there's no way Calderone would have planted someone here that long ago."

"I don't care how long he's been here," Jonah said. "He's one of Calderone's."

"How do you know?" Ruger asked.

"Run that tape back to where he puts his arm out the window. No . . . a little more . . . more . . . There!"

"What is it? What do you see?" Ruger asked.

Jonah put his hand on Thomas's shoulder and pointed to the image frozen on the screen. "Can you enlarge that?"

Thomas moved the mouse over the picture, clicked once, then twice, then again, until maximum enlargement had been achieved.

"Any more and I'll lose the image," Thomas said.

"That's good enough," Jonah said, then looked at the picture again. What he saw only reinforced his belief. "Do you see that?" he asked.

Ruger leaned forward. "Looks like a tattoo."

Jonah nodded. "You can't see all of it, but I know what it looks like. It's a python swallowing an eagle. The python is Calderone's totem, so to speak. The eagle represents the United States. Everyone who belongs to the Calderone organization bears that tattoo."

Ruger stood back and stared. "Are you sure?"

"Oh, yeah," Jonah said, and took off his shirt and then turned around, giving them a full view of his back. "Undercover work has its own set of drawbacks. As you can see, some of them are permanent."

"I'll be damned," Ruger said. "But how does that explain the man's presence here? It can't just be a coincidence. Or maybe he was a part of that life until he immigrated? After all, he's pushing fifty. Sooner or later a man gets too old to run and gun."

Jonah pulled his shirt back over his head

and was tucking it back into his pants when Ruger's last statement soaked in.

"Fifty? If that man is pushing fifty, then I am, too. What's his name?" he asked.

Ruger looked back at his notes. "Felipe Sosa."

"Have you checked his papers?" Jonah asked.

Ruger turned to his men. "Did we?"

No one answered.

"Go find him," Ruger ordered, then Jonah grabbed him by the arm.

"No, wait!" he said. "I don't know what kind of switch Calderone has pulled, but I'd bet my retirement that the man cutting Blaine's grass is not Felipe Sosa, and alerting him to the fact that we know that might end our chance to find Evan. I say let him be, but watch him. Find out where he lives, who he makes contact with . . . that kind of thing. He might be the key to getting us to Evan."

Ruger grabbed his phone and headed out of the room as Jonah turned toward the monitor, once again staring long and hard at the man's face. To his knowledge, he'd never seen him before, but that didn't mean the man hadn't seen him. He had to be careful — to make sure he kept a low profile. He thought about another disguise, and the moment he did, he realized that the way he looked now was his best disguise. Calderone had never seen him without long hair and a beard. Unless they were face-to-face, he doubted he would be recognized. Still, he wasn't going to take chances.

"Run the rest of that tape," Jonah said. "Let's see if there are any other little surprises to be had."

Outside, on the grounds of the Blaine estate, the man calling himself Felipe Sosa was wielding a pair of clippers on the ornamental shrubbery along the graveled pathway. He wore a floppy straw hat and loose-fitting denims, and hummed to himself as he worked. Although he knew what had happened inside the big house, it changed nothing about what he'd been hired to do. He snipped and clipped while trying not to make eye contact with anyone carrying a badge. Even though his gut instinct had been not to come back to work after the incident, he didn't have the luxury of making that decision for himself. If he'd been a no-show, he would have been automatically put on the suspect list. Then the authorities would have come looking for him, and that would have been a disaster. The last thing he wanted to do was produce his papers or his green card. He was fifteen years younger than the real Felipe Sosa, who'd been eating beans and tortillas when he'd drawn his last breath, but he'd been assured by the man who'd smuggled him into the States that, to the white men, all Latinos looked alike. So he did his work without fuss, moving about the lush and elaborate landscaping like a small brown bird, unaware that he'd already been made.

The noise level on the cell block was secondary to the smell. It offended every one of Miguel Calderone's senses and pissed him off to no end — and he had but one man to thank for his change of abode. Jonah Slade.

He slapped the flat of his hand against the wall of his cell and then laid his forehead against his bunk. Alejandro. His first son. His best son. Dead by Slade's hand.

Pain roiled in his belly like a snake, coiling and then striking — first at his heart, then blinding him to everything but the need for revenge. Procuring a good lawyer and concentrating on his own trial had taken a back seat to avenging Alejandro's death, and the means by which to do it had come when he needed it most. He owed his informant, a hit man who called himself The Snowman, more than he could ever pay. When he got out of prison — and he knew he *would* get out — the Snowman could name his price. Everyone knew that he, Miguel Calderone, was a man who kept his word. He'd vowed to make Jonah Slade pay, and pay he would. Before Slade died, he would watch his own son bleed out before his eyes. It was this vow that kept Calderone from going insane.

"Hey, Calderone! You got a visitor. Come with me."

Calderone looked up. The guard at the cell door was an intimidating son of a bitch. Calderone had hated him on sight, but for now, he played their game. More was gained by patience than panic. He held out his hands, refusing to acknowledge by expression or word that the handcuffs the guard placed on his wrists were too tight, or that the leg irons they put around his ankles were too small. He let himself be led meekly to the visitor area. The guard was merely a gnat in the soup his life had become. He would not lower himself to small pains when there were bigger issues at stake.

He was led to what appeared to be an interrogation room, which was where prisoners were allowed privacy with their counsel. Assuming it was his lawyer, he hid his surprise when he saw the nun waiting for him on the other side of the table. Hindered by the handcuffs, it was difficult to make the sign of the cross, but he did so without thinking.

"Sit here," the guard said, and shoved him into a chair, then turned his gaze to the nun. "You sit there. No touching. Understand?"

"Yes, my son, and I thank you," the sister said, smiling benevolently at the guard, who backed away, only to stop just inside the closed door a short distance away.

Calderone glanced over his shoulder, gauging the distance between himself and the guard, then shrugged and nodded, as if to acknowledge the guard's presence. When he turned, his back to the guard, he allowed himself a brief moment of recognition before playing out the game. It was his woman, Elena.

"Sister . . . you have come to pray for me?"

The nun nodded, took out her rosary and then bowed her head. Calderone leaned forward, lowering his voice and his head. Although they were not touching, there was less than a foot between them.

"You have news for me?" he asked.

The nun nodded while continuing to run her fingers along the rosary beads. To the guard, it appeared as if she was praying.

"It is done," she said.

"And the Padre . . . how is he?" Calderone asked.

The nun's fingers paused on one small bead, and then she shook her head slightly from side to side.

"Alas . . . not to be found," she said softly.

Calderone's heart skipped a beat. "And do we know why?"

"No, *señor* . . . we do not. But we search for him."

Frustration made Calderone careless. "It doesn't work without him," he hissed.

The guard shifted at the door. The nun began to pray a little louder. To her relief, the guard stayed, seemingly satisfied by what he heard.

"All that can be done is being done," the nun said, then kissed the cross, and for the first time since Calderone sat down, lifted her head and looked up. "I miss you, Miguel. I miss our nights together and your lips at my breast. Please tell me this will soon be over."

"Elena . . . my beautiful Elena. How fares our child?"

"She is well . . . missing her papa."

Calderone sighed. The woman was a whore, a *puta* . . . but she'd stolen his heart just the same. When she'd borne him a child, he'd taken her into the *hacienda* as if she were his wife. She'd enjoyed all the privileges of being the *padrone*'s woman without benefit of the church's blessing, and that would never come. Even a man like Calderone had his limits, and marrying a woman who had fucked other men for money was one of them.

"Give her my love," Calderone said. "Tell her I will see her soon, and tell Juan Carlos not to let me down . . . understand?"

"Yes, Miguel . . . I understand."

She stood abruptly and looked at the guard. "I am done here," she said.

The guard moved toward Calderone, took

him by the arm and all but dragged him out of the room. Calderone didn't look back. It wouldn't do to cast a longing and lustful look at one of Christ's brides.

4

Jonah came out of the makeshift conference room and started up the stairs. He'd just identified a man who might be their first real lead to finding Evan, but he wasn't sure he was going to tell Macie. They didn't want the gardener alerted to the fact that he'd been made, and the more people who knew, the less likelihood they had of pulling it off.

As he reached the top of the stairs, he heard a flurry of footsteps, and stopped and looked down. Ruger was heading for the front door with a cell phone to his ear. There were two agents right behind him. The urge to go with them was strong. He wasn't used to being out of the know, and it made him antsy, but he couldn't be an active part of the search without compromising the investigation.

Just as the men exited the house, he heard another door opening behind him. He turned just as Rosa exited Macie's bedroom, leaving the door ajar. Her head was down, and she was dabbing at her eyes with a handkerchief as she took the back stairs. Jonah frowned. What now?

Macie sat on the side of the bed, staring at

the floor. She'd tried sleeping, but every time she closed her eyes, she kept seeing herself walking into her father's office, hearing the gunshots on the tape and turning toward the sound, then seeing Felicity's lifeless body falling headfirst into view and thinking that the blood splatter on the wall looked like an abstract painting. She didn't know that one of the bullets had hit an artery in Felicity's body, or that the arterial spray had lasted only as long as her heart had been beating. She didn't know that the moment the spray had stopped, so had her sister's heart. All she'd seen was her sister lying headfirst down the stairs and the blood pooling under her head.

She drew a deep breath, then exhaled on a sob, wondering if it had hurt to die. Felicity never could stand pain.

God . . . this was a nightmare.

Wiping a shaky hand across her face, Macie took the ice bag from her head and laid it on the nightstand. The pain in her head had faded to a dull throb. If only the ache in her heart would subside as easily.

She heard footsteps coming down the hall and looked up just as Jonah walked in. His stride was long and hurricd, his voice almost angry. And then he spoke, and the question was almost absurd in content.

"What's wrong?" he asked.

Hysteria bubbled, threatening to explode.

"You have to ask?"

"Rosa came out of your room crying."

Macie sighed. "Oh, that . . . I was talking to the funeral director about Felicity. She wanted to be cremated. I was . . . I had to . . ."

"Never mind," Jonah said. "I understand."

Suddenly Macie's composure broke. Tears rolled unchecked down her face as sarcasm filled her voice.

"How nice for you. I wish I could say the same."

Taken aback, Jonah did what any normal person would do. He defended himself.

"Damn it . . . don't do this."

Macie's voice was now close to a shout. "Do what? Do what? What have I done?"

"Make me the bad guy."

Shame came quickly, replacing anger. Macie's face crumpled. He was right. She was taking her grief out on him. She reached toward Jonah, but he stepped back, and when he did, her heart dropped. The words she'd spoken in haste and anger had obviously ruined their shaky truce.

"Jonah . . . please . . . I'm sorry," Macie said. "It's all this . . . this . . . Oh God, it's a nightmare, and it's making me crazy."

Jonah wouldn't look at her — couldn't look at her. Not without breaking, but he was finding it more and more difficult to remain objective where Macie Blaine was concerned. Every instinct he had was to keep her at arm's length. Her sister had been beautiful, intriguing — and as deceptive as the devil. The same blood ran in Macie's veins. He needed to keep his distance, keep his head and find his son. No more. No less.

"Yeah, sure. Forget it."

The lack of emotion in his voice said it all. With a few careless words, she'd destroyed their tenuous relationship. She needed it and him more than she could say.

"Jonah, I —"

He took another step backward. "I need to make some phone calls."

"Rosa is serving dinner in about an hour."

He paused. There was no way to get out of that. He was staying under this roof. He had to eat. With her.

"All right."

"Jonah?"

The quiver in her voice slowed his exit. Reluctantly he stopped and looked back.

"Don't be mad at me."

The tears in her eyes undid him. "I'm not mad at you, honey," he said gently. "Just at the situation, okay?"

"Promise?"

He almost smiled. "Yeah, I promise."

"See you at dinner?"

"Yes . . . at dinner," he said, and then headed for his room. It was past time to check in with the director and, if he was in a good mood, ask him a favor.

⋆ ⋆ ⋆

It was getting dark. The only piece of furniture in the room where Evan was being kept was a cot-size bed. The mattress was old and dirty, but not as dirty as the floor. After hours of frustrated pacing and tugging at the boarded-up windows with no success, Evan was hungry. Considering what he'd endured, he would have thought bodily needs would have ceased, but they had not. Frustrated and desperate to quench his thirst, he braved angering his captors by pounding on the door.

"Hey!" he yelled. "Bring me some water!"

He waited for a moment and then repeated the demand, this time pounding harder. Within seconds, the door came open. Startled, Evan staggered backward and then fell. He found himself looking up at an armed man from a sitting position, and feeling foolish and vulnerable.

"You keep quiet," the man said, and poked at Evan's belly with the barrel of an assault rifle.

"I just want some food and water," Evan muttered.

The man sneered. "Why waste food and water on a boy who is already dead?"

For a moment Evan was so frightened he couldn't speak. But then he remembered what they'd already done to his mother, seeing his grandfather crumpling onto the floor. Evan stood abruptly, startling his captor enough that he took a defensive step back.

Evan held his arms out to his sides, making his chest a perfect target. "If you want me dead, then do it! You've already killed the rest of my family, so what are you waiting for?"

The armed man shoved the barrel of the rifle into Evan's belly.

"We wait for your *padre*. You sit," he ordered, motioning toward the bed.

Evan frowned. "I'm not Catholic. What does a priest have to do with it?"

"No, no. Your father . . . not a priest."

The notion was so ludicrous to Evan that before he thought, he threw back his head and laughed.

It was the last thing the armed man expected. He struck out at Evan, using the butt of the rifle on Evan's chin. This time, when Evan fell, he didn't get up.

"Laugh now," the bandit said.

Tasting blood, Evan stifled a groan and then reached for his face, wincing as he tested his jaw to see if it would still open. When it did, he couldn't resist adding, "Fine. I never said you weren't in charge, but it won't change the fact that my so-called father doesn't know I exist. We could pass each other on the street and never know it."

"You lie," the man said, and threatened to hit Evan again.

Evan shook his head as he pulled himself upright.

"Beating the crap out of me is not going to change the truth. Someone in your organization messed up big-time, because the man never knew I was born." Then he held his breath and waited, all but daring the man to hit him again.

To his surprise, the man cursed and left abruptly, slamming the door behind him as he went. Evan raced to the door but was too late. The lock turned just as he grasped the doorknob.

"Bring me some water! Water! I need water!" he yelled, and slapped the door over and over with the flat of his hand.

Shaken by despair and trying not to think about the pain in his fingers, he leaned against the door and tried not to cry. Moments later, the lights went out, and he realized the faint hum he'd been hearing all afternoon had ceased. Whatever had been powering the electricity had been shut off. He spun quickly, peering into the shadows in the ever-darkening room, and then moved toward the bed.

It was the sound of the generator coming back to life that brought Evan out of a deep, dreamless sleep. With that came the acknowledgment of pain in his jaw, swollen and burning fingertips from his earlier attempt to escape, and something else — something he'd never experienced before in his life — true hunger.

He rolled over on the cot and then swung his legs to the floor, telling himself that hunger was secondary to the fact that he was still alive. The overhead light had come on the moment the generator had started, ironing the shadows from the room, and as it did, he saw the tray of food by the door. But elation turned to shock when he saw a large rat only a few feet away from the tray, lying motionless on the floor. He jumped to his feet and then knelt by the tray. There were bite marks on the fruit where the rat had nibbled, as well as a trail of breadcrumbs from the tray to the partially eaten roll beside the rat.

He stood abruptly, then toed the rat with his shoe. Its limp body rocked gently beneath the nudge, then fell back into a supine position. Evan stepped back in shock. Poison? They were going to poison him? What kind of madman did this? If they wanted him dead, why hadn't they killed him at the house? Why drag him so far away just to do the deed?

Evan glanced back down at the tray, then picked up the piece of partially eaten fruit and sniffed it, trying to discern a sinister smell. Instead the scent of crisp, sweet apple filled his nostrils and made his belly grumble.

The urge to taste it was strong. It would be easy — so easy just to give up. He had no one to live for except himself. Then he remembered his aunt Macie. He wondered if she was okay, or if they'd made her a victim, too.

He dropped the apple back on the tray, then picked up a large bottle of water that had been knocked over during the rat's foray. He eyed it closely, then ran his fingers around the seal, checking to see if it had been broken. He was overjoyed to find it had not. Thirst overcame hunger as he unscrewed the lid, taking comfort from the pop when the seal broke.

The water was tepid, but to Evan, it couldn't have been better as he tilted the bottle and drank greedily. It wasn't until he'd downed almost a pint that it dawned on him that this might be all he would get. Reluctantly he lowered the bottle, replaced the cap and set it down on the floor by his bed. As he did, he glanced toward the door leading into the small bathroom and knew, despite his disgust, he was going to have to make another visit.

But when he got inside, the job of unbuttoning his fly became such an issue that he forgot the stench. The raw places on the tips of his fingers were trying to scab over, while the splinters under his nails had started to fester under the skin. His hands were puffy and sore.

By the time he was through, the scabs had cracked and bled, and he was shaking from pain. Instead of rebuttoning his jeans, he opted to take them off and tossed them on the end of the bed, leaving him dressed in dark, navy blue boxers that looked like gym shorts. He looked down the length of his legs, noting several dark, purpling bruises, and had no memory of how they had come to be there. He wondered if his upper body had fared the same and took off his T-shirt to see. There were none he could see on his belly, but there were several smaller ones on his arms. He guessed they'd happened during his abduction, or when he'd been carried as they'd moved from van to van.

He started to put his T-shirt back on and then impulsively tossed it on the bed with his jeans. The air in the room was close. The last thing he would do was get cold during the day. Tonight — if he was still alive — he could put them back on to sleep.

His belly rumbled, and he glanced back longingly at the tray of food, then gasped with surprise. The rat was up and staggering toward a hole in the floor near the corner of the room. At that point Evan realized the food had been drugged, not poisoned, but it changed nothing for him. Whether it killed him or just put him to sleep was immaterial. He wasn't going to do anything that would make him any more vulnerable to these people than he already was. He stood, watching until the rat all but fell into the hole, and then he crawled back onto the bed and pulled his knees up under his chin. He wouldn't let himself think of the man who'd fathered him. He couldn't afford to hope that the man would somehow find out what had happened and come to his rescue. And so he sat, and as time passed, he slumped over onto his side and fell asleep.

But in his dreams, his father came, kicking in doors and dragging him to freedom with guns blazing. When he woke, the room was hot and airless, and his body was covered in sweat. He had no idea how long he'd been sleeping, but the tray of partially eaten food was no longer on the floor. Instead there were a couple of cans at the foot of the bed where he'd been lying.

He shuddered, thinking of them watching him as he slept, and then hunger overcame revulsion as he grabbed the cans — one was a can of peaches, the other a can of Vienna sausages — both opened by a tab-top. He popped the top on the Vienna sausages and then peeled back the lid. The aroma almost made him cry as he thrust two fingers into the can and pulled out the first tiny wiener. In less than a minute he'd emptied the can. A minute or two later, he'd emptied the can of peaches the same way; then he lifted it to his lips and drank what was left of the juice.

Only after he'd finished his makeshift meal did he take a long drink of water. He sat for a moment, wishing he had more, and then picked up the two empty cans and walked over to the corner of the room and dumped the empties into the hole in the floor. It was the first time in his life that he'd "done the dishes," but the irony of it was lost on him.

The same morning: Bel Air, California

Jonah stepped out of the shower and was reaching for a towel when he heard a knock on his door. Wrapping it around himself toga style, he strode through the room, leaving wet footprints behind him as he went. It was Macie, holding a breakfast tray. At that point he realized he should have been wearing more than a towel.

"Uh . . ."

"I brought your breakfast," Macie said, and sailed into the room without waiting for an invitation. She set the tray down on a table, then plopped down in one of the chairs and picked up a piece of toast from his plate and took a big bite. After the cold shoulder he'd given her at dinner last night, she'd made up her mind to change his attitude.

Jonah watched her small white teeth sinking into the bread and glared. She was daring him to react, and he knew it. What angered him most was that his reaction was not one of anger but of lust. He thought about slapping that damned toast out of her hand and taking her there on the floor beside the table. At that point he accepted the fact that his emotions were getting out of hand. Just because he lusted, that did not mean she mattered. She was a beautiful woman, soft in all the right places, and he was in need of a physical release. Nothing more. But then she took another bite, her small pink tongue flicking out to catch an errant crumb lingering on the edge of her lower lip, and he snapped.

Cursing beneath his breath, he dropped the towel where he stood, then turned and walked to the closet to get some clothes. She'd invaded his space. He would be damned if he would let her call the shots.

Macie saw the towel drop and still couldn't believe what he'd done. She swallowed quickly to keep from choking and told herself she should look away, but it was impossible. The sight of all that bare skin and muscle was too intriguing not to view.

She inhaled slowly and then leaned back in the chair, looking at him as she might have a priceless work of art. The tattoo on his back looked lethal and yet oddly beautiful. His legs were long, the muscles well-defined. His shoulders were wide, his hips narrow, and there was a defiance in his stride that she had to admire. He had called her bluff and then some, so she accepted the inevitable. So she would be careful never to play poker with Jonah Slade. So what.

Then he turned around.

Macie's gaze centered on the lower half of his body, just as he'd known it would, so he waited until she lifted her gaze.

"Well?" he drawled.

Macie stood. "The toast needs more butter," she said, then tossed her hair with a lift of her chin and walked out the door without saying another word.

The door shut with a distinct thump. Jonah grinned. She had more guts than he'd given her credit for. She'd not only called his bluff, but she'd ignored the challenge, which was the distinct opposite of what Felicity would have done. He dressed quickly, then downed his food, and as he did, he wondered if he was selling her short by blaming her for her last name.

Macie was standing on the terrace, watching three men clipping the intricate hedge that formed the boundary between the clay-surfaced tennis court and the pathway that led to an Olympic-size pool. It had been years since she'd been here, so she didn't know them by name, and as she watched, it occurred to her that they could even be undercover police.

The thought that her family home had become the scene of a crime seemed absurd, but she only had to walk back in the house to know it was true. Despite the presence of so many federal agents, the place was absent of life. She leaned forward, bracing herself against the waist-high rock wall surrounding the terrace, and dropped her head.

That was the way Jonah found her.

He was still harboring a grudge when he walked out on the terrace, but the moment he saw her, his attitude changed. Staying pissed off at Macie would be like kicking a dying dog. The last thing she needed was another piece of grief. He took a deep breath.

"Ruger said you wanted to go see your father."

Macie jerked and then turned. "I didn't know you were there."

The despair on her face hurt his heart. What hurt even more was that he was responsible for some of it.

"There's something I need to say," Jonah said.

Macie waited.

"This morning I —"

"No. Wait," Macie said, interrupting what he'd been going to say. "I was taunting you. You called my bluff, and rightly so." Then she took a deep breath. What she was about to say went against everything she'd learned from Declyn Blaine, which was to never show your weaknesses. "Chalk it up to the crush I used to have on you. Not only was it a stupid thing to do, but the timing couldn't have been worse. We have to focus all our energies on finding Evan. As for visiting my father, I would never expect you to do that."

Jonah didn't know whether he was glad she'd given him an out, but the subject was obviously changed.

"You're right. I don't want to see the son of a bitch, but you're not going alone."

"Agent Ruger said he'd have a couple of agents accompany me to the hospital."

"Never send a bunch of feds to do what one Company man could do with his eyes closed."

Macie smiled before she thought. "Ah, so that competition I've always heard about really does exist."

"Only in theory," Jonah said, then held out his hand. "Truce?"

Macie didn't hesitate. "Truce," she said softly, and felt the gentleness in his touch as his fingers curled around her wrist.

As they entered the house, Jonah paused momentarily and looked over his shoulder toward the trio of gardeners clipping the hedge. They were too far away for him to see their faces, and he wondered which one was the man calling himself Felipe Sosa, or if they were any closer to finding out where Calderone's people had taken his son. Instead of following his instincts to beat the information out of the man and then nail his sorry hide to the floor, he followed Macie into the house and then escorted her to the hospital to see Declyn Blaine.

A trustee was mopping the floor outside Calderone's cell. Not only could Miguel hear the intermittent slap of the wet mop against concrete, but he could smell the industrial-strength disinfectant. It offended his soul.

He thought of the beauty of his *hacienda* and of the dark-eyed women who had warmed his bed — of the satin sheets and fine wines, and of the laughter of his children. It was lost to him here, but not for long. Miguel Calderone was a man, not an animal to be locked up in some cage. He would get out, but not before everything was set in place. He was going to take great pleasure in watching Jonah Slade's son die. He would cut the heart right out of his chest while it was still beating and take great pride in watching Slade's shock turn to agony and despair. Then he would kill Jonah Slade, too. But not before he'd suffered as he himself was suffering now.

The trustee was closer now. Calderone could hear him humming beneath his breath. He rolled over on his bunk to face the wall and began to breathe from his mouth until the man had passed. Then he heard a word that he had not heard since he'd been taken from his country.

"Padrone."

It was little more than a whisper, but he heard it just the same and immediately rolled to a sitting position on the edge of the bunk. The trustee never looked his way as he swung the wet mop from side to side along the floor, and for a moment Miguel thought he must have imagined what he'd heard. Then the man paused, put the mop head into the bucket and sloshed it up and down. When he pulled the mop out and slapped it back on the floor, it made a loud, wet splat. The guard at the end of the cell block never bothered to look up. It was then that the trustee stepped closer to the cell.

"There is a problem with the boy," the trustee whispered.

Calderone jumped to his feet, certain that he was being set up.

"I don't know what you're talking about," he whispered.

The trustee paused, took a handkerchief from his back pocket, and wiped sweat from his face and then the back of his neck. At that moment Calderone saw the tattooed head of a python just above the trustee's collar. This time, when the trustee spoke, Calderone listened without fear.

"He says his father does not know he exists. He says they would pass on a street and be strangers to each other."

"How can this be?" Calderone asked.

The trustee shrugged and stuffed his handkerchief back into his pocket, then doused the mop head into the bucket again.

"I am sorry, *Padrone*. That I do not know, but they ask for further instructions."

Calderone hesitated, but only for a moment. "Tell them to contact the Snowman. He will know what to do. I want Slade found and taken to the boy. Lock them up together and then wait for me."

The trustee looked up then, for the first time meeting Calderone's gaze. In that moment Calderone recognized a man who'd been a runner in his organization — a man they'd long since thought dead.

"When I go, *Hermano,* I take you with me."

"No, *Padrone,* it is too late for me. I am already dead."

Before he could explain himself, the guard yelled. The man ducked his head and went back to his task.

Suspicious, the guard walked the length of the block, but when he got to Calderone's cell, he saw nothing but the man's back as he lay curled up on the cot, snoring softly. Just because he could, the guard hit the bars with his riot stick, then grinned when Calderone rolled abruptly and fell off the bed.

He was still chuckling to himself as he walked away, unaware that Calderone was smiling, too. He knew something that the guard didn't know, that in the hours to come, he would be the one to have the last laugh.

5

Cedars-Sinai hospital was a massive and imposing structure, sitting on acres of prime land between Wilshire Boulevard and Melrose Avenue. It had been years since Macie had been here, but her memories of it were anything but favorable. Although the finest doctors in the country were on staff, there had been no way to save her mother from the cancer that had invaded her body. The day her mother died was the last day Macie Blaine had ever felt safe.

Until Jonah.

She looked over at the man behind the wheel of the car and knew that it would have been far more difficult to come here had it not been for his presence. And while she understood his reluctance to trust her, it still hurt — more than she would have expected. She sighed and then shifted her gaze to the road before them.

Jonah sensed her scrutiny but chose to ignore it, instead, glancing into the rearview mirror, as he had off and on since leaving the Blaine estate. The two agents Ruger had sent along with them were still there — a vivid reminder that this was anything but a social call. Traffic slowed at the light, and he slowed down with it, angling the car into the turning lane.

"This is a damned big place," Jonah said, as he turned south off Melrose. The edifice of Cedars-Sinai rose above the concrete like a man-made mountain, stretching in every direction over the length of several city blocks.

"It's one of the best medical facilities in the country," Macie said, and then added, "My mother died here."

There weren't many things that touched Jonah anymore, but those four words did it. Her quiet, nearly emotionless remark was more poignant than anything else she could have said. He thought of the skinny little redhead she'd been, with her braces and unruly hair, and wondered how many nights she'd cried herself to sleep.

"I don't think I knew that," he said. "Sorry."

"It was a long time ago."

"How old were you?"

"Eight." Then she pointed toward a sign on their left. "If we park here, it will put us closer to the critical care unit."

Jonah hurt for the child she'd been. Now he knew why she and Felicity had been so close, and what a difficult decision it must have been for her to take his side against her family. He wanted to tell her how much he appreciated what she'd done, but now just didn't seem like the time. Instead he wheeled into the parking lot and began the task of trying to find a place to park. A couple of minutes later, an SUV backed out of a parking place and Jonah took it.

He pulled into the space and started to get out when he realized the car carrying the two agents had stopped directly behind him. One of them got out and approached the driver's side of the car. Jonah rolled down the window.

"What's up?" he asked.

"My partner is parking. Please wait until he joins us. We're taking no chances on another abduction."

Macie shuddered and then glanced nervously around the huge parking lot.

"I never thought of that. What makes them think it would happen again? Is there something they're not telling me?"

"Not that I know of," Jonah said, then added, "Don't worry. If they come after anyone else, it will be me."

He said it with such nonchalance that for a moment Macie couldn't think what to say. Before she could gather her thoughts, the agents were at the car and escorting them toward the building. As they stepped up on a curb, Jonah's hand was suddenly at her elbow, steadying her step. She glanced up.

His eyes were hidden behind sunglasses, but she could see the rest of him, and he looked just fine, in his dark blue slacks and white shirt. She couldn't help thinking that the years had been kind to Jonah Slade. His hair was still thick, dark and bone straight, and he walked with his chin tilted just the tiniest bit upward, as if readying himself for the next blow life might deal. She shuddered slightly, remembering all too well what he looked like beneath his clothes, and wished they'd met again under different circumstances.

"Like what you see?" he asked, and then silently cursed his flippant attitude toward her. He'd already had this conversation with himself. Why in hell couldn't he leave her alone?

Macie flinched. She hadn't meant for him to catch her staring. Then she surprised him as well as herself by answering truthfully.

"Yes, actually, I do, but that's not the point. Were you serious?"

"About what?" he asked, as he hurried her past a sprinkler system.

"Why would they want to take you hostage, too?"

"So I could watch my son die."

Macie stumbled.

Jonah caught her and then glanced down. Her face was colorless, her expression blank.

"Macie?"

She looked up at him, her pupils wide with shock. "God . . . oh, God. I never thought

. . . it didn't occur to me that . . ."

"Let it go," Jonah said.

Macie grabbed his arms, her fingers digging into the muscles beneath his shirt.

"But you might be in danger, and I've dragged you out here in plain sight."

"I'm always in danger, and that's only one of the reasons why I'm so mad at your father for fostering the lie that led me to believe Felicity had aborted our child. Men who live the life I live don't usually have families. It not only makes them vulnerable, but it puts their loved ones in danger of retaliation."

"I'm so sorry," she whispered.

"You have nothing to apologize for," he said sharply. "Now, let's get inside. The agents are waiting."

Macie let herself be hurried into the hospital, but as they entered the lobby, the hair suddenly stood up on the back of her neck. She told herself it was nothing but the sensation of coming out of the heat into air-conditioning, but she was too afraid of what she might see to turn around and look.

Jonah had felt the same thing. Almost immediately, his warning system had gone on alert. As they crossed the lobby, he took Macie by the elbow on thc pretext of courtesy, but what he really wanted was control. If he had to throw her down or grab her and run, he didn't want to be reaching for her when the bullet had already left the gun.

Macie looked up at him again, but he didn't acknowledge the look. He was too busy eyeing the people between them and the elevator.

There was an elderly couple sitting near a large potted plant, and a woman with three young children who looked like she was ready to give them away. There were two teenagers slouching against a wall. One had green-streaked hair and a lot of body tattoos, which made Jonah nervous. The other one's hair was about an inch long and fire-engine red, and he was sporting a considerable number of body piercings. Jonah couldn't tell if they were male or female or one of each, and he wondered what kind of parents let their kids run like that. Almost immediately, the thought brought him up short. He had no business judging anyone for how they raised their kids when he'd left his own without benefit of a father for fifteen years. Even though he hadn't known, he couldn't rid himself of the guilt about Evan.

As they neared the elevators, a young woman suddenly got up from her seat and started across the lobby. Jonah was still eyeing the psychedelic twins when she stood, but when he saw the agent to his left step in front of him with his arm outstretched, he reacted instinctively and put himself between Macie and the girl.

The girl looked up just as the agent appeared in front of her. When he thrust out his arm in a gesture of defense, she let out a cry of alarm and immediately dropped her bag. The contents went everywhere. A lipstick rolled across the floor, while an assortment of papers and tissues went flying.

Macie felt as if she'd been blindsided. One moment they'd been walking toward the elevators, and the next thing she knew she was staring at Jonah's back. Then everyone was talking and apologizing, and the woman was almost in tears.

"What happened?"

Macie turned around and found herself face-to-face with a good-looking man in his early thirties. His smile was friendly, his question innocuous.

"I don't know. Just an accident, I think."

He nodded, eyed her with obvious appreciation, then walked away just as Jonah turned around.

"I'm sorry, Macie, I didn't hear what you said."

"Oh, that's all right. I wasn't talking to you," she said.

"Who *were* you talking to?" he asked.

Macie frowned. "Some man . . . I guess he was just curious about the spectacle we managed to make of ourselves."

Jonah yanked off his sunglasses, quickly scanning the room.

"What man, Macie? I don't see any man?"

"I don't know, Jonah . . . just a man. Now can we please just get to the elevator?"

But Jonah obviously wasn't satisfied with her answer.

"What did he ask you?"

"He asked me what happened. I told him I didn't know. He smiled at me and walked off. You turned around. End of story."

"He smiled at you?"

Macie rolled her eyes. "Yes. And if I had been interested, I'm pretty sure he would have had a lot more to say." Then she added, "It may be hard for you to realize this, but it's not the first time a man's shown interest in me."

Then she shifted her purse to her other shoulder, tilted her chin and strode toward the elevators.

Jonah eyed the sexy sway of her hips beneath her pale pink slacks and sighed.

"I'm out of here, boys," he said to the agents, then had to hurry to catch Macie before she got on the elevator alone.

The two agents finished picking up the woman's belongings, apologized again and quickly followed.

The woman clutched her bag closely to her chest, watching until the doors went shut; then she walked out of the lobby. She went down the walk, dodging the sprinklers and admiring the view as she headed for the parking lot. A few moments later a bright red sports car pulled up beside her. She opened the door and slid in. The man behind the wheel was smiling as he leaned over and kissed her square on the lips.

"Smile, Gloria, we're out of the woods."

Gloria James glared at her husband, Donny, her lower lip jutting angrily as she reached for her seat belt.

"We never would have *been* in the woods if it wasn't for your little 'habit.' Did you plant the bug like he told you?"

Donny's smile slipped. He didn't like to be reminded that his penchant for "nose candy" had put them on the edge of bankruptcy, and he especially didn't like to be reminded that his dealer had been going to kill him. The fact that he'd been forced to beg Dominic Cosa for his life still made him weak in the knees, but that was all behind them now. Dominic had given Donny a picture of a woman and told him that if he would plant a bug in her purse, they would be even. It had taken two days of sitting in that damned hospital lobby before the woman had made an appearance, but their diligence had finally paid off. Now they were even with the world.

"Sure, baby . . . it's all over." He put the car in gear and headed for the street. "What do you say to a fresh start? We could move within the week. Where would you like to go?"

Gloria's glare deepened. "With you? Nowhere."

"Now, baby, that's no way to be. I told you. Once I let Dominic know the job is done, we're square with the world."

"I don't trust him, and I don't trust you," she said. "Just take me home. I need to think."

"What? Are you talking about divorcing me?" he asked.

"Yes."

This wasn't what he'd expected to hear her say, but the longer he thought about it, the more he liked the idea. This was just what he needed. A true fresh start. No one to answer to but himself. Just like the good old days.

A short while later, they pulled into their driveway. Gloria looked over her shoulder at the green Jag parked in the street in front of their house.

"There's a strange car parked in front of our house, but no one's in it."

"It's Dominic's."

Gloria James got out of the car, still staring at her husband in disbelief.

"He's in our house? That motherfucking drug dealer is in our house?"

Donny felt a little nervous about the fact himself, but he wasn't going to let her know. It was all about losing face, and he'd lost all he was ever going to lose in this deal.

"Why don't you tell the whole neighborhood, Gloria?" he drawled, and then headed for the house without looking to see if she was following.

Dominic Cosa was sitting in Donny's favorite chair, drinking a wine cooler from their own refrigerator, when Donny walked in the door. It pissed him off, but considering the muscle Dominic had brought with him, he was in no position to say so. Instead he took the positive approach and greeted Dominic with a wide grin.

"It's done," he said, and then brushed his hands together as if dusting them off. "Took a couple of days for her to show, but it was a piece of cake."

Dominic set the wine cooler down on the table as he got up, straightening the tail of his sports coat and smoothing down his hair with the palms of both hands as he stood.

"You are sure it was Mercedes Blaine?"

"Yeah, sure I'm sure. She looked just like the woman in the picture, and she had escorts, just like you said she would."

"How many?"

"Three. Feds, I guess. Two suits and a tough-looking guy who was probably a bodyguard. I didn't stop to get introductions."

"Where is your lovely wife?" Dominic asked.

"Outside."

"Is she coming in?"

Before Donny James could answer, they heard the sound of a car engine starting, then, a few moments later, the sound of tires squealing against pavement. He sighed.

"Doesn't look like it," Donny said.

"Pity," Dominic said, and then shrugged. "Ah, well. All in due time." He picked up his wine cooler and then headed for the door.

"We're even now, right?" Donny asked.

Dominic paused and then turned. He looked at Donny James with something close to disdain, then nodded.

"Almost," he said, then looked at the bodyguard who'd come with him.

Donny's voice rose to a squeak of disbelief. "Almost? What do you mean, 'almost'?"

Then he saw the look that passed between Dominic and his man, and knew that his fresh start was over before it had begun.

The muscle pulled a gun from beneath his jacket and calmly attached a silencer to the barrel while Donny began to cry.

"Dominic . . . please! Don't do this! You told me this would square us up. You don't have to kill me. I'll get the money to you somehow. Just give me a little time."

Dominic Cosa lifted the wine cooler to his lips and downed the last drops, then blotted his mouth with his handkerchief before answering.

"Begging does not become you," he said.

Donny went to his knees — not because he thought prayer would help him, but because he was too scared to stand. "Dominic . . .

please. You promised."

Dominic Cosa smiled and then started to laugh.

"That just shows how stupid you are, Donny James. You can never trust a drug dealer. I lied."

There was a popping sound, not much louder than the sound of a cork popping from a good bottle of champagne, and then it was over. Donny James was lying on his back with a bullet hole in the middle of his forehead. Most of the back of his head was now missing, but it no longer mattered. Donny wouldn't be needing it anymore.

Dominic walked out of the house with his driver beside him. He paused at the side of the house, lifted the lid to Donny's trash can and laid the empty wine cooler bottle on top of several others inside the bag. He wasn't addicted to the drugs he pedaled, but there were other things that kept him high, one of which was playing games with cops. It gave him a buzz to think of the DNA and fingerprints he was leaving behind, knowing full well that the police would never think that one more empty bottle was more important than all the others inside the trash bin. He shifted the contents slightly so that the bottle was no longer on top, then smiled as he closed the lid.

"It's good to keep things tidy, isn't it, Joey?"

"Yes, boss, but what about the woman?"

Dominic squinted thoughtfully. "I think if she's smart enough to get the hell out of that punk's life, then she's smart enough to keep her mouth shut. What do you think?"

"I think you're the boss, that's what I think," the man said.

Dominic's smile widened as he patted the behemoth's arm. "That's what I like to hear. There's a lot more between your ears than muscle, my man."

As they reached the car, Dominic paused, staring up and down the street, but he saw nothing and no one that put him on the alert. He smoothed the palms of his hands on either side of his hair and then straightened the front of his jacket.

"Let's get out of here, Joey. Our work here is done."

Moments later, they were gone.

After several phone calls back home without an answer, Gloria, who was no fool, feared the worst. And since she would automatically be the number one suspect in the killing of her husband, she went straight to the police and told them everything.

Jonah was sitting beside the pool, watching Macie slice through the crystal clear water with vicious strokes. She'd been like this ever since they'd left Cedars-Sinai. He didn't know what had transpired between her and her father, and truth was, he didn't care. What he did know was that Declyn Blaine had recovered consciousness, taken a turn for the better, with a good chance of a complete recovery.

There was a part of him that wished the old bastard had died. Felicity was dead, and while he didn't want to think about it, Evan might be, as well. Logically he accepted the fact that it was Miguel Calderone who had given the order to destroy Jonah's life, but he couldn't see the justice in Declyn being the only person to survive, when it was his lie that had put everyone else in danger.

However, he'd kept those thoughts to himself and waited for Macie to comment on her father's recovery. Instead she'd come out of the critical care unit as if she were being chased. He'd started to ask her what was wrong, but the expression on her face was enough to make him keep his questions to himself. He didn't know what had gone on inside that room, but he was guessing it hadn't been good.

So now he sat in the midst of opulence and luxury, watching a leggy redhead working out her frustrations in the water, and tried not to think of more interesting ways in which they could pass the time. The minuscule two-piece swimsuit she was wearing left little to his imagination, which was already in high gear. He watched her reach the end of the pool, then turn and kick off as ably as an Olympic swimmer, and thought about joining her. He thought about swimming alongside her and wondered if the anger in her strokes would heat the water as quickly as it heated his blood. He thought about pulling her out of the water and letting her work out her frustrations on him — in his bed. Even if she was a Blaine.

Instead he sat without moving, watching without talking, studying the woman she'd become, and knew the world as he'd known it was unraveling. Being forced to sit on the sidelines while others solved his problems rankled.

He didn't know Macie had stopped swimming until he saw her coming toward him. Her body was as sleek as the Thoroughbred she was, and lust hit him like a fist to the gut. He needed to move, but he couldn't — or wouldn't. A part of him wanted the confrontation he felt coming. Then she was standing in front of him — so close that the water on her body was dripping onto his legs.

"Don't you want to know what he said?" Macie asked.

Jonah took a slow breath and then stood, willing himself to look only at her face. He could smell the chlorine from the pool on her hair and body. He looked straight into her eyes and saw his reflection. Without thinking, he reached for her.

"He told me I wasn't welcome here," she said. "He told me to go home." Then she grabbed a beach towel from the back of a chair and began toweling herself off with vicious swipes. "He knows Felicity is dead." Then she turned away, and as she did, her shoulders slumped in defeat. "He told me to get out of his house."

Jonah sighed. So much for keeping his hands off her body, but after what she'd just said, he couldn't go where he wanted to go.

"Come here," he said softly, then wrapped his arms around her and pulled her close against him. The water from her body soaked the front of his shirt and pants, but it didn't matter. Nothing mattered but holding Macie.

She leaned against him, taking strength from the tenderness in his touch.

"He can't make you leave."

"I know, but it still hurt to hear it said."

"He's a bastard, and don't expect me to apologize for saying that," Jonah muttered.

Macie managed a small chuckle. "No apology expected." Then she turned in his arms until they were facing. "I'm getting you all wet."

"I can think of worse things," he said gruffly.

Macie looked up, her gaze lingering on his mouth longer than what would be considered polite.

"Jonah, I —"

Before she could continue, Ruger strode out of the house and onto the terrace.

"There you are," he said. "I've been looking for you two. We've got a problem."

Macie turned abruptly. "What? Have you heard from the kidnappers? Is it about Evan?"

"No. It's about you," Ruger said, then looked at Jonah. "Tell me exactly what happened at the hospital today."

For a moment Jonah went blank; then it hit him.

"It was that thing in the lobby, wasn't it? I knew something was hinky with that."

"What thing in the lobby?" Macie asked.

"Miss Blaine, I need to see the contents of your purse."

"But I —"

Jonah took her by the elbow and hurried her into the house.

"Don't argue, Macie, just hurry."

The anxiety in Jonah's voice hastened her steps. By the time they reached the second floor, she was running. Her purse was on the floor, near her chair and reading lamp. She picked it up and quickly dumped the contents onto the bed.

Ruger began sorting through the items one at a time.

"What are you . . . ?"

Jonah put his hand over Macie's mouth

and quietly shook his head, then leaned down and whispered against her ear.

"Don't ask, just follow my lead."

Macie's heart was hammering against her chest as she nodded.

"What time will Rosa be serving dinner?" Jonah asked.

Macie clasped her hands against her belly, staring at the federal agent as he began taking apart everything in her purse.

"Miss Blaine?"

Jonah's hand slid beneath the heavy weight of her wet hair and gently squeezed her neck. She tore her gaze away from Ruger and looked up.

"I'm sorry . . . what did you say?"

"I asked what time Rosa will be serving dinner."

"Oh. Right. Seven o'clock, unless you'd like me to have her hold it. If you're not ready, I can give her a call."

"No, that will be fine with me. I'll notify the others and meet you downstairs."

"Yes . . . all right," Macie said, and wondered why they were playing this game.

Jonah made a big deal out of opening and then closing the door. To anyone who might be listening, they would now think Macie Blaine was alone.

Immediately he went to the bed and began helping Ruger sort through the remaining items. Macie stood to one side, watching in disbelief. Moments later Jonah picked up a ballpoint pen and started to unscrew it. Before he could take it apart, Macie grabbed his arm and shook her head, mouthing the words, "It's not mine."

Jonah looked at Ruger, who hesitated, then nodded. Carefully, Jonah unscrewed the pen and started to pull it apart. The tiny listening device that fell out onto the bedspread was smaller than a pencil eraser.

Macie's lips parted, then went slack.

Jonah watched the color fade from her face and knew she was going to be sick. She beat him to the bathroom by seconds. He held her while she threw up, then wiped her face with a wet cloth. When they came out of the bathroom, Ruger was gone.

"What's happening?" Macie whispered.

"Someone bugged you. Probably the man who came up behind you in the lobby."

"My God," Macie said, and dropped onto the side of the bed. "Why me? What do I have to do with this?"

"Probably nothing, but knowing Calderone like I do, he's just covering all the bases."

At that point Ruger came back into the room.

"How did you know about the bug?" Jonah asked.

Ruger glanced at Macie, as if deciding how much he was going to say. Macie caught the look and frowned.

"I have a right to know what's going on," she said. "Granted, I have no experience in this kind of terrorism, and I've been scared and sick to my stomach every day since this mess started, but I'm tougher than I look. So spit it out. Who bugged me and why?"

Ruger looked at Jonah.

"Tell her," Jonah said.

"Okay, but we don't know much. What we do know is the guy who put the bug in your purse was named Donny James. According to his wife, who was the woman who dropped her purse to create the diversion, he owed a lot of money to a drug dealer. The story was that if he did this little job, the dealer would wipe out Donny's debt. Donny's wife didn't have a lot of choice in the matter but went along with it just the same. However, when they got home, she says the dealer's car was parked in front of their house. She panicked and left the premises, then later tried to call their house. Trouble was, Donny didn't answer. Fearing the worst, she went to the police, knowing that if Donny turned up dead and she went missing, she would be the first one to blame. She's also in fear for her own life, since she knows about the deal that was made between Donny and his dealer."

"Damn," Jonah muttered. "But what does this have to do with Macie? Why would some L.A. drug dealer want to bug her . . . unless . . . Ruger, what's the dealer's name?"

"Dominic Cosa."

Jonah flinched. "A tall, skinny Latino with a bad complexion . . . always smoothing down his hair with his hands?"

"I don't know about the hair bit, but according to his rap sheet, he's six feet, two inches, and one eighty, with a pockmarked complexion."

Jonah slapped the bedpost with the flat of his hand and then cursed.

"What?" Ruger asked.

"His mother and Calderone's mother are sisters."

"You know that for a fact?" Ruger asked.

"I ate with the man. I watched him get drunk with Calderone. I saw him walk away from Calderone's party with a young prostitute and later come back alone. One of the shepherds on the Calderone estate found her body the next morning. He's bad news, and he'd do anything Calderone asked."

"What are we going to do?" Macie asked.

"Pretend we don't know about the pen. It was a stupid move on Calderone's part. Women change purses all the time, and pens quit writing. When they don't get anything further on their wire, they'll figure it out for themselves."

Before Macie could comment further, the telephone rang. She thought about just letting it ring, but there was always the chance the kidnappers would call.

"Hello?"

"May I speak to Mercedes Blaine?"

"This is she."

"Miss Blaine, this is the Deloach Crematorium. Your sister's ashes are ready to pick up."

"Yes, all right," Macie said. "But I can't do it today."

"That's fine. Just come by at your convenience. Someone will be here to help you. And may I say again, we are so sorry for your loss."

Macie's stomach was in knots. She needed him to stop talking now. This was more than she could take.

"Thank you," she said, and hung up the phone.

"Who was that?" Jonah asked.

Macie turned around. She had picked up the beach towel that she'd carried upstairs with her and was clutching it against her belly, as if to keep her from coming apart. Water was still dripping from her hair and onto the carpet.

"The crematorium. Felicity's ashes are ready to be picked up." She took a deep breath, willing herself to stay steady. "I would appreciate it if you two would leave now."

Ruger eyed Jonah and then was gone, but Jonah hesitated.

"Are you sure you don't want me to —"

"Get out," Macie said, but when he didn't

move, her voice rose. “For God’s sake, Jonah, what do you want? Do you want to see me beg? I need to be alone.”

“No, that’s not what you need,” he said. “But I’m leaving just the same.”

He left, quietly shutting the door behind him, and the moment hc was gone, Macie knew he was right. She didn’t want to be alone. She wanted Jonah. But that wasn’t going to happen. Ever.

6

The wheel inside the hamster cage was spinning wildly as Arnold, the fat, brown and white rodent, ran and ran on his way to nowhere.

It was an odd pet for a man who traveled like the Snowman traveled, but as a child, he'd always wanted one, although his parents had refused. Even though he was nearing forty-seven, he took perverse pleasure in the fact that he could now do what he damn well pleased.

The home where Arnold, the hamster, resided bordered on understated elegance, although his cage was fairly mundane. The interior decorator had been leaning toward a Mediterranean influence with both furniture and accessories, and he'd almost made it, but for the garish piece of sculpture in the foyer that the Snowman had insisted on displaying. It was a replica of a huge gargoyle with bulging eyes, gaping nostrils and fangs for teeth. The designer had been appalled by the request and begged him to desist, but the Snowman had been adamant, claiming it represented good luck, that it would protect him and his home from evil spirits, so the piece of statuary had stayed.

The irony of it was that, as the Snowman well knew, his own evil was far worse than any imagined spirit that might exist. When the phone beside the hamster cage began to ring, it startled the hamster to the point that it fell off the wheel. Distracted by the sudden change of scenery, it scurried to the feed bowl and began to eat, while, outside, its owner was busy climbing out of his pool to answer the call.

Water dripped from his finely honed body as he crossed the terrace to the wet bar. A towel was lying on the bar, and he picked it up first, briefly drying his face and hands before answering the call.

"Yes?"

"Snowman . . ."

The man tensed.

"Yes?"

"You have a package on your front step."

He hung up the phone without saying another word, slipped into a pair of espadrilles so as not to leave wet footprints on the floor and strode through the house. As promised, there was a large packet on the step. He picked it up and then went back into the house, quickly shutting the door before the woman across the street had time to wave hello.

He opened the packet as he walked. There were two pictures and a small, hand-printed note inside.

Find Jonah Slade but do not alert him. Instead, call this number for further instructions.

He laid the note aside and then picked up the pictures. One was of a bearded man with his hair pulled back in a ponytail. In the picture he was standing beneath a banana tree holding an assault rifle. The other was of the same man, but the long hair and beard were gone, and he was wearing a suit. Had he not known it was the same man, it would have been difficult to believe.

He studied the pictures for a few seconds, then laid them on top of the note and picked up a box of hamster food before going to the cage. He poked his finger through the tiny bars, smiling as the hamster nibbled at his fingers.

"Hey, Arnold, how's my little buddy? You smell supper, don't you, guy?" He opened the cage, took out the feeding dish and filled it up, then refilled the water, as well. "Looks like you're going next door to stay with Jennifer again. You like that, don't you, guy?"

The Snowman had never intended to be someone who killed men for money, but along the way, the occasional marijuana cigarette had turned into a need for something stronger and harder. With that addiction had come problems that he couldn't control. He'd made friends in all the wrong places and owed favors to people who could ruin his world. Rather than admit to himself he was in so far over his head that he'd already drowned, he'd chosen to bend laws, which had then evolved into out and out breaking them. By the time he killed his first man, he was immune to the guilt and dwelled only on the relief he felt, knowing that, once again, he was the one in charge and the people he owed were, for the time being, off of his back. Added to that was the growing numbered Swiss bank account held by a dual identity that was also his.

Given his true nature, it made no sense that his fondness for the hamster was real, but it was. When he had to go away, which was often, he paid his neighbor's ten-year-old girl to care for Arnold. It was an amiable arrangement, even though he was getting tired of the chase.

Reluctantly he shut the door to the cage, made a call to his neighbor for Jennifer to come get his pet, and then went to change clothes.

The next morning

Evan moaned in his sleep, fighting against an unexpected pressure on his shoulder.

"Boy. Wake up. You wake up now!"

Startled by the sound of a voice, he sat up and then scooted back against the wall, putting himself as far away from his captor's reach as possible.

The guard shoved a tray of food in Evan's lap, then pointed.

"You eat now."

The scent of warm tortillas and beans made Evan's stomach ache and his mouth water, but eating their food wasn't something he was willing to do. He had no control over what was happening to him except for this.

"You eat it," he said, and shoved the tray away.

The guard frowned. The boy had been in captivity for three days now, and except for a couple of small cans of food they'd given him earlier, he had yet to eat. He kept the water they gave him, but little else. But the guard had his orders. Keep the boy alive and healthy. He didn't want to think about what would happen to him if something happened to the boy before the *padrone* gave the word. Frustrated, he shoved his gun in Evan's face.

Evan was so light-headed and weak from lack of food that he'd gotten past the point of fear. His only weapon against them was not eating. They wanted him to eat. But they were going to kill him? To hell with them all.

"So shoot me," he muttered, and leaned forward until the barrel of the gun was resting against his forehead.

Suddenly frightened that the gun might go off, the guard yanked the gun back and slapped Evan instead.

Evan's head snapped backward, thumping

sharply against the wall. The coppery taste of fresh blood was in his mouth, and he could feel a sharp pain where his tooth had cut the inside of his lip. Without saying a word, he leaned over the side of the bed and spat. A splatter of blood and sputum landed near the guard's shoe. He resented the hell out of the man for bringing tears to his eyes, but he wouldn't let them see his fear — not anymore.

"You can beat me. You can shoot me. You can do whatever the hell you choose, but you can't make me eat. You doped the food, you son of a bitch, and I will not make myself any more vulnerable to you than I already am. Understand?"

The guard set the tray down on the floor with a thump and stomped out of the room. The walls vibrated from the impact as the door slammed shut. Evan staggered to his feet, took the bottle of water from the tray, then carried the remaining contents to the hole in the floor. With one last lingering sniff, he dumped the food into the hole. At least the rat is getting fat, he thought, then moved back to the bed and crawled in, wincing as his hands took too much of his weight.

Three of his fingers were horribly swollen. He knew they'd gotten infected from the splinters beneath his nails, because they were seeping a thick, bloody pus. All he could do was pour a little water on them from time to time and then ignore the pain. Moments later he rolled over, curling up into a fetal position and willing the pain to a deeper part of his consciousness.

He could hear metal panels of the roof popping in another part of the building and knew the wind must be rising. He thought of all the carefree days he'd spent in the sun and surf, vaguely aware that this kind of evil was in the world but never imagining that it would invade and destroy his life, and wished to God he could turn back time. He would never take life for granted again.

Somewhere in the distance he heard the sound of an approaching car engine. Someone was coming. He stood with his ear to the door, listening until he heard voices. They were faint, but close enough that he could just make out the words.

"What do you mean, he isn't eating?" the man asked.

"Just what I say," the guard answered.

"Why not?"

"At first we drugged the food. It was only to keep him sleeping. But somehow he knew. Now he won't eat."

The man laughed. "So he's smarter than you. What else is new, buddy?"

Evan gritted his teeth. He recognized the guard's voice, but not the other one, although he would swear the man was an American.

He wasn't speaking Spanish, and he didn't have an accent.

"Why did you come?" the guard asked.

"You tell the *padrone* that I'm on the job."

"Yes. I will tell him."

"Good man," the stranger said. "Oh, and, buddy? Don't take any wooden nickels."

"What?"

The man laughed. "It's just an American saying."

A few moments later, Evan heard the sound of a car engine starting, then driving away. He tracked the sound as it disappeared into the distance and decided that he must be in an isolated place. Not once since they'd brought him here had he heard traffic or sirens or anything that would lead him to believe they were anywhere close to civilization.

He pushed himself away from the door and crawled back onto the bed. When he finally closed his eyes, the tears he'd been holding back welled and spilled out from under his lashes. He needed a miracle.

Finally he slept in the small, airless room and dreamed that he was home.

Dominic Cosa had made a mistake. He'd underestimated Donny James's wife. Not only had she gone to the police, but she'd fingered him. He could get rid of her now, and he was tempted. But it would not undo the damage that had already been done. His lawyer had assured him that what the police had was purely circumstantial. The woman had assumed the car was Dominic's, but she hadn't seen the tag. She had not seen Cosa inside her house. She had not seen him come out, nor had she heard the gunshot that had killed him.

But there was plenty of evidence that Donny had been a user and his wife had been present when Dominic had ordered Donny to plant the bug on Macie Blaine. In accordance with his lawyer's wishes, he was lying low, not taking phone calls, not making phone calls. Truth was, he was more afraid of his cousin Miguel's anger than of going to jail, and that was why he was packing, and why he had a chartered plane waiting at LAX. Miguel Calderone did not suffer fools, and what Dominic had done was not only foolish but careless.

"Joey!" Dominic yelled.

Moments later, Dominic's bodyguard appeared in the doorway.

"Carry these bags downstairs. I'm ready to leave for the airport."

But Joey didn't move.

"What's wrong with you?" Dominic asked.

"I'm real sorry, boss, but you ain't goin' nowhere," Joey said, and pulled a gun from the holster beneath his jacket.

Dominic was stunned. "What the hell are you saying?"

"I can't let you go, boss. I got my orders."

Dominic felt the floor tilting beneath him. This couldn't be happening. Not to him. Miguel wouldn't do this. Would he? They were family.

"You got orders? Bullshit! Miguel would never do this to me. Who told you to do this?" he yelled.

"You know who, boss. We all take orders from the *padrone*."

"I don't believe you," Dominic said. "Miguel would not kill his own blood kin."

Joey shrugged. "I don't know nothin' about that. All I know is I got my orders."

Despite what he'd told Joey earlier, the man was big and dumb and single-minded. He could do only one thing at a time, which was why he made a good stooge. Give him an order, and he latched on to the words like a bulldog with a bone. If someone had told Joey to take him out, then it was over. At that point, Dominic panicked.

"Listen to me, Joey. For once in your life, just think. Someone is tricking you. Miguel is in a Federal prison. There is no way he could still be giving orders when he's behind bars."

"Sorry, boss, but you know that's not true. It's plenty easy to run the business from inside. It's done all the time."

Dominic's underarms started to sweat. To his shame, he heard himself beg.

"Don't do this, Joey. I got money. Lots of money. Let me go. Just let me go."

Joey took the silencer out of his pocket, just as he'd done at Donny James's house, and screwed it onto the end of the barrel with quiet precision.

"There ain't enough money to hide me from the *padrone,* and you know it, boss. . . ."

Dominic couldn't believe this was happening. Not to him. He took a step forward, his hands outstretched.

"Come on, Joey. You know me. How many years we been together, huh? You can't do this. Not to me. You know you can't."

Joey pointed the gun. "Just stand still, boss. I'm real good. Trust me, you won't feel a thing."

Dominic thought of all the things he'd planned to do in life and still hadn't done. Somewhere along the way he'd meant to get married. His *madre* wanted grandchildren. He'd kept putting her off, telling her someday it would happen, but his someday was never going to come, and all because he'd misjudged a woman.

He took a deep breath and then sighed. His Eden was coming to an end. Dominic Cosa's paradise was over because he'd made an error in judgment. He'd expected that a weak man like Donny James would be married to a woman who was just as vulnerable, but he'd been wrong — so wrong. Joey was right. He'd made the mistake, and in this business, mistakes got you killed.

Suddenly a calm came over him — an acceptance of the inevitable. He straightened his jacket and then palmed his hair with both hands before holding his arms out to his sides.

"Okay, Joey. Do it right, and no hard feelings."

Joey smiled. "Thanks, boss. I knew you would understand."

The sound of Dominic's skull exploding from the back made more noise than the shot itself, but Joey had been right. Dominic Cosa never felt a thing. He was dead before the bullet that passed through his body hit the wall behind him.

Joey unscrewed the silencer, dropped it back in his pocket, holstered his gun and walked out of the house without looking back. He didn't feel anything — not even remorse. It was, after all, only business.

It was nearly three in the morning, and Jonah still hadn't slept. The knot in his gut was tightening. Hour by hour, the helplessness of the situation was making him crazy. Miguel Calderone was in a Federal penitentiary, locked behind a mountain of concrete, iron and steel, and yet his presence was as real as if he were here in the room with him. He got up from the bed and began pacing the floor. He should have killed him. He'd witnessed the atrocities that he'd committed. When the choppers arrived and the fire fight started, he should have killed him then. God knows he'd thought about it. It would have been so easy. Bullets were flying, men were dying. All he would have had to do was —

The scream came without warning, almost stopping his heart. He bolted for the door and out into the hall. One of Ruger's men was already halfway up the stairs.

"What the hell was that?" the agent asked.

"I think it came from Macie's room," Jonah said.

The agent pulled his gun and followed Jonah across the hall. Just as Jonah got to the door, he heard a moan and then what sounded like a muffled sob. He opened the door and then stepped inside. There was a night-light on in the bathroom. It shed enough light for the men to see that Macie was obviously in the throes of a nightmare. She was rolled up in her covers and curled into a fetal position. Even in the dim light, Jonah could see her trembling.

"I've got this," he whispered.

The agent nodded, holstered his gun and went back downstairs, leaving Jonah alone with Macie. Jonah closed the door, then moved to the side of her bed. He switched on the lamp and patted her shoulder.

"Macie . . . honey . . . wake up. You're

having a bad dream."

The unexpected voice, along with the pressure of a hand on her shoulder, woke Macie instantly. Blinded by the light, she tried to sit up but was too wound up in the covers to move. When she realized it was Jonah, she sank back against her pillows in shock.

"What's happened? What are you doing here?"

"You screamed."

"Oh, Lord," she mumbled, and swiped her hands through her hair, roughly combing it away from her face. Her voice quavered, then broke, as she started to talk.

"I was dreaming about Felicity. They were putting her into the crematorium, but she was still alive. I kept telling them to stop, but no one would listen."

Jonah sat down beside her, then, without asking, scooped her into his lap. When she tucked her head beneath his chin and pulled his arms around her as she might have a blanket, he sighed. God. She felt so damned good in his arms.

"It was only a dream, Macie. You know it wasn't true."

She nodded, but she couldn't help but add, "It just seemed so real."

"Yeah, dreams can play with our fears in a way nothing else can." Then he leaned his cheek against the top of her head and closed his eyes. Her hair was like satin against his cheek, and she smelled sweet — so sweet.

Macie sighed, taking comfort in Jonah's presence and willing her mind to a better place than where it had been.

Several minutes passed without either one of them speaking. Jonah thought she'd fallen back to sleep and was just at the point of laying her down when she spoke.

"I didn't eat dinner, did you?"

Jonah grinned. "Yes. When you didn't come down to eat, Rosa seemed pretty ticked off. I was afraid to tell her no."

Macie leaned back and looked up at Jonah's face. "I'm sorry," she said.

"For what?"

"For having that fit. I was just so upset about what Declyn had said to me, and I took it out on you. I'm sorry . . . really sorry."

"Apology accepted," Jonah said. "Now, about the dinner you didn't eat. I'm guessing you're hungry."

She nodded.

"Is it permissible to raid the kitchen?"

"It never used to be," she muttered.

"So what are we waiting for?" he asked.

Macie stared at him, silently mapping that face for the time when he would no longer be in her life.

"You," she said softly. "I was waiting for you."

The words hit him like a fist to the belly,

and it was one of the few times in Jonah Slade's life when he was at a loss for words. He was afraid to read something deeper into her statement, but before he could think what to say, Macie wiggled her way out of his lap and grabbed a sheer blue robe from the back of a chair.

"So, are you coming with me?" she asked, as she headed for the door.

Jonah stood, and in that moment, he knew that if things had been different, he would have followed her to the ends of the earth.

"Yeah, I'm coming," he said, and swallowed past an odd lump in his throat.

Macie strode toward the stairs, her floor-length robe billowing out behind her as she walked. Her hunger had suddenly dissipated, but she would never have admitted it. The little deceit was nothing if it meant she was going to spend a quiet hour in the middle of the night with the only man she'd ever loved. Then she snorted beneath her breath at the drama of her thoughts. What she'd felt for Jonah had been a childish crush. What was happening to her now was completely different. Before, she'd dreamed of gentle touches, soft smiles and tender kisses. Her limited experience with boys had never let her imagination past that point. But now she knew him as a man. She'd seen him naked. She'd seen the power in his body, and she was no longer an innocent child. She'd known the overwhelming surge of sexual climax, and thinking of him naked between her legs, his body hard, his skin slick with sweat as he rocked against her, made her weak at the knees. There was where her true hunger lay, but tonight it would not be fed. She was going to have to settle for a sandwich instead.

And while they were digging into Rosa's leftovers, the Snowman was letting himself into Jonah's apartment.

The Snowman was tired. Flying back and forth from coast to coast got old, especially when you were catching the red-eye, but a job was a job. He picked the lock on Jonah Slade's apartment, then let himself inside and was halfway across the foyer and heading for the living room when something rattled off to his right. He pulled his gun and froze, half expecting to see Slade himself. He slowed his breathing and waited. As he stood in the darkness, he heard another, less distinct, sound and frowned. He knew that sound. He'd heard it . . .

He grinned. He'd just pulled a gun on the ice maker dumping ice in Jonah Slade's refrigerator.

Jumpy bastard.

Quietly he checked the kitchen. As expected, it was empty. He moved down the small hallway, noting the two doors opposite each other and stopped. He took a step to the right and cocked his head toward the door, listening for any sounds of occupancy, but heard nothing. Gripping the gun a little harder, he leaned against the door and turned the knob. It swung inward on silent hinges to reveal a Spartan bedroom partially lit by a night-light beside the bed. The bedclothes had not been disturbed, although there was an imprint on the spread, as if something had been set there after the bed had been made. The closet door was closed, and from where he was standing, he could see the towels neatly folded on the rack in the adjoining bathroom.

It was obvious Slade was not here.

He stepped back into the hall and opened the other door. Slade had made an office out of the second bedroom. There were two computers, a fax and a copy machine, as well as a couple of printers. File cabinets lined one wall. He tugged on one of the drawers. It was locked, as were all the others.

Now where did he go from here?

The longer he stood there, the more certain he became that he knew where Jonah Slade was. What had happened to the Blaines was all over the news. It seemed plausible that someone had contacted him about his son's kidnapping. Slade might not have known about the boy before, but he surely did now.

The Snowman smiled. "If it was *my* son, I know where I'd go."

7

Jonah stood at his bedroom window, staring down at the grounds below and watching two of several groundsmen on riding lawn mowers, who were in the process of keeping the lawns of the Blaine estate neatly mowed. Another gardener was on his hands and knees in a bed of flowers, carefully weeding, while yet another wielded a pair of hedge clippers. Jonah leaned closer to the glass, wondering which one was the man masquerading as Felipe Sosa, and what Ruger and his men had found out about him and his habits. He'd asked more than once, but Ruger had consistently hedged his answers.

Jonah frowned as he shoved his hands in his pockets. Last night had been hell, and the longer he stayed here with Macie, the worse it was going to be when he left. He hated to admit it, but she'd gotten under his skin. Her beauty, coupled with her vulnerability, made him feel things he hadn't felt in years. As for his son, he wouldn't even let himself think of what Evan must be enduring. He couldn't. Not and remain objective about what had to be done.

He watched as the gardener with the hedge

clippers paused, then took off his wide-brimmed straw hat and mopped his brow with the back of his shirt sleeve. As he did, Jonah realized it was the man from the video — the man who was calling himself Felipe Sosa. The fact that he was still on the premises was proof of how omnipotent Calderone considered himself to be. Control was everything to the man, and he was willing to sacrifice anyone to maintain it. If the impostor knew how expendable he was to the cartel, he would most likely have disappeared at the same time the kidnapping had occurred. It remained to be seen what his part in the attack had been, but Jonah would bet his life it was prime. For that reason alone, he could easily have killed him without a second of concern. But that wouldn't help find Evan.

However, Jonah held a trump card.

Himself.

He was willing to give Ruger another forty-eight hours, and then he was going to take matters into his own hands. Jonah knew how to blend into the underworld. He'd done it countless times before. With the right word to the wrong people, he could let himself be found, and if his theories were correct, he would be taken directly to Evan. The problem would be in getting them both out alive.

A knock at his door broke his concentration. He called out as he turned.

"Come in."

It was Macie. She was quiet and pale, her expression blank. Her black, ankle-length, short-sleeved dress was of a sheer, gauzelike fabric, revealing a darker slip dress beneath. She'd left her hair down, framing her face in a veil that was the color of new copper. Her shoes were nothing but a few strips of black leather fastened to a nearly flat sole. The only color she'd added to the ensemble was a thin wash of bronze lipstick.

"You look beautiful," Jonah said. "What have you been doing?"

"I've been on the phone to Chicago, trying to iron out some problems at the company. It isn't easy to do it long distance, but for now it's okay."

"What do you do?" Jonah asked.

"I own an import business. It's time-consuming but lucrative."

Jonah looked at her with new respect.

"I don't think I knew that," he said. "Good for you."

She shrugged. "I'm ready to go."

Jonah was so struck by her appearance that it took him a few moments to answer. Then he remembered. The crematorium. Today was the day she was going to pick up Felicity's ashes.

Hell. Well, there was no other way but to get this over with. He walked toward her. When he stopped, he was close enough to hear the soft inhalation and exhalation of her breath. She smelled of gardenias, and despite her carefully applied makeup, he could tell she'd been crying.

Despite his better judgment, he brushed the backs of his fingers against her cheek, then sighed. Soft. So soft. When he bent down and kissed the side of her face, he heard a quiet, almost indistinguishable sob. He wanted to say something that would alleviate her pain, but there was nothing to be said other than the mundane things that must come.

"Ruger is sending a couple of men with us."

She nodded.

He hesitated, then added, "Macie?"

She swallowed, struggling to find a way to talk without screaming.

"Yes?"

"You're not doing this alone. Lean on me. Let me be strong for you. It's not much, but right now, it's all I can do." Then his voice lowered perceptibly, an indication of how deeply he was affected by what she was going through. "God only knows how badly I need to do something."

She shuddered, then momentarily rested her forehead against his chest, inhaling the scent of his cologne and feeling the power of his heartbeat against her skin.

Strength? Right now she had none.

Leaning on Jonah? It was something she would gladly do for the rest of her life. However, she would take what she could get, and if today was all it would ever be, then it would have to be enough.

"Thank you, Jonah, more than I can say." Then she flattened her hands against his shirt and pushed herself away. "Let's go. The sooner this day is over with . . ."

She didn't finish her sentence, but she didn't have to. Jonah knew what she meant. Dying was easy. It was the living who had to struggle with the loss.

"Do you have everything you need?" he asked.

Macie looked at him, thinking to herself that as long as he was at her side, she would never need anything else, but she didn't say so. Instead she patted her handbag.

"Yes, all the papers are here."

He took her hand in his and gently squeezed her fingers.

"Considering everything that's going on, what you're wearing probably doesn't mean a damn, but just for the record, you take my breath away, Macie Blaine."

Macie looked up at him then. A slight shiver ran through her when she saw the look in his eyes. Dear God. If only — She shivered and pushed the thought from her mind.

"Thank you," she said. "Felicity always liked pretty things. I did it for her."

He held out his hand. She took it without hesitation, letting herself be led down the stairs, past the place where her sister had died, then out of the house and into the sunlight. Just as she started to get in the car, she stopped and turned, curiously eyeing the grounds and then the massive, three-story mansion.

"Macie . . . what's wrong? Did you forget something?" Jonah asked.

She stood for another moment, still staring around the area, then shrugged.

"I guess it's nothing."

"What?"

She looked up. "I know it's weird, but I just had the strangest feeling I was being watched." Then she grimaced. "That's stupid. Of course I'm being watched — by all kinds of police officers, right?"

Jonah had managed to stay alive this long by trusting his instincts, so he wasn't one to ignore anyone else's. Without thinking, he put himself between Macie and the house, and quickly opened the car door.

"Get in," he said shortly.

Macie obliged, only afterward realizing the urgency in his voice. Agents Sugarman and Carter were in the front seat, with Carter behind the wheel. Jonah leaned in the window and said something to Carter in a voice too low for her to hear. She watched as he got into the back seat beside her. As they were driving away, she saw a trio of men come out of the house.

"Jonah?"

He looked down at her and then took her hand, holding it as if to reassure himself that she was still there.

"Yeah?"

"What's going on? What did you say to the men?"

"You said you felt as if you were being watched. I just told them what you said. Instinct is what keeps us alive, and in this business, we don't ignore anything."

"Oh."

"It's probably nothing," he said. "Just being careful, you understand."

"Yes, of course," Macie said, but she was lying. She didn't understand any of this. They were supposed to be investigating her sister's murder and her nephew's abduction, not behaving as if she was about to be the next victim. Something was wrong, but they were keeping her in the dark. Her resentment grew as the ride went on. She watched the two men in the front seat. One of them was on a cell phone constantly, but when she leaned forward slightly, as if hoping to overhear what was being said, he clammed up. That only reinforced her belief that she was the last person to know what was being done. It not only hurt her feelings, it was making her mad.

A short while later they exited the residential area of Bel Air and pulled onto a freeway. She leaned forward and tapped the driver on the shoulder.

"There's a more direct route," she said.

"Yes, ma'am," Carter said, and kept driving.

Jonah touched her shoulder to get her attention.

"It's okay, kiddo. Just a little evasive driving."

Kiddo? Disgusted that she was being placated with smiles and pats on the back, Macie leaned back against the seat and closed her eyes, too drained to notice the evasive maneuvers the agent was taking as he drove.

But Jonah noticed, and more than once ran his hand down the front of his jacket, taking comfort in the bulge of the holster and handgun he could feel beneath.

When they finally arrived at the funeral home, Macie had fallen asleep. Jonah, however, was a bundle of nerves. He'd stared intently at the driver of every car that passed them on the freeway, and now that they had parked, he was loathe to let her out of the car. Calderone had ordered a hit on Felicity, thinking she was his woman, even though they'd never married. If Calderone had any indication of what Jonah was beginning to feel for Macie, then her life was in danger, as well.

Macie roused, then sat up. Agent Carter, who'd been driving, turned around.

"Miss Blaine, would you mind sitting in the car for just a few moments while my partner checks out the area?"

Flustered that she'd fallen asleep, she didn't realize the implications of what he'd just said until both federal agents got out of the car. She shifted where she sat, absently running a hand through her hair while waiting as she'd been told. It wasn't until she saw Sugarman take a stance by the car while Carter started toward the building that she realized something was amiss. She scooted toward the edge of the seat.

"Jonah . . . what's going on?"

"They're just being careful."

She sat for a moment, staring out the window at the perfectly manicured lawns and the sidewalks lined with stately palms. On the surface, everything looked so calm, so ordinary, and yet ordinary was no longer a part of her world. The longer she sat, the angrier she became. Her sister was dead, her father in a hospital clinging to life, her nephew missing and enduring only God knew what, and here she sat, hiding in the back seat of a car. Suddenly she snapped.

Before Jonah knew it, the door was open and Macie was getting out.

"Wait! Damn it, Macie, you can't —"

She shut the door in his face, smoothed

her hands down the front of her dress and then lifted her chin as Sugarman turned, then started toward her.

"Miss Blaine, you need to wait."

She held up her hand, stopping him where he stood.

"Don't come any closer," she said.

"I'm sorry, ma'am, but I've got my orders."

"Fine, but they didn't come from me, and you need to stay right where you are. I'm tired of being afraid. I'm tired of having people I don't know in every corner of my home. I'm going into that building and coming out with what's left of my sister, and you can wait right here or go home."

The agent eyed her nervously, then looked toward Jonah for guidance as he got out of the car.

"Sir, Ruger will have my —"

"I'll go with her," Jonah said.

Macie turned on him. "You're just like the rest of them," she said. "This is my family that's been decimated, and I'm the one who's being kept in the dark. I ask questions and get half-assed answers that don't make any sense. You want me to cooperate? Tell me the truth."

Jonah stood without flinching, taking the brunt of her anger while knowing it came from despair. He also knew he wasn't going to tell her a damned thing more than she already knew. If she knew the depths of

Calderone's capabilities for evil, she would go mad thinking of Evan in his grasp. He would take any amount of her anger not to let that happen.

"The truth? What truth? I can't change what's already happened, and no one knows where Evan is. If they did, don't you think I would move heaven and earth to get him back?"

For a moment Macie's expression registered nothing of what he'd just said, then she pivoted sharply and started up the walk.

Jonah glanced nervously over his shoulder, giving the area one last scan, then took off after her.

Macie knew in her heart that there were good reasons for the things they weren't telling her, but it wasn't the secrecy that troubled her as much as her feeling of helplessness. She'd been in charge of her life and her career for many years now, and quite successfully. Being dependent and treated like an incompetent was not only insulting, it was unnecessary, and today it had all come to a head. She knew Jonah was right behind her, but she wasn't slowing up and she wasn't waiting — not anymore. She was the only one left in her family who could function, and by God, she wanted justice, even though all she was going to get today were her sister's ashes.

Jonah got as far as the lobby of the funeral

home before Macie turned around. They stared at each other for a long, silent moment; then Jonah held up his hands in a gesture of defeat and took a single step back.

Macie's lips thinned, the only sign of her determination to do the rest of this alone, and walked away.

Jonah didn't entirely understand what had set her off, but he could tell by the look in her eyes that she was serious. He respected guts and determination, whether they came from a man or a woman. Right now, watching the length of Macie's stride and the unyielding stiffness of her posture, he knew, for the first time in his life, he was falling in love. At that point he sat down in the nearest chair he could find and tried not to think of what that reality meant.

One minute flowed into another and another, until twenty minutes had passed. Patience had never been his strong suit, so when he finally saw her coming, he bolted to his feet, then forgot what he'd been going to say.

She'd stormed into this place like an avenging angel, but somewhere between then and now, she had shattered. When he saw the small gray urn she held clutched to her chest, he knew. He took a step toward her, then stopped as she came toward him.

She paused, as if suddenly remembering that he was there, and looked up. There was no question on her lips, no expression in her eyes. She was just waiting.

Jonah started to touch her, but the subtle shift of her shoulder told him it was not okay. Instead he moved toward the door, then held it open as she walked through. Both Carter and Sugarman were waiting near the front walk. When they saw her, Sugarman automatically fell into stride beside her, while Carter hurried to the car. Jonah paused on the steps, giving the surrounding area a final sweep before following. When he was about halfway down the walk, the skin suddenly started to crawl on the back of his neck and he knew, the same way Macie had sensed back at the house, that they were being watched. Automatically his hand brushed the pocket of his sports coat. The gun was there — but where the hell was the enemy?

By the time he got to the car, Macie was safely inside. He slid into the back seat beside her and then tapped Carter on the shoulder.

"Get us out of here," Jonah said.

Carter swiftly obliged.

A few moments later, a dark gray car pulled out of an obscure driveway and into traffic, taking care to stay far enough behind the car in which Macie was riding so as not to be observed.

The two men in the car were pros. They had their orders, and taking out a couple of feds and a bodyguard to get to Macie Blaine was just part of the plan. They talked casually as they continued surveillance, confident that at the next stop they would make their move.

It was Jonah who spotted the car. What startled him was that he recognized the driver. The last time he'd seem Jorge Vega, he'd been running for cover from the DEA. It gave him chills to think that he'd walked right out of the funeral home in plain sight of a man he'd played cards with every night for months. Granted, he'd had long hair and a beard, but Vega was no fool.

He leaned forward and tapped Sugarman on the shoulder.

"We need some backup. Call Ruger and have him send some men to intercept. We're being tailed."

Sugarman reacted to the news without question, quickly relaying what Jonah had told him, as well as their present location and destination.

Carter tightened his fingers around the steering wheel.

"Do you want me to lose them?"

Jonah glanced out his window, watching the side view mirror on the passenger side of the car to see if they were still there. They were. Then he glanced at Macie. They could easily lead the men into a blind and take them down, but it was too dangerous with her along.

"No, just make sure we don't get where we're going until we know our backup is in place."

Carter nodded.

Jonah glanced into the mirror one more time and then leaned back against the seat. Macie seemed oblivious to what was going on, but he wasn't sure.

"Macie . . . honey?"

She shuddered, then blinked, as if coming out of a trance. Her fingers tightened around the small gray urn as she turned her head.

"Felicity taught me how to braid my hair. Did you know that?"

Jonah laid a hand on her knee, feeling the warmth of her skin beneath the sheer black fabric.

"No, I didn't, but that's a good memory to have."

A sigh passed her lips, and then she nodded and looked away.

"Macie, look at me."

It was a struggle for her to focus, but there was something in Jonah's voice that pulled her back.

"What?"

"Back at the estate . . . when you thought someone was watching you?"

"Yes?"

"You were right."

That penetrated the miasma of her grief. She gasped and started to turn around when Jonah stopped her.

"Don't look back."

Her heart started to pound.

"What are we going to do?"

"Right now, nothing. By the time we get to La Jolla, Ruger will have taken care of the problem, okay?"

"But —"

He put a finger against her mouth, silencing her.

"Trust us."

"I have no other choice," she said harshly, and then looked away.

The next few minutes seemed endless. Twice Vega got so close to them that there was only a single car between them, and each time Jonah feared that this was where the other men were going to make their move. He had no idea what they were planning, but with the technology available today, it would be a simple thing to take out an entire car and its passengers without ever stopping. But each time he readied himself for a fight, they would drop back. He didn't know what they were up to, but it couldn't be good, and the closer they got to La Jolla, the more nervous he became. Frustrated, he leaned forward again, tapping Sugarman on the shoulder.

"Where the hell is our backup?"

Sugarman's cell phone was against his ear as he turned and grinned.

"The cavalry has arrived. Look behind us."

Macie was the first to look as she got up on her knees and peered through the back window. Four city police cars and a half-dozen unmarked vehicles had just cut off a dark gray sedan, bringing it to an abrupt halt in the middle of the street. As they continued to pull away, she watched in disbelief as policemen spilled out of the vehicles with their guns drawn and dragged the two occupants out of the sedan.

Jonah saw the look of disbelief on Vega's face and grinned. For the first time since they'd walked out of the house, Jonah began to relax. They would find out more later. The only thing that mattered was Macie's safety.

Then Carter spoke up from the driver's seat.

"Miss Blaine, we're almost there. Is there a particular place you want to go, or is anywhere on the water okay?"

Macie turned, immediately recognizing the area.

"What about a boat?" Sugarman added, aware that she intended to spread her sister's ashes in the Pacific. "If you want, we can have one —"

"Just get me to the beach," she said. "I'll take it from there."

A short while later, Carter pulled up to the

curb of a walkway overlooking the ocean. Immediately he and Sugarman got out. Carter opened the door for Macie, while Jonah slid out on the other side. At the same time, Sugarman's cell phone rang.

"Sugarman," he said briefly, then listened intently without commenting. When the caller was finished, Sugarman smiled as he looked up. "Yes, sir, and thank you for letting us know."

"Was that Ruger?" Jonah asked. "Is everything okay?"

"More than okay," Sugarman said. "Ruger said to tell you that you have a good eye. The tail was a good one. It was two of Calderone's men, right down to the tattoos. They were carrying guns, and they had a picture of Miss Blaine."

Jonah's stomach knotted. "Did they say why she'd been targeted?"

"They aren't talking," Sugarman said.

"Damn."

The door slammed shut on the other side of the car. Both men turned just as Macie stepped up on the curb.

"I'm going down to the beach," she said. "Would it be possible to please give me some space?"

Both agents looked at each other, then nodded.

Macie clutched the urn a little closer to her breast and started walking toward a stairway that led down to the beach. Jonah hesitated for a few moments, then began to follow.

Sensing his presence, she paused and turned, frowning slightly when she realized he wasn't going to stay at the car with the agents.

When she stopped, so did Jonah.

She arched an eyebrow questioningly.

He tilted his chin.

The silent standoff lasted just long enough for a strong gust of wind off the ocean to snake beneath Macie's hair and lift it away from her neck. The skirt of her dress billowed slightly, then plastered itself against her body, and still he waited.

Still frowning, she turned around and resumed her trek, accepting Jonah's presence without comment.

There were sixty-four winding, twisting steps to the bottom of the cliff. When Macie reached the sand, she paused and stepped out of her shoes, then continued barefoot toward the water, thinking to herself that the sand was warmer than the wind coming off the Pacific. To her right, a pair of seals were sunning on a line of rocks, their coats wet and sparkling in the sunshine from the spray of the crashing breakers. Overhead, a flock of seagulls rode the air currents. Every now and then one would break rank and dive toward the water or the shore, squawking loudly as it came. A pelican was floating on the water a few yards off shore, like a big white cork bobbing on the end of a fishing line.

Macie's eyes filled with tears. It seemed idyllic — the kind of day that Felicity would have loved. A few moments later, she ran out of sand. Another step and she would be within reach of the ebb and flow of the water. She looked down at the urn, then stepped forward into the ocean, gasping once from the shock of the cold, then took the second step, then another and another, until she was knee deep in the Pacific.

The waves were stronger here, pushing and pulling against her legs like cold, urgent fingers, demanding that she follow the power. The horizon was blurred now, too far away to see through tears. The urn she'd been carrying felt heavier than it had, as if Felicity were urging her from beyond the grave to release her in the only way Macie knew how.

Macie's hands were shaking as she removed the lid, but she couldn't look down. Without hesitation, she turned until the wind was at her back. Then she tilted the urn.

Instantly the ashes spilling out of the opening were swept up in a small gust of wind and carried out onto the water. Macie caught a brief glimpse of the ash floating on the surface as it became part of the sea. She watched as the waves carried it away, and still she stood, the urn held fast in her hands.

Jonah was on the shore, waiting for her to

come in, when he saw the wave coming. He called out to Macie, but it was too late. It hit her waist high. The urn fell from her hands as she staggered under the onslaught.

He cursed beneath his breath and, without removing his shoes, dashed in after her. She was pale and shivering when he reached her. He put one hand under her knees and the other around her waist and scooped her out of the water. Without saying a word, he started back toward the shore.

Macie wrapped her arms around his neck, clinging to him as if she were a child, only vaguely aware that she was no longer in the water.

Jonah carried her to the bottom of the steps, where Carter and Sugarman were waiting, and put her down long enough to stuff her shoes into his pockets. Then he slid an arm around her waist, and between the three of them, they got her up the winding stairs and into the car without incident.

Before backing away from the curb, Carter looked over his shoulder at the woman huddled in his back seat.

"Is she going to be okay?"

Jonah glanced down. Her clothes were sodden and plastered to the lower half of her body. Her skin was pale, her lips blue from the chill of the Pacific.

"She has to be," he said shortly. "Just get us home."

8

The long drive back from La Jolla had been nerve-racking. Jonah began to relax only after Carter turned off the main highway and began driving up the road that led to the Blaine estate. All the way from the beach, he'd had visions of a second pair of Calderone's men coming out of nowhere and finishing what Vega had failed to do. He shifted slightly, ignoring the discomfort of his wet shoes and pants to look down at Macie, who was motionless in his lap. He tried not to think of that quick wit and vital personality coming undone and concentrated on just getting her home.

The road leading up to the mansion was a winding two-lane, bordered on both sides by towering trees and heavy undergrowth. While the growth was a way to maintain privacy, it was also good cover for someone with ill intent on his mind.

The media crews that had appeared when the news of the murder/kidnapping broke were still camped out in a small cul-de-sac a short distance from the main gate of the estate. Carter sped past without acknowledging their presence.

Then, in spite of the two on-duty officers,

an overzealous reporter spied Macie in the back seat of the car and immediately broke ranks. He grabbed a video-cam, slung it on his shoulder and ducked under the barrier behind which they'd been standing.

"Miss Blaine! Miss Blaine!" he yelled.

"Floor it, Carter," Jonah muttered, and tightened his grip on Macie as the car shot forward, leaving the reporter in the proverbial dust of their exit.

"I hate reporters," Carter said, as he negotiated the turn into the main gate.

Aware of nothing but the warmth of Jonah's body and the security of his embrace, Macie had curled in on herself, holding on to sanity by shutting out everything else.

Jonah looked at her again. Although her eyes were closed, he could tell by the sound of her breathing that she wasn't asleep. She'd simply withdrawn.

He touched her face. Her skin was pale and clammy, but what bothered him most was that she hadn't stopped shaking since he'd dragged her out of the water. Carter had driven like a man possessed, taking the I-5 coastal highway north to L.A., but Jonah feared it hadn't been fast enough.

"We should have called a doctor," he muttered, more to himself than to the agents.

"Already done," Sugarman said, as Carter pulled under the grand portico and killed the engine.

Seconds later, Jonah was out of the car and carrying Macie inside. Ruger met them in the foyer.

"What happened to her?" he asked.

"Hell if I know," Jonah said. "Exhaustion. Emotional breakdown. You name it. All I know is, she hasn't said a word since we left La Jolla."

"Why is she wet?" Ruger asked, then looked at Jonah's pant legs and frowned. "Hell of a day to go for a swim, don't you think?"

"Where's the doctor?" Jonah asked.

"Upstairs."

Jonah looked up at the winding staircase, then down at Macie.

"Need some help?" Ruger asked.

"No," Jonah said, then shifted his hold on her, tightening his grip as he started up the stairs.

Moments later, he was in the hallway and striding toward her room. He kicked the door open and carried her to the bed, then started taking off her dress.

"Señor . . ."

He turned around. Rosa was standing in the doorway.

"Help me get these wet clothes off her," he said.

She hastened toward the bed, muttering beneath her breath. When she saw Macie, she crossed herself, then began tugging at her slip.

"Where's that doctor?" Jonah asked.

"In the sitting room down the hall."

"Go get him."

Rosa left, carrying the wet dress and slip as she went, leaving Macie nude except for a wisp of bra and panties. Jonah grabbed a coverlet from the foot of the bed and quickly covered her, then rushed into the bathroom and began running warm water into the tub.

When he came back into the room, a portly man in a three-thousand-dollar suit and a bad comb-over was leaning over the bed with a stethoscope to Macie's chest.

"Doctor?"

"Anson Schultz, at your service," he said without looking up. "What happened to her?"

Jonah briefly outlined the circumstances leading up to Macie's collapse, while the doctor nodded occasionally, continuing his examination. A few moments later he looked up and then past Jonah's shoulder.

"Tub's going to run over," he said.

Rosa gasped, then dashed past the men, quickly turning off the water.

Dr. Schultz straightened up, then took the stethoscope from his ears and dropped it into his bag.

"Her vital signs are fine. I'll leave something to help her sleep, but other than that, I think she's going to be all right."

"She hasn't stopped shaking," Jonah said.

The doctor shrugged. "She's cold, also a

little shocky. A hot bath and something warm to drink should do the trick. Just make sure she doesn't take any alcohol with the sleeping medicine. Not a good combination, you understand."

Less than impressed with the man and his bedside manner, Jonah frowned.

"Anything else?" he asked.

The doctor looked down at her again, eyeing the pale skin and wet hair, then up at Jonah.

"Maybe someone could stay with her tonight . . . a nurse . . . or that housekeeper, perhaps?"

"She won't be alone," Jonah said, and took the sample packet of sleeping pills the doctor handed him.

Moments later, Rosa came back. "The water, *señor* . . . it is ready."

"If you have further need of me, I can be reached at this number," the doctor said, and handed Jonah a card.

"I will see him to the door," Rosa said, then looked at Jonah. "Should I come back to help with the bath?"

Jonah shook his head.

She hesitated once, as if contemplating the impropriety of such a thing, then shrugged and left with the doctor in tow.

Once they were gone, Jonah shut the door, then moved to the bed and sat down. He cupped the side of Macie's face.

"Macie . . ."

She opened her eyes.

He smiled.

"There you are," he said softly.

"I didn't go far."

"I know." He patted her cheek and then stood. "You need to get in the tub while the water is hot."

"Yes."

"Do you need any help?"

She looked up at him then. "No."

The tremble in her voice was enough that he would have walked on hot coals to do anything she asked.

She drew a slow shaky breath, then threw back the covers and swung her legs over the side of the bed.

"There's not much left to the imagination, is there?" she said, as the air hit her near naked body.

"My imagination has been working overtime for a while now, but the real thing far surpasses anything I might have dreamed about you." Then he took her by the hands and pulled her upright before kissing the side of her cheek. "You are a very beautiful woman, now come get in the tub."

She hesitated for a second, then unhooked her bra and stepped out of her panties, dropping both where she stood. Her steps were slow but steady as she walked into the bathroom.

Jonah stood and watched her until he was sure she was safely seated in the water, then took a deep breath.

"Macie?"

"Yes?"

"I'm going across the hall to get some dry clothes."

There was a moment of silence, followed by a rather poignant question.

"You're coming right back?"

"Yes."

He pivoted sharply and got the hell out of the room. By the time he reached his bedroom he was shaking, but not from cold. He was hard and hurting and in serious want for Macie Blaine. It had taken every ounce of willpower and good sense that he had to walk out of her room before he made an ass of himself, and he had less than five minutes to get himself together before he saw her again.

His fingers curled into fists as he kicked off his shoes. With angry jerks, he yanked off his wet socks and pants and dropped them on the bathroom floor as he stepped into the shower. Without waiting for the water to warm, he turned on the faucets and leaned into the jets. Gritting his teeth, he welcomed the rush of cold on his body. Something had to stabilize this ache he had for her, and a cold shower should do it.

It didn't take long for the water to get

warm, but by the time it had, he was already rinsing off the soap and turning off the taps. He'd promised Macie he wouldn't leave her alone for long. Keeping that promise was the least he could do.

He dried quickly, then pulled on a pair of sweatpants and a T-shirt before hurrying back to her room. He knocked once, then, when he heard no response, opened the door and walked in.

"Macie?"

"What?"

"Are you okay?"

"No . . . but I will be."

"Do you need any help?"

"No."

"Is there anything I can get for you . . . some clean clothes . . . a dressing gown?"

"No . . . but thank you."

It wasn't much, but he heard what he needed to know. At a loss as to what to do next, he picked up the remote control and then sat on a bench at the foot of the bed. The first program that came on was a news channel. Curious as to what was going on in the world, he leaned back, resting his elbows on her mattress, and tried to concentrate on what the news anchor was saying, but it was difficult. He kept picturing the long-limbed perfection of Macie's nude body. It wasn't until the news anchor started talking about the local news that Jonah's attention shifted.

"On to local news . . . Sources at Cedars-Sinai Hospital tell us that the status of billionaire power broker Declyn Blaine has been updated from critical to serious. Meanwhile, the authorities are still searching for Evan Blaine, the billionaire's fifteen-year-old grandson, who was kidnapped during the attack that left Blaine fighting for his life. Declyn Blaine had only two children, Felicity Blaine, who was killed at the time of the attack, and Mercedes Blaine, who owns a very successful import-export business in Chicago, and who is now in the city, cooperating fully with the authorities in an effort to find her nephew.

"While we have not been able to interview Miss Blaine, she was seen today coming out of a local mortuary, presumably with her sister's ashes."

Jonah cursed. He hadn't seen any news crews. Where the hell had they been? Then he frowned, knowing that with today's technology, a telescopic lens on a state-of-the-art video camera could record almost anything. As the man continued to speak, Jonah returned his attention to the broadcast.

"This news footage was taken only a short time ago, a few hours after her exit from the mortuary. We at this station sympathize with her grief. From all accounts, the earlier speculation about her being under heavy guard seems to be true, as evidenced from this tape."

Jonah stared at the screen in disbelief. There was Carter at the wheel, then the camera zooming in on Macie's face, highlighting her grief for the world to see. He cursed. The little bastard back at the front gate had probably sold that piece of footage for a dandy profit, which seemed, to Jonah, as honorable as selling bones from the dead for souvenirs.

"According to a police spokesperson, there have been no demands made for Evan Blaine's ransom. Friends from the private school that he attended have made up their own posters and are placing them in public buildings all over the city, with plans for statewide distribution this weekend. If anyone has any information regarding the whereabouts of this young man, you are asked to call the Los Angeles police department or the state branch of the Federal Bureau of Investigation. The numbers are at the bottom of the screen."

The picture that Evan's classmates had put on the posters had obviously been taken at the end of a winning soccer game. His hair was in classic disarray and sticking damply to his forehead. He had been hoisted onto the shoulders of his teammates, his fist thrust upward in a gesture of victory. Jonah stared at the picture on the screen until he thought he would throw up, then grabbed the remote and turned off the TV. He closed his eyes as he stifled a groan. He'd seen an entire album of photographs, from the time Evan was a baby to spring break of last year on a trip to Cancún.

Now this.

The smiling picture they kept flashing on the television seemed oddly obscene, as if Evan was laughing at his own fate. But Jonah knew different. If the boy was still alive, he would be incapable of laughing.

Suddenly he felt the mattress dip behind him, and then smelled the fresh, sweet scent of soap and shampoo. It was Macie. He turned around. She was looking at him, her eyes red-rimmed and shadowed. He tore open the packet of sleeping pills that the doctor had given her and then went into the bathroom to get a glass of water. When he came back, she was sitting up in bed.

"I don't need those," she muttered, but she put them in her mouth anyway and downed them with a half glass of water.

"I'll leave you to —"

Macie grabbed his hand.

"Please, stay with me, at least until I fall asleep."

He set the glass down on the nightstand and then slid onto the bed beside her.

"Do you want to talk?"

She leaned back, using a pair of pillows and the headboard as a resting place, then eyed him curiously.

"About what?"

"Anything. Today? Last week? Your business? Your friends? I don't know, Macie . . . you're the one who will be talking."

She pinned him with a hard, cool stare. "I'd rather talk about you," she said.

Instinctively his guard went up. His lifestyle wasn't a topic for conversation. He looked at her, trying to temper what he was going to say with a smile.

"If I told you, then I'd have to kill you."

She snorted. It was a most unladylike sound, which made Jonah's grin widen.

"Oh, bull," Macie said. "Surely you have friends you can talk about. Don't you have a hobby? What's your favorite thing to eat? Since you live near Washington, D.C., are you a Redskins fan? Talk to me, Jonah. Tell me something ordinary before I go out of my mind."

"Damn, woman, you asked me everything but what's my sign?"

"I already knew that," she said. "You're a Gemini."

"Witch."

"I've been called worse. So talk. Surely you can come up with something. These pills will kick in before long, and then you'll be off the hook."

"Fine. Yes, I have a best friend. His name is Carl French. As for hobbies, I can't say that I have any, although I enjoy the water and I like to fish."

Macie settled down beneath the covers and folded her arms across her breasts. Now they were getting somewhere. She needed an ordinary conversation, like one would have with a dinner companion. It made the horror of this day a little bit easier to handle.

"Deep sea or freshwater fishing?" she asked.

"Either, although if I had to pick just one, I guess it would be the sea. I like the endlessness of the horizon. Keeps me from feeling hemmed in."

She frowned slightly, contemplating the implications of what he'd just said. Hemmed in. She wondered how many times he'd come close to dying in that damnable job of his. No wonder he liked thc frccdom of the sea.

"Do you have a boat?" she asked.

"No, but I always thought I'd like to get one."

Macie thought about Jonah, picturing him on the open sea, standing on the deck with feet apart, bracing himself against the pitch and roll of the water.

"Then I think you should."

He shrugged. "Maybe one day . . . if I live long enough to retire."

"Don't say that," she mumbled, then yawned and closed her eyes. "Don't ever say anything like that again."

Her eyelids were getting heavy. There was something else she wanted to say to him, but her thoughts wouldn't focus.

"Stupid pills . . ."

Then she took a deep breath, rolled onto

her side and sighed.

It was the last thing Jonah heard her say. He waited until he was sure she was sound asleep before he leaned forward. Her breath was soft on his cheek, her lips parted slightly. Her hair was a tangle of red on the white pillow slip, and despite the heavy fan of her eyelashes, he could see the lingering shadows of grief beneath her eyes.

"Sleep well, sweetheart," he said softly, and then kissed her.

It took every ounce of willpower he had to get up and walk away, but there were things he needed to know.

Downstairs, Ruger was fielding the information gained from the arrest of Samuel Vega. He looked up as Jonah walked into the room.

"Tell me something good," Jonah said.

"Snickers candy bars," Ruger said, and then shrugged. "Sorry. I get this way when I start losing sleep."

"Samuel Vega. Tell me about him. Has he talked? What did he say when they confronted him about having Macie's picture in his car?"

"Not a damned thing," Ruger said. "He's not talking, and neither is the thug who was with him. Also, they produced permits for the guns they were carrying. You're not going to like this, but unless we come up with another reason they're going to release them tomorrow."

Jonah's belly knotted. It was what he'd feared. "Let me guess. They have no reason to hold him."

Ruger nodded.

Sarcasm was thick in Jonah's voice. "Well, hell. What were we thinking? We should have let him blow her head off first, then his ass would be ours." He kicked at the leg of a chair and then shoved his hands through his hair. "Christ almighty! Sometimes this crapshoot of a legal system we have makes me want to throw up."

"I know, I know," Ruger said. "But you and I both know it's the truth. Technically, he hadn't broken any laws, and it's not illegal to carry someone's picture. He had just as much right to be on that highway as anyone else. At least that's what his lawyer is claiming."

"This so-called lawyer . . . his name wouldn't by any chance be Abraham Hollister?"

Ruger's eyebrows arched; then he nodded. "You know him?"

"I know *of* him," Jonah said. "Calderone always bragged that money could buy anything, especially the best lawyers." Then he took a deep breath, making himself calm. "So where do we go from here?"

Ruger shuffled a handful of papers into a file, then laid it aside.

"Back off, Jonah. You're not going anywhere, and we're doing all we can."

Frustrated, Jonah lowered his voice and moved closer to Ruger.

"Damn it, man. Look at this from my point of view. I have a son in mortal danger, and it's all because of me. I need to do something. I can't just stand on the sidelines and be satisfied with the same little bits and pieces of bullshit information you tell regular parents. I'm not regular. I'm a Company man, for God's sake. Use me."

Ruger glanced over his shoulder, then back at Jonah.

"You know I can't," he said. "I'm sorry as hell, but that's just the way it is."

"What about that gardener? The one I saw on tape. What do we know about him? Has he made contact with anyone who —"

"He goes home. He comes to work. He goes home. He comes to work," Ruger said. "He's so clean, he squeaks when he walks."

"There isn't a man in Calderone's organization who's clean," Jonah argued. "He knows something. Give me an hour alone with him. I'll make him talk."

Ruger's nostrils flared in anger as he poked a finger against Jonah's chest.

"That's just what I mean," he said sharply. "It doesn't work that way here."

Jonah jerked as if he'd just been hit on the chin. His eyes narrowed angrily, and his voice grew even softer.

"What the hell are you insinuating?"

Ruger sighed. "Damn it, man. Don't make me say it. You know what I mean. I'm bound by rules. I can't beat information out of a perp, no matter how much I might want to, and I can't make someone disappear, no matter how much the bastard needs killing."

"And I can?" Jonah asked.

Ruger met Jonah's gaze without flinching. "You tell me," he countered.

Silence stretched between the two men until it was razor thin. One wrong breath — one blink too many — and the thread of civility that kept them from punching each other in the nose would break.

It was a call from one of Ruger's men that got his attention. He turned to answer the question, and when he turned back, Jonah was gone.

"Guess that answers my question," Ruger muttered, and went back to work.

He didn't know that Jonah had gone straight to his room, or that he was making a call to his boss. The secretary put his call through immediately, which told him that the deputy director had been waiting for contact.

"Sir . . . I need a favor," Jonah said.

"Ask."

"I need a list of everything that Calderone ever put money into — from the time he cut the strings on his mama's apron to the day we locked him behind bars. If he owns a piece of land in California, I want to know where it is. The same goes for businesses. I know Calderone has holdings here. I just don't know all the locations. Also, I need one of our people on the inside. I need to know what's going on. Agent Ruger is a good man, but he's got his orders, and they don't include me. I was thinking maybe Carl French."

"Yes."

Jonah relaxed. Finally something positive. "Thank you, sir. I owe you, big time."

"When it comes to our families, there are no favors to be returned. Understood?"

"Understood," Jonah said.

"Expect French before morning."

"Yes, sir, and thank you."

Jonah was very relieved when he disconnected. So Ruger wouldn't let him in on their investigation. Fine. He would work one of his own, with one of his own.

Satisfied that for now he'd done all he could do, he wandered out of the command center, following the scent of cooking into the back part of the house.

He found the kitchen, then Rosa and a small Chinese man who was stirring something in a pot on the stove. This, he assumed, was the cook.

Rosa saw him and gasped.

"*Señor* . . . you did not have to come in search of me. I would come to you. How can I help you?"

"I don't need to be waited on," Jonah said, and then softened his words by adding, "something smells very good. How long until dinner?"

"You go sit in the dining room. I will bring your food."

"I can eat in here," Jonah said.

Shock spread across her face as she grabbed him by the arm and shooed him out of the kitchen.

"No, no. I bring to you."

"Fine," he said. "But keep something hot for Macie. She's still sleeping."

"Yes, yes," she said, nodding vigorously as she hustled him out of the kitchen.

Reluctant to eat alone in the splendor of the formal dining room, he waited until the food was served, then took his plate and moved out to the terrace beyond a set of oversize French doors. He sat down in one chair, using another as a foot rest, and took his first bite.

The food was hot and spicy and reminded him of Bangkok. He ate with relish while watching a lone gardener on a riding lawn mower at the back of the estate. He watched while the man finished his task, then started toward a toolshed. Suddenly the urge to look the man in the face overcame his good sense. If it was Calderone's plant, he wanted to see him face-to-face. He set his plate aside, and when the man rode the lawn mower into a nearby shed, he got up and walked off the terrace.

The air was thick with the scent of fresh-cut grass and the fragrance of the flowers he was passing. It reminded him of summers on his grandfather's farm in Illinois, and for a few moments he wished to God he was still that little boy, hurrying to the barn to help his Poppy with the milking. But reality was too ugly to ignore, and the fantasy of Poppy's farm quickly faded.

Just as he walked up to the shed, the gardener walked out. Jonah recognized him immediately, and he could tell by the expression on the man's face that he had scared him.

Felipe Sosa was just getting used to his stolen name and new career as a gardener. There had been several times in the past few days when he had wished it was not all a lie. He liked working with his hands and helping things grow. It was a far cry from the makeshift cocaine factories scattered about Colombia.

He had just finished mowing the last of the grounds and was thinking about talking the maid, Rosa, out of an ice-cold lemonade when he found himself face-to-face with a man he'd never seen. His first instinct was to reach for his machete, but then he remembered it was back in his village, so he made himself smile instead, adopting a subservient attitude as befitting a man of his means in a place such as this.

"*Señor,* there is something you need?" he said.

Jonah stared at him for a long, silent moment and saw not only the fear but the guilt. It was then that he knew. The man who called himself Felipe Sosa might not know where Evan was, but he was a link to the people who did.

"No, just taking a walk," Jonah said, then shoved his hands in his pockets and continued on past the shed as if the tennis court in the distance had been his destination after all.

Felipe nodded, then hurried toward the house. Halfway there, something made him stop and look back. The man was standing under the shade of a large mimosa tree. From the way he was standing, Felipe knew he'd been watching him all along. Suddenly his thirst for the lemonade was gone in his desire to get away. He hurried to the garages, retrieved his old pickup and drove away. Not until he'd cleared the main gates and lost himself in the busy traffic did he breathe a quiet sigh of relief.

Later, while Sosa was heating up beans and tortillas, Jonah was in a small salon off the main library. He had one picture album in his lap and another on the table beside him that he had yet to view. He turned the pages slowly, his gaze lingering on the snapshots of his son. The longer he looked, the more his hate for Declyn Blaine grew.

9

While Jonah was wallowing in regret, Miguel Calderone was being led to the visitors' room for a consultation with his lawyer. His step was jaunty, almost defiant, in spite of the leg irons and chains. He expected good news.

Abraham Hollister was fidgeting as he waited for his client to show up. Representing criminals was his chosen profession, but there were days, like today, when he wondered if going into the greengrocer business with his father might not have been wiser.

A few moments later, Hollister heard footsteps outside the door and quickly stood up. But it wasn't from politeness as much as in deference to the man who was the largest contributor to his retirement fund. Seconds later, the door opened and Miguel Calderone entered, followed by one of the guards. Hollister nodded cordially as he stood on one side of the long table. Calderone took a seat opposite him.

"Mr. Calderone . . . I trust you are well?"

Calderone's upper lip curled. "As well as can be expected in such a hideous place."

Hollister nodded, as if in total understanding, when in fact he was not. Except for the times when he was forced to come to places such as this to confer with his clients, he had never had the pleasure of the accommodations, and for that he continually thanked God. He started to speak, then noticed the guard was still in the room.

"We require privacy, sir," he said shortly.

The guard stood his ground. "I've got my orders."

Hollister gestured at the room in which they were sitting. "And Mr. Calderone has his rights, not the least of which is privacy with counsel. As you can see, there are no windows in this room, and I've already been searched, so I'll trouble you to step outside . . . and close the door behind you."

The guard hesitated, well aware that the lawyer was within his rights to make such a demand, then turned and walked out of the room.

Calderone waited until he heard the lock turn in the door, then he looked at Hollister.

"You have news?"

Hollister frowned, then put a finger to his lips, as if to indicate silence.

Calderone shrugged. "What more can they do to me, arrest me?" Then he laughed aloud at his own joke as Hollister sat down with a thump.

"I don't know how long we have, so I'll

make this quick. Your dog . . . the one who's gone missing . . . is nowhere to be found."

The analogy to Jonah Slade was not lost on Calderone, but the message was not what he wanted to hear. He bolted to his feet, a curse yet to be uttered, when Hollister waved his hands, gesturing for Calderone to calm.

"This is not possible," Calderone said. "I sent my best man."

"Yes, well, obviously his best wasn't good enough. The report I received was that your dog is gone, and no one seems to know where." Then he added, "Appearances can change. You saw him as one thing, others might see him as another."

The reference to the man's undercover work was obvious, and the truth rankled. It was true that Calderone had known the man only as Juan Diego Rivera, a Mexican-American mercenary. And it was also true that he had no idea what the man looked like beneath his long hair and beard, but thanks to the Snowman, he did know his name. And the Snowman had assured him that he could identify Jonah Slade, no matter what his disguise. But now this. It was not to be borne.

Calderone closed his eyes in frustration, and as he did, he flashed on the sight of Alejandro's head bursting from the impact of the bullet. He moaned, then closed his eyes and started muttering beneath his breath.

The flesh on the back of Hollister's neck

began to crawl, but he stayed his ground. When Calderone finally looked up, Hollister was prepared for almost anything but Calderone's smile and ensuing shrug. In a way, that response was more frightening than the fit he'd been about to throw only moments before.

"So he's gone," Calderone said. "But his pup is not. Tell Elena to go ahead with the rest of the plan. She'll know what to do. And when she comes next, you must come with her."

Hollister frowned. "Do you think that's wise . . . trying to pass her off as a nun? If she's found out, everything is going to blow up in our faces."

Calderone's smile widened as he leaned across the small table. Hollister's nostrils flared as he smelled the man's breath and wondered if the devil himself would smell any worse.

"You do what you're told," Calderone said, then added, "and make sure the prison doctor has been taken care of."

For years, Abraham Hollister had ignored the evil in Miguel Calderone because his greed was greater than the sum of his fears. But right now, what he saw in Calderone's eyes was enough to make him sick. It was all he could do to keep his seat.

"Of course," Hollister said, and began shuffling papers from the table back into his briefcase. "I'll be in touch."

Calderone leaned forward, his voice barely above a whisper. "Tell them to take good care of that pup. I will be the one to put it down."

Hollister nodded, then strode to the door and gave it a quick thump. Seconds later, the guard was inside and escorting Calderone back to his cell.

All the way back to his hotel room, Hollister kept fighting an urge to throw up. He wondered how far he could run on the money he had, and how long it would take to get lost enough, then shook off the thought. There was no need dwelling on the impossible.

No one ever escaped from the *padrone*.

No one.

Ever.

The only escape from Miguel Calderone was in death, and Hollister wasn't ready to take that trip.

The rat was back, sitting at the foot of Evan's bed while Evan sat in the corner of the room, watching the rat's beady eyes and nose whiskers twitch as it nibbled on a crust of bread left from the untouched tray near the door.

Evan called him Howard, although he wasn't sure of the rodent's sex. It might be a Harriet, for all he knew, but he didn't want to find out that his first time sleeping with a female had turned out to be with this damned rat. The humor of the situation kept him sane when he wanted to let go. Already weak from lack of food and certain he had fever, it would be so easy to give up.

Instead he pulled his knees up under his chin and then rested his forehead against them, making himself ignore the tins of food on the tray and the single plastic spoon. It was his kidnappers way of assuring him that the food was no longer drugged, but it had become a point of honor that they would not control what he did. They obviously wanted him to eat. There had been numerous confrontations with the same dark-skinned guard over just that, but Evan stood his ground. He'd seen their faces, so it stood to reason they wouldn't let him live. While he didn't understand why this had happened to him, his refusal to do what they wanted was his only weapon.

Suddenly there was a sound at the door.

"Leaving the sinking ship?" he muttered, as Howard bailed off the bed and ran for the hole in the floor.

Moments later the door opened, but it wasn't the guard who came in. It was a woman, and from the look on her face, she was pissed. She glanced down at the tray, then across the room at him. The left corner of her mouth turned up in a gesture of disdain right before she kicked the tray and its contents. Cans went flying, as did the tray itself. When she started toward him, the plastic spoon crunched beneath the sole of her boot.

Evan flinched at the sound, then dragged himself to an upright position. A wave of dizziness washed over him, but he pushed it back, making himself focus on the hate in her eyes.

"You!"

Her demand for his attention was full of anger. Evan lifted his chin, bracing himself for whatever came next.

"You will eat now."

"Or you'll kill me?" Evan drawled. "Go ahead and get it over with."

The woman slapped his face. The force of the blow sent him reeling back against the wall. The male guard dashed into the room, yelling something in Spanish. Evan got just enough of the conversation to learn that they were supposed to be keeping him safe. She turned on the man, her hand on the handle of a knife that she wore on a belt around her waist. Moments later, the man ducked his head and left.

Evan waited, wondering why she had power over these men, wondering if she was the one behind the murders, and wondering why.

The woman picked up a can of peaches, popped the tab top and thrust it under his nose. Suddenly her voice was soft and crooning, the tone she might have used if coaxing a small child to eat.

"Smell this, *niño?* Is good, *verdad?*"

Saliva flooded his mouth. He had to swallow before he could talk.

"Probably," he said.

She smiled. "Then you eat."

"No."

A frown split the smoothness of her forehead, right between her eyebrows. She pushed the can toward his mouth. He shoved it away, spilling the contents onto the floor between them. Her anger spilled with it, as she grabbed at the hilt of her knife.

"Is this it?" Evan asked. "Was that to be my last meal? Are you to be my executioner?"

It was the disdain in his voice that stayed her hand, coupled with a reminder of what would happen to her if she ruined her *padrone*'s plans for personal revenge.

"Why you not eat?" she asked. "It is not tainted."

"I see your face," Evan said.

The frown deepened. "I do not understand," she said.

What was left of Evan's defiance suddenly rose and flooded over. Within seconds, he was shouting. His words brought a pair of guards running into the room, but by then he didn't care.

"You don't understand? *You* don't understand? No, you stupid bitch . . . I'm the one who doesn't understand. You killed my mother. You killed my grandfather. And you let me see your faces. Kidnappers do not reveal themselves to victims that they plan to let go. Get it? This place stinks . . . just like you people. You're going to kill me sooner or later. Maybe I prefer it to be sooner."

The woman's face flooded with rage. She understood enough English to know she'd been insulted several times over. At that moment, the last thing on her mind was displeasing Miguel Calderone. She grabbed for her knife, but the guards grabbed her instead, dragging her kicking and screaming out of the room. The door was pulled shut. The lock was turned. Suddenly Evan was alone again. He glanced toward the hole in the floor.

"Hey, Howard, you can come out now. The witch is gone."

But the rat chose to make no appearance, and Evan chose to sit down before he fell. He slid downward, his butt thumping solidly as he hit the floor. The scent of peaches was now mixed with the ever-present dust and the constantly growing stench of body waste accumulating in the tiny bathroom.

He wasn't sure, but it was either his third or fourth day in hell, and he wondered how much longer before it was over.

* * *

Sometime during the night he awoke, stiff and cold from sitting on the floor. With considerable effort, he finally rolled over on his hands and knees and crawled to the bed. There was a scuffling noise somewhere beneath it, but it didn't even fazc him.

When he was a kid, he used to dream of monsters hiding under his bed, waiting to come out and eat him, but now he knew that to be false. The real monsters were on the other side of the locked door, waiting to steal his breath.

With a soft, muffled sob, he closed his eyes and rolled up in a ball. Within seconds he was asleep and dreaming of a man who looked like him, and who came in a wall of dust and flame, kicking in the door while slaying all the monsters. And in the dream, Evan knew him and called him Father, and all was right with the world.

It was dark now. Jonah had given up waiting for Carl French to arrive but was too heartsick to sleep. He walked past the command center in Declyn Blaine's office and wondered what the old son of a bitch would say if he saw his antique cherry-wood tables littered with all the electronic equipment and files that the feds had accumulated.

Earlier, he'd heard Ruger calling the hospital. Not only was Blaine still on the mend, but he'd been taken out of intensive care and put into a private room with a round-the-clock nurse to tend to his every need.

The knowledge that the least innocent person in this whole affair was probably going to be the one to survive only served to resurrect old anger and hate. Suddenly the need to see Macie overwhelmed him. He started up the stairs, taking them two at a time, and then hurried into her room.

She was sitting on the side of the bed, holding a picture of Felicity and Evan. When she saw Jonah, she shoved the picture in a drawer on the nightstand, then stood.

"Macie . . . I —"

"Hold me," she begged, and walked into his arms.

"Jesus," he said softly, and pulled her close, tunneling one hand beneath the tangle of her hair and cupping her neck, while centering his other hand in the middle of her back.

She was so close, and still not close enough. Her pulse was rapid — almost too rapid. Her breath was coming too fast, and it felt as if she was swaying on her feet.

"Macie . . ."

She moaned softly, so softly he almost didn't hear the sound.

"Look at me, baby," he said softly.

Macie shuddered, then lifted her head.

"Take a deep breath and then exhale slowly."

"But I —"

"Please . . . for once, just do as I say without arguing."

Macie leaned forward and closed her eyes, then rested her forehead against the breadth of his chest.

One deep breath in.

One slow breath out.

Then she repeated it again and again until the floor began to settle beneath her feet.

"Better now?" Jonah asked.

She nodded.

"Would you like something to eat? I could call Rosa and have her bring you a tray."

Silence. Then a shifting of her body that brought her closer within his embrace. He waited for her to answer. It didn't happen.

"Macie?"

Then she looked up. "Lock my door."

"But why —"

She put her hand on his mouth, silencing his question before he could finish, then stared straight into his eyes.

"Jonah, if I asked you to do something for me, would you?"

Jonah's head was reeling. The softness of her skin, the fullness of her lower lip, that sleepy, half-awake look in her eyes, made him want. Made him want her. Made him want her hard and fast. Even though he knew he was going to say yes, the skin suddenly crawled on the back of his neck, as if warning him against what was to come.

Still, he nodded.

She sighed then, as if relieved by his answer.

He felt the warmth of her breath and wanted to kiss her again, just as he had before. But she was no longer asleep, and the familiarity seemed awkward. It had already occurred to him that he'd bedded one sister and given her a child. That he was attracted to this one as well seemed wrong. He waited for her to continue, then frowned when a lengthy silence began.

There was a slight crease between Macie's eyebrows, and her chin had begun to tremble. He heard her breath quicken as she lifted her hand and laid it on his cheek. He closed his eyes and leaned into her touch. When he felt the brush of her mouth against his lips, he jerked.

"Jonah . . ."

"What, baby?"

"Make love to me."

It was a question right out of the best dream he'd ever had and the last thing he had expected her to say. He looked down at her, studying the intensity of her expression. His first instinct was to take her to bed without questioning the gift, but his conscience wouldn't let him take advantage of what he considered a request that came out of her distress.

"Do you think that's wise?"

She frowned. "Do you mean . . . wouldn't I rather be a good girl and take the rest of the sleeping pills the doctor left? If so, then the answer is no. As it is, I've already spent too many days with grief and death. You don't have to pretend you care for me. Just help me remember what it feels like to be alive."

Jonah felt as if she'd punched him in the gut. Her honesty hurt in a way he wouldn't have believed. There was no denying he wanted her, but touching her now in that way, when she was so vulnerable and so hurt, was wrong — plain wrong.

Still, he leaned forward, centering a kiss on her mouth that left them both aching and wanting more. Reluctant to turn loose of her, he trailed kisses down the side of her cheek, then nuzzled her neck just beneath her ear. For the rest of his life, he knew the scent of lilac-scented shampoo was going to make him want to cry.

"God . . . Macie, I —"

She tensed, and he felt it, and in that moment he changed what he'd been going to say.

"Damn," he muttered, then cupped her face with both hands. "I should have the guts to tell you no, but I don't. God forgive me, but I can't pretend I don't want you."

She smiled, then reached for his hand to lead him to bed.

"Wait," he said, and then added, "you've got to promise me something."

Macie's heart was still hammering from the kiss they'd shared. Right then she would have promised him whatever he asked.

"Anything."

"In the morning . . ."

"Yes?"

"Don't hate me . . . or yourself."

Her eyes darkened. "Oh, Jonah . . . don't you know?"

"Know what?" he asked.

"I could never hate you. Before, you only saw me as a child, but I was thirteen and falling in love . . . in love with you. You were my first love, Jonah. When you left and never came back, it broke my heart. I don't know what I feel for you now, but I can guarantee it's nothing close to hate."

Guilty that he'd been so oblivious to a girl hovering on the edge of womanhood, he cupped her face and then feathered a kiss across her brow.

"Forgive me, sweetheart. I didn't know." Then he thrust his fingers into her hair, letting the weight and the silken tangles of it pull him farther away from sanity. "If I was cruel to you, forgive me. I didn't mean it. When I left, I was blindsided by what Felicity told me and hurting in a way you could never understand."

"Then make it up to me now," Macie

begged. “We can pretend, just for tonight, that there’s nothing more important than the pleasure of each other.”

Jonah tore himself away from her long enough to turn the lock on her door. He turned around, then stopped, still giving her the time and the distance to change her mind.

Instead she began to take off her clothes. Seconds later, she was naked and waiting.

One minute Jonah felt as if he’d been stomach-punched, and then his heartbeat hit an all-time high. He crossed the floor in two strides, lifted her off her feet and then laid her on the bed. For a long, silent moment he stood there, staring at the beauty of her body and the hunger in her eyes.

“Jonah, please . . . I ache for this . . . and for you.”

He kicked off his shoes, then tore off his clothes. Moments later, he was beside her, then above her.

Macie wrapped her arms around his neck.

“I promise,” she said softly.

He rose up on one elbow and then rolled his tongue around the tip of one of her nipples.

“Promise what?” he asked.

She arched off the bed with a groan, then dug her fingers into his shoulders, trying to remember what came next. When he circled her belly button with the tip of his finger, she gasped, then blurted out the words.

"That this doesn't have to mean anything."

Jonah paused momentarily, then slowly shook his head.

"No, Macie . . . it's too late for that. It already means something . . . you mean something . . . to me."

Suddenly he was at the foot of the bed and Macie was watching him crawl between her legs. When his head dipped and she felt the heat of his breath on her belly, she closed her eyes and gave herself up to his touch.

Jonah had accepted why this was happening. Macie wanted the sexual release as a means to forget, but he wanted her to remember — to remember, so that for the rest of her life, the thought of making love brought his face to her mind.

Seconds turned into a minute, then another and then another. Macie was trembling beneath him, begging in a choked whisper for release, but he wouldn't let her go. Each time he felt her muscles starting to tense, he would slow down, then pull back, leaving her hanging on the edge of completion.

Suddenly he raised his head and slid a hand between her thighs.

There was a moment of cognizance when she felt his fingers center on that tight, swollen bud, and then everything began to blur. It felt as if her body had started to hum, like a perfectly balanced engine running on full throttle.

He watched her eyes losing focus, heard her breath coming in short, fast gasps. When she suddenly bucked beneath his stroke, he knew she was coming undone.

Macie called out his name, or at least she thought she did, although there was nothing but the unbearable pleasure and the man who was making it happen.

One wave of the climax washed over her, frightening in its intensity.

The second wave came, peeling back the layers of social propriety and leaving her raw and waiting for more.

The third wave came and took her high, then let her fall — all the way back into Jonah Slade's arms.

The last tremors were still rocking her sanity when he lifted himself up and thrust hard between her knees. Suddenly that which had been ending took on a new life. Like the upswing of a kite that was catching a new wind, the climax she'd been riding began to recoil.

"Oh God . . . oh, Jonah . . . I don't think —"

She smelled the musk from the heat of his body, then felt his breath next to her ear.

"Macie."

She opened her eyes just as their bodies slammed against each other.

"Feel that?" he grunted.

She tried to answer, but the words only came out in a groan.

He thrust again, harder and higher.

"Wrap your legs around my waist," he muttered.

She kept trying to tell him that she couldn't even feel her legs, but the words wouldn't come. Then, somewhere within herself, she found the strength to do as he asked.

Macie locked her ankles around his waist, and as she did, it not only shifted his power, but the angle of their joining. Within seconds, she knew she was lost. It was there all over again — the need to die and be resurrected in his arms. Screaming his name in her mind, she reached above her head, grabbed the headboard of the bed and let the climax come. It ripped through her in shock waves, shattering both modesty and inhibition.

When Jonah felt the internal tremors of her climax ebbing and flowing around him, he tried to hold back, to prolong this sweetness, but it was impossible. With a deep, aching groan, he spilled into her, rocking back and forth until there was nothing left of him but the aftermath of a miracle.

"Baby . . . ah, baby," he said, then took her in his arms and rolled, pulling her close against his chest and raining kisses into her hair.

Macie was dumbstruck. She'd asked him to help her forget, but the request had backfired. That would never happen. Making love with Jonah had been more beautiful and yet more frightening than anything she'd ever experienced. She lay close within his embrace, wondering at the complete and utter stupidity of her sister to have had a man like this and given him up for money. From their first kiss, Macie knew she would have given away her last dime just to keep him. But what they'd just done hadn't come out of love — only need. It broke her heart to think of the years to come and how lonely she was going to be. This had been the best she would ever have, and with the best man she'd ever known. The day he left her, a part of her was going to die. It wasn't something she looked forward to, but it was something she'd already accepted.

"Jonah . . . I —"

"Don't talk," Jonah said, then brushed the thick tangle he'd made of her hair away from her face.

Macie sighed, then nodded. He was right. There was nothing left to be said. They'd already said it all — with their bodies.

Once, in the night, Jonah woke and wondered if Carl French had arrived, but he didn't care enough to let go of Macie to go see. Later, he dreamed he was in a huge warehouse of a room, and everywhere he looked there were babies. Babies in boxes. Babies in cribs. Babies on the floor on pallets. And somewhere he could hear one baby crying. Only one. And he knew it was his. In the dream, he was running from one baby to the other, farther and farther down the vastness of the warehouse, searching for the source of that one tiny voice. But the farther he went, the fainter the child's cry became. Then, suddenly, he could no longer hear it.

Jonah gasped, then sat up with a jerk. Beads of sweat dotted his forehead, and when he reached up to wipe them off, he realized his hands were shaking.

"God in heaven," he muttered, then slid out of bed, careful not to wake Macie.

He staggered to the bathroom and began splashing cold water on his face, trying to wash away the remnants of that dream. It had been so real. He reached for a towel and began to dry off, telling himself that it was only a dream — that it wasn't a portent of things to come. He wouldn't let himself believe that it was some sort of fatherly instinct warning him that Evan had just died.

"Jonah?"

He turned around. Macie was standing in the door.

"I didn't mean to wake you," he said, and then turned away, busying himself with hanging up the towel so that she wouldn't see the fear on his face.

But she'd seen that and more.

"Jonah! What's wrong?"

He swallowed around the knot in his throat, and when he turned around, he was smiling.

"Nothing but a bad dream," he said, and reached for her. "Come back to bed."

She went, but not because she believed him. She went because, this time, he was the one who needed to forget.

10

Macie came to slowly, waking in lazy increments, then stretched languorously, savoring everything, including the tenderness between her thighs. Last night had been incredible and, at the same time, frightening. She was falling in love with him all over again, and there was nothing she could do to stop it.

She reached out to the other side of the bed and, as she did, realized it was empty. Disappointed, she opened her eyes and then saw the note on his pillow.

The covers fell to her lap as she sat, leaving her bare from the waist up. Her eyes were still sleepy, her hair a mess. She looked like a woman who'd been thoroughly made love to, which she had. With a heartfelt sigh, she opened the note.

I wanted to wake up with you this morning, but Carl French has arrived. Come find me.

J

The fact that he hated leaving their bed as much as she hated waking up alone made her feel better. She pressed the note against her lips, then got out of bed and went to shower. All the time she was dressing, she felt a constant urge to rush. If she remembered correctly, Carl French was not only Jonah's best friend, but he also worked for the CIA. She couldn't help but hope that this was a good sign. Maybe there was a break in the case regarding Evan. Dear God, if only that could be so.

Choosing a pair of white slacks and a pale pink DKNY T-shirt, she dressed without once looking in the mirror as Felicity would have done. After pulling her hair back and fastening it with a tortoiseshell clip, she stepped into a pair of thin-strapped silver sandals and hurried downstairs.

Rosa was dusting the furniture in the foyer as Macie reached the main floor. When she heard Macie's footsteps, she turned around and smiled.

"Good morning, Miss Macie. Would you like some breakfast?"

"Just some coffee and toast."

"In the dining room?" Rosa asked.

Macie shook her head. "Would you please bring it to the library instead?"

Rosa nodded, then hesitated. "Miss Macie, may I ask you a question?"

"Of course."

"The *niño* . . . Mr. Evan . . . do they have any leads?"

"I'm on my way to find out. If there's any good news, I'll be sure to let you know."

"Thank you, Miss Macie. He is a fine, strong boy. Just like his father, I think."

When Rosa's gaze suddenly shifted before she hurried away, Macie knew that Jonah must be behind her. Wondering what the "morning after" would be like with this man, she stilled a frisson of nervousness and turned around.

His expression was unreadable until she looked into his eyes. At that point, she let out the breath she'd been holding.

"Jonah?"

He slid a hand beneath the weight of her hair and gently squeezed the back of her neck.

"I'm sorry," he said softly.

"For what?"

"I didn't want you to wake up alone."

She realized she had no idea how to respond to that. She wanted to throw herself into his arms, to tell him that last night had been the most amazing night of her life, and that she was falling in love. Instead she nodded and managed a smile.

"Thank you for the thought, though."

When he didn't offer anything else to the conversation, Macie wanted to scream. The formality between them felt almost insulting. From the way he was behaving, last night had been nothing to him except what she'd asked for: a favor he'd agreed to fulfill. If that was the way he wanted to play it, then she was more than up to the task.

"You told me to find you, but obviously

you've found me. You said Carl French was here? Did he bring any good news?"

Jonah frowned. What the hell had he done to turn her off like this? There was a sudden formality between them again that he flat out didn't like. He didn't want her cool and courteous. He wanted her the way she'd been last night, under him and on fire. But what he wanted apparently wasn't one of the options.

"Yes, he's here. Would you like to meet him?"

Macie noted that he hadn't answered the last part of her question. Fine, if that was the way he wanted to play it, she would ask the guy herself.

"Yes, thank you, I would."

"He's with Ruger," Jonah said.

When Macie started toward her father's office, Jonah surprised himself as much as her by taking her arm, then turning her around.

"What are —"

Macie never got the rest of the question said. Jonah cupped her face with his hands and then kissed her.

The sensation of that mouth on her lips, hard and demanding, yet coaxing every sensual feeling in her body into an all-out alert, was staggering. She was on the verge of a moan when he turned her loose.

"Just so you know. . . . Just so you remember," he said softly.

Macie touched her fingers to her lips. They were only slightly moist, and trembling just a little bit. They didn't feel hot or scarred, but she felt as if she'd been branded.

"I remember everything just fine," she muttered. "But what is it you want me to know?"

Jonah started to answer, then stopped. Silence lengthened between them.

"Jonah?"

Finally he sighed. "Never mind. If you don't already know, then it does no good for me to tell you."

With that enigmatic remark, he took her by the elbow and led her to Ruger and French. She spotted the stranger almost immediately and was taken aback by his open, friendly manner when he saw them come in.

"Hey, buddy, I wondered where you'd gotten off to," Carl said, then grabbed Macie's hand and shook it before she could offer. "Miss Blaine, I assume. I'm Carl French." Then he added, "So sorry for your loss."

Macie nodded as she watched him talking. Although she wasn't the type of woman to make snap judgments about people, she liked him. His personality was in direct contrast to what she would have expected an agent with the Central Intelligence Agency to be. Then she chided herself, guessing that she'd seen too many movies. CIA agents were just people, too, only with a few more survival skills than the ordinary citizen. At least that was what she told herself as she shook his hand. Then she looked in his eyes and saw depths that his ready laugh and quick smile only thinly disguised. She wasn't used to dealing with people who were something other than they presented themselves to be. She wondered why she hadn't had the same reaction to Jonah, then decided it was because she'd known him much longer, and at a time when he had not been a Company man.

Unlike Jonah, Carl was stocky and not much taller than Macie. He wore his curly blond hair clipped close to his head, and had a pair of wire-rimmed glasses just above a small bump on his nose. And, like most of the men in the room, he carried a cell phone in one hand the way most people would have carried a pen. She took a step forward, shortening the distance between them, then lowered her voice just enough to make her question disarming.

"So, Agent French, do you have any news regarding my nephew's abduction?"

"Please, call me Carl. As for news, I'm afraid I don't have anything new to add except a list of Miguel Calderone's holdings in California. We're checking them out right now."

"Holdings . . . as in companies?"

Jonah slid a hand on Macie's shoulder. "He's got to be holding Evan hostage somewhere. Eliminating the obvious locales is a place to start."

"But how do we know if Evan is still in the state? He could be anywhere, right?"

Carl started to fidget but was saved from answering when Ruger called him to the phone.

"Excuse me," he said quickly, and hurried to the other side of the room.

Macie turned around. "Jonah? What do you know that I don't?"

He shrugged. "Not much, and only because I've been up longer than you."

"What do you mean?"

"Carl brought some intel with him that we didn't know before."

"Intel? What's that?"

He smiled slightly. "Sorry for the spy-speak. Sometimes I forget there's another world out here. Intel is intelligence, information. Okay?"

"Oh, of course. I wasn't thinking. So what did he have to say?"

"The reason we think Evan is still alive and in California is that some of our people have seen unusual activity in the Calderone cartel. There are at least a half-dozen of Calderone's most trusted people who are no longer in Colombia. A couple were spotted entering Central America, then three more were seen at the Mexican border. Carl said that four of those five are now known to have crossed the border into California. As far as we know, they're still here. Also, his woman and his surviving son, Juan Carlos, have disappeared from the Colombian plantation, although the child Calderone fathered with the woman is still there. If she went somewhere without that little girl, that tells us that she's probably doing some dirty work for Miguel. God knows she's capable of it. Carl also said the authorities have been notified at the Federal penitentiary where Calderone is being held, although nobody's really concerned. With today's technology, it's virtually impossible to stage a prison break."

"Okay, so because some of Calderone's people are in California, you think they're with Evan?"

He shrugged. "It's a better than average guess that they're the ones who staged the abduction and are holding Evan hostage. And what safer place to hold someone like Declyn Blaine's grandson than on your own property?"

Macie needed to believe.

"So you think Evan is still alive?"

Jonah didn't want to give her false hope, but he'd been around Calderone long enough to know that there was a twisted sort of logic to everything the man did.

"Look at it this way, honey. If Calderone

had intended to kill Evan without making some kind of statement first, they would have shot him when they shot Felicity and Declyn. And since we've heard nothing, and there have been no demands, then it only stands to reason that he's waiting."

"For what?"

"That's the tricky part. My guess is it has something to do with me."

Macie's heart skipped a beat. "How will we know? What —"

"Don't. Second-guessing a madman will turn you into the same thing. I don't know what to tell you, baby . . . but I do know it won't be much longer, okay?"

The tenderness in Jonah's voice was almost her undoing.

"I want Evan back. He's all I have left of Felicity. But I don't want anything to happen to you, either."

He touched her face, then lightly brushed a thumb across her lower lip. She thought he was going to kiss her, but instead, just dropped his hand.

"If it's humanly possible, we'll make this all right."

Macie frowned. "I don't know how. This is so dangerous. They're nothing but butchers."

"But I *do* know," he said.

"I don't understand. How can you be sure?"

"Because it's what I do."

"Oh." There was a moment of silence, then she shuddered. "God."

Before Jonah could reassure her, Carl yelled at him from across the room.

"Hey, Moby, come here a minute, will you?" Carl called.

"Yes, okay," Jonah said. "Be right there."

"Why did he call you Moby?" Macie asked.

Jonah grinned. "It's a little complicated, but you'd have to know Carl. Moby is short for Moby Dick. The whale, right?"

"Yes, but —"

"Now what's my name?"

"Jonah, but —"

He started to grin. "You're doing good. In the Bible, remember the story of Jonah?"

"Yes, he was swallowed by a . . . Oh, good grief, a whale. But that doesn't make a bit of sense," Macie said.

"Well, I said you have to know Carl."

Macie smiled.

"You should do that more often," Jonah said.

"What?" she asked.

"Smile. It looks real good on you, lady."

"I haven't had a lot of reasons to smile lately," Macie said.

"Hey, Jonah!"

Carl was yelling now.

"Yeah, coming," Jonah said. "Are you all right now?"

"I'm fine. I'm going to have some toast

and coffee, then call the hospital. I need to go check on Daddy today."

"Don't leave this house without me," Jonah warned.

Macie frowned. "Are you thinking there's a possibility of another incident like the one we had yesterday?"

"There's no way of knowing, but we don't want to take chances, okay?"

"Okay."

"There *is* another option."

"Like what?" Macie asked.

"We could put you under protective custody until all this is over."

Macie looked around at all the law enforcement people.

"What do you call this?"

"I'm talking about a safe house, Macie. A place where only a very few people know where you are. You would be under guard at all times until this is over."

"No."

"Maybe you should just think about —"

"No."

She turned angrily and strode out of the room. Jonah cursed beneath his breath as he moved to the conference table where Carl and Ruger were waiting.

"What took you so long?" Carl teased.

"Just shut up," Jonah muttered, then turned to Ruger. "What do we know about the gardener?"

Carl looked up. "What gardener? I needed you to run down this list — see if you recognize any locations."

Ruger wanted to tell Jonah to back off, that they were doing their job just fine, but the truth wasn't that simple. They weren't doing just fine. Unless they got a break in the case, they had nowhere else to go.

"We know he's not really Felipe Sosa, and we know he's living in Sosa's house. He comes to work. He goes home. The only time he uses the phone is to order food. We could pick him up, but all that would do is alert Calderone's men that we're on to him."

"Son of a bitch," Jonah said.

"Hey!" Carl said, abandoning the list of Calderone's holdings.

Both men looked at him.

"I repeat — what gardener?"

Jonah shoved his hands into his pockets. "One of Calderone's men. He's outside right now, pruning the goddamned rosebushes. Probably laughing behind our backs and thinking he's fooled us good. I'd lay odds he had a hand in getting the killers through security to the main house, but we can't prove it. And Ruger's right. If we pick him up, there's no telling what might happen." Then he looked at Ruger. "You're still keeping a tail on him?"

"Twenty-four/seven."

"And you'll let me know if —"

Ruger stifled an urge to sigh. "Yes."

There was way too much condescension in Ruger's voice. It ticked Jonah off, and he didn't bother trying to hide it.

"You get pissed off all you want at me, but I have a hell of a lot more at stake than you do. I would very much like to have my first visit with my son not be at a goddamned funeral home. So let's drop the antagonism and get real. When I ask you a question, all I want is an honest answer. If you need me, call. I intend to be out today. Macie wants to visit her father."

He nodded at Carl. "See you later," he said, and headed for the door.

"Take Sugarman and Carter," Ruger said.

Jonah didn't bother to answer. He just kept walking. His heart was aching, and he felt as if he was losing his mind. Standing back and letting others be in control of his world was almost impossible for him to maintain. He kept thinking of Evan, wishing he'd known him before, wanting him to believe he wasn't alone.

Stay strong, kid . . . stay strong. I swear to God, I will find you.

Back in the command center, Carl's eyes narrowed thoughtfully as he watched his friend's angry exit.

"You pissed him off," Carl said.

Ruger shrugged. "He's a loose cannon. I don't feel comfortable trusting him with all the information. After all, it's not as if he's a normal father whose child has been kidnapped. The man has skills that are illegal in every country in the world, for God's sake. If he goes off half-cocked, he could ruin the entire rescue attempt and get his son killed."

"Do you know where the boy is? Are you planning a rescue attempt?"

Ruger's face flushed. "No, but —"

"Then I don't think there's any danger of anything being ruined, now is there?"

Ruger sighed. "You guys stick up for your own, don't you?"

Carl smiled and shrugged. "Are you feds any different?"

Ruger hesitated, then chuckled. "No, I don't guess we are."

"Then cut the man a little slack."

"Yeah, okay," Ruger said, then reached across the table for his half-empty coffee cup and downed what was left. "Damn . . . I hate flavored coffee," he said, shuddering slightly.

Now that he'd mellowed Ruger out, Carl moved his motives for being there up a notch.

"So what's with this Samuel Vega guy? Is he still in custody?"

"They're going to spring him today," Ruger said. "Don't have enough to hold him."

"Hmm . . . mind if I have a go at him before he hits the streets?" Carl asked.

"He's not talking," Ruger said.

Carl grinned. "Oh, I don't know. I have a real winning way about me. How about it?"

Ruger gave the blond charmer a cool, studied stare, then finally chuckled.

"What the hell. Go for it. Just remember, if he talks, you have to share."

"It's a deal," Carl said, and left before Ruger could change his mind.

A half hour later he was at the L.A. County jail, waiting to talk to Vega. When the man appeared, he was handcuffed and belligerent.

"Who the fuckin' hell are you?" Vega said.

Carl smiled. "I'm Carl French, Mr. Vega. Why don't you have a seat? I thought we'd have a little chat. Would you like a cigarette? Maybe a soda or some coffee?"

The man's attitude began to shift as Carl continued to offer small perks. Finally he shrugged.

"A coffee. Colombian, of course, and I would like a cigar."

Carl stifled a smirk. "Coming up," he said, then eyed the guard. "Sir, if you would be so kind as to pass on Mr. Vega's requests, we would both be very grateful."

The guard had already been coached to adhere to the agent's wishes, so he stepped outside the room long enough to request the desired items.

Carl took a seat across the table from the

man and then leaned forward, well aware that moving into the man's personal space made him seem more accessible.

"So, while we're waiting, I'd like to talk about that little incident yesterday. What was that all about, anyway?"

Vega's expression changed, taking on a much-injured air.

"You tell me," he said. "I am driving down a street, minding my own business, when your cops pull me over and arrest me. They accuse me of stalking. They accuse me of attempted this and possible that. But it's all a lie."

Carl frowned sympathetically. "Probably a case of mistaken identity. Maybe your car looked like another they were searching for. Maybe you looked like another man who's wanted for some felony."

Vega thumped his doubled-up fists on the table. The handcuffs rattled noisily, alerting the guard, who took a couple of steps forward.

Carl held up his hands. "It's okay. It's okay," he said. "Mr. Vega is understandably upset." He turned back to the prisoner. "So I'm assuming your lawyer is working on your release?"

"Damn right," Vega said. "Say . . . you never did say who you are."

"Sure I did. My name is Carl French."

Vega frowned. "No, man . . . I mean, *who the fuck are you?*"

"Oh, that," Carl said, and took out his ID just as the door opened and Vega's coffee and cigar were delivered.

"Son of a bitch," Vega said, and scooted backward in the chair, as if he'd suddenly gotten too close to a fire. "What's going on here?" he shouted, and swept the coffee off the table onto the floor.

"Now look what you've done," Carl said, and waved away the guard, who was about to grab Vega by the collar and haul him out of the room. "Fresh Colombian. Nothing better, and it's wasted." Then he leaned forward, and the smile slid off his face. "Just like you're going to be when we turn you loose."

Vega's features were contorted with rage. "I want my lawyer. You have no right to question me like —"

Carl took a small tape recorder out of his pocket, turned it on and set it on the table between them.

"You need to get your facts straight, Samuel Vega. After I leave, you are going to be released without any further contact with your lawyer, while your buddy stays locked up nice and tight."

Vega's swarthy complexion went from red to pale. He jumped out of the chair.

"You can't do that to me!"

"Do what?" Carl said. "We're just turning you loose, as you requested."

Vega started to shake. "You son of a bitch!

You know what will happen to me."

Carl's smile disappeared. "I'm sorry. I'm not following your complaint. You have assured us that you are completely innocent of trying to kill Mercedes Blaine. The fact that you had her picture in your car and were seen following her from several different locations was pure coincidence, right? And since you're innocent, nothing will happen when we turn you loose."

Vega cursed, sputtered, then sat down with a thump. Sweat was running out of his hair and down the sides of his face, and he kept swallowing over and over, as if he were trying to choke down something caught in his throat.

"Is there something you want to say?" Carl asked, then stood up and leaned forward.

Instinctively Vega leaned back. All the amiability in Carl French's behavior was gone.

"Like what?" Vega muttered.

"What were you supposed to do to Miss Blaine?"

Vega shrugged. "I wasn't going to do anything to her."

Carl straightened up and started toward the door.

"Release him," he told the guard.

Vega jumped up. "No. Wait."

Carl kept walking.

Vega followed. "Wait! Wait! I will tell what I know."

Carl stopped. "That's better."

"But you have to protect me," Vega said.

"No, I don't," Carl said. "Sit down."

Vega sat.

"Who sent you after the Blaine woman?"

"I got a call. I do as I'm told," Vega said.

Carl frowned slightly. "That's not what I'm asking, Mr. Vega. I'll start over, and I'd better get the right answer or I'm out of here . . . and so are you."

The last of Vega's attitude crumbled.

"One more time. Who do you work for?" Carl asked.

Vega looked down at the floor. "The *padrone*," he mumbled.

"I'm sorry. I didn't hear you," Carl said, and scooted the tape recorder closer to Vega. "Could you speak a little louder."

"The *padrone*. I work for the *padrone*."

"Just for the record . . . how about a name?"

"Calderone," Vega said, then looked up. "Miguel Calderone."

"And he told you to do what to Miss Blaine?"

"Get rid of her."

"What about the boy?"

Vega frowned. "What boy? There was no boy with her."

Carl reached across the table, and this time he grabbed a fistful of Vega's shirt and yanked the man to his feet.

"Don't fuck with me, you sorry little bastard. Tell me where Calderone is holding Evan Blaine or the deal is off."

Vega started to shake. "I swear . . . I don't know anything about that."

"You lie. Everyone knows about it. It's been on the news for days."

"No, no, that's not what I meant," Vega said. "I meant that I don't know where he is. I had nothing to do with that. I swear."

Carl could tell the man was telling the truth, but he hid his disappointment. He motioned to the guard.

"I'm done with him. Take him back."

Vega eyed Carl nervously as he stood.

"You are not going to give me up? You promised me, man. Remember that."

Carl just stared. "I promised you nothing. You're the one who did all the talking."

He stood without moving as Vega was led from the room, cursing him with every step. He turned off the tape recorder and dropped it in his pocket. He would give it to Ruger later. Right now he was going to swing by Cedars-Sinai Hospital and see if Jonah and Macie were still there. He would not hide any evidence from Ruger, but his first allegiance was to Jonah, and he was going to tell him everything he'd learned.

The Snowman was coming out of a coffee shop when his cell phone rang. He took it out of his pocket, glanced at the caller ID and then frowned.

"Hello," he said shortly.

"You have not called in."

The accusation in the man's voice made the Snowman's frown deepen. "I've been busy," he said shortly. "Tell the *padrone* that I've found Jonah Slade. Ask him what he wants me to do next."

"This is good news," the man said.

"I always deliver," the Snowman said. "And just for the record, I don't like being pressured, understand?"

"Just for the record, you can be replaced," the man countered.

For a second, the Snowman froze. He knew all too well what Calderone and his men were capable of. Then he snorted lightly, taking care that it was heard on the other end of the line.

"Maybe," he said. "But not easily. I await further orders."

He was the first to disconnect. It gave him a sense of control, which was good, because right now, his life was seriously fucked.

The men guarding Evan were worried. They couldn't make the boy eat, and he was getting weaker by the hour. The *padrone* had told them to keep the boy healthy and in one piece until his arrival, but they didn't know how to do that. Not even the *padrone*'s woman had been successful, and her powers of persuasion were well-known within the organization. She was the perfect partner for a man of Calderone's personality — a female counterpoint of selfishness and evil. But not even she knew how to keep the boy alive, and she had left in a huff, not wanting to catch the backlash should the boy succumb before Calderone could mete out his revenge.

Now the guards were left with a quandary. How to keep someone alive who believed that his days were already numbered? As he'd done twice a day since they'd arrived in this place, Evan's guard prepared a tray for the boy and carried it to his room. As always, the boy was curled up on the bed with his back to the door, as if offering up his vulnerability with a quiet defiance. The guard set the tray down on the floor, then rattled the bed frame.

"You eat now," he said. "It is good."

Evan didn't move.

The guard threw up his hands in defeat, and shut and locked the door.

On one level, Evan had heard the guard's entrance, as well as his exit, but mentally he'd moved into a place where no one could touch him. He'd thought more than once that he was starting to hallucinate, but at other times he convinced himself they were only dreams. Now, though, there was one recurring image that kept staying in his mind.

While he'd never seen his father's face or heard his voice, somehow he knew the voice he kept hearing was that of his dad. And all he kept saying was the same phrase, over and over and over.

Stay strong. Stay strong.

He hadn't decided whether he believed it or not, but he wanted to. God, how he wanted to. With the words echoing in his mind, he rolled over, then sat on the edge of the mattress. His head was swimming, so he leaned forward, lowering his head between his knees until the vertigo stopped. Once he thought he could stand, he got to his feet, staggered to the tray and then carried it back to the bed.

With painful and shaking hands, he finally popped the top of a snack-size can of peaches. The simple aroma seemed more wonderful than anything he'd ever had in his life. He lifted the can to his mouth and drank off the juice, then, because his hands were too sore to hold the spoon, he tilted the can again and proceeded to eat the contents in three bites.

Almost immediately, his stomach protested, growling in protest at the appearance of food after such a long drought. He set the empty can back on the tray and eyed the small can of Vienna sausages, then thought better of it. No sense making himself sick. He had enough to deal with without adding vomiting or diarrhea.

He set the tray on the bed, then lay down in front of it, taking some comfort in the fact that he'd pulled himself out of the depression and was taking a positive step toward saving himself. Now all he had to do was trust the voice he kept hearing and pray that it wasn't a figment of his imagination.

11

Macie sat in the back seat, staring blankly at the back of Federal Agent Sugarman's head as he leaned over to say something to Carter, who was, as usual, driving the car. She wouldn't let herself think past the moment and the comfort of leaning against Jonah's shoulder as the car took a sharp right turn. She was thankful her father was improving, but she dreaded another confrontation with him.

Jonah sensed her nervousness but was under the wrong impression, thinking she was concerned about Declyn's progress. He glanced into the front seat at Carter and Sugarman, then clasped her hand and lowered his voice as he spoke.

"Don't worry. Ruger said your dad has been moved out of intensive care into a private room. That's a good sign, right?"

Macie nodded, then curled her fingers into fists.

Jonah had spent too many years reading body language not to know something besides the status of her father's health was on her mind.

"Macie . . . ?"

"What?"

"It's not his health that's bothering you, is it? You don't really want to be here, do you?"

Macie shrugged, then turned away to stare out the window.

"Honey . . . talk to me."

"From the time I was small, my father and my sister were my world. They fed off each other, and I was perfectly happy to settle for being the other child. Everything I did in life was to make sure they approved of my decisions. When I 'meddled' in Evan's life, as Declyn called it, they not only shut me out, they disowned me." Her voice started to shake. "It wasn't losing the inheritance that mattered. I've made plenty of money on my own. It was losing the only people with whom I shared blood. You know what I mean?"

"And all because of me. Did I ever say thank you?"

Macie looked at him then, her eyes swimming with tears. "No, but now would be a good time, I think."

Jonah's gaze slid from her eyes to her mouth as he tilted her chin. He heard the catch in her breath as he leaned down. A moment later, his mouth was on her lips. It was a brief but tender kiss that reminded them of their passionate joining and the bone-melting climax that had followed.

Jonah very much wished they were somewhere other than the back seat of a car being driven by two Federal agents. Finally, and reluctantly, he broke contact.

"Macie?"

"Hmmm?"

"Thank you very much for making sure my son knew I hadn't abandoned him."

With her heart still pounding from the kiss, Macie managed to nod. Jonah leaned back, his eyes narrowing as he read the expression on her face. Along with the passion roused from their kiss, he saw something more. Suddenly he knew.

"You're royally pissed off at Declyn, aren't you?"

Macie's eyes widened in surprise. "How did you know?" Then backtracked by adding, "I shouldn't be. This isn't the time to . . . I mean, after everything that's happened, I should be elated that he's still alive."

"But you think the wrong person died, don't you?"

Again Macie was stunned by his observations.

"You must be one hell of a spy."

He shrugged. "I've been thinking it for days."

"The better he feels, the more hell I'm going to catch," she said.

Jonah frowned. "I don't want to see the bastard, but I'll go in with you if it will make you feel any better."

She sighed. "No, but thank you just the

same. I'm not afraid of him by any means, but with him in such fragile condition, I can't bring myself to yell back at him, even though I want to."

"I don't have any inhibitions about it," Jonah said. "If you need backup, remember I'm nearby."

She managed a smile, then told herself to relax.

Sugarman looked over his shoulder. "We're almost there. Carter's going to let us out at the front entrance and then go park the car. I'll accompany you to Mr. Blaine's room. Carter will meet up with us there."

"Thank you," Macie said. "I won't be there long."

"It doesn't matter, Miss Blaine. We're happy to help."

Macie leaned back, bracing herself for what was to come.

A few minutes later they were walking into the hospital lobby. Macie felt Jonah's focus shifting to bodyguard mode, which made her remember the last time they'd been here. It also dawned on her that she couldn't even remember what the man who'd bugged her purse looked like. It seemed surreal to realize that becoming a cohort in Calderone's revenge had gotten him killed. However, this time as they crossed the lobby, they reached the elevator without incident. As the car stopped on the floor where Declyn was hospitalized, Macie's stomach lurched. For a moment she thought she might throw up, but then Jonah slid his arm around her shoulders and the feeling passed.

As they started down the hall, Macie had a feeling of déjà vu. It took her a few moments to figure out why; then she realized that the floor Declyn was on now was the same floor on which her mother had been when she died. She swallowed around the sudden knot in her throat, then took a deep breath as they stopped to acknowledge the seated guard outside Declyn's door.

"Hey, Watts, how's it going?" Sugarman asked.

Watts nodded. "Good. The old man is gaining ground." Then he glanced at Macie. "Sorry, Miss Blaine. No disrespect meant."

"That's quite all right," she said, and started into the room, then looked back at Jonah.

"If you need me, I'll be here," he said.

Macie took a deep breath and walked into her father's room.

Declyn Blaine was, by nature, a self-centered, insensitive man. To find himself naked beneath a well-washed and backless hospital gown that countless other patients had worn was the height of humiliation. Add to that the fact that each day total strangers were doing everything for him from washing his body to wiping his behind. It made him furious. Not only was he weak as hell and in constant pain, but he was grieving to the depths of his soul. He'd seen his daughter murdered and his only grandson kidnapped. When the bullets had ripped through his own body, he'd been sure he was dying.

But fate, it seemed, had other plans.

The first word out of his mouth had been "Evan." And then he'd heard Macie's voice. It had taken him a few moments to remember that he had banned her from his life, and he vaguely remembered a few mumbled words about vultures circling a dying body. Then he'd asked about the ransom demand, and she'd told him there hadn't been one, and that they'd had no contact with the kidnappers whatsoever.

It was then that true fear had begun to seep into his soul. A man like him made enemies. It came with the power plays and takeovers. There were some who claimed that for every dollar he'd made, he made a new enemy, too. Drunk on the victory of another business success, he had laughed. But he wasn't laughing now. There was only one reason for a kidnapping other than money, and that was revenge.

He'd felt Macie's hand on his brow, and in his doped and fevered state, he'd pushed it away and blamed her, instead of himself, for what had happened. It was the last important thing he remembered until this morning, when they'd moved him into this private room. The nurses ignored his angry outbursts and met his demands without so much as a raised voice. For the first time in his privileged life, Declyn Blaine was frightened of the future. So when he heard the voices outside his room, he was afraid of the news they might bring, but when he saw Macie walk in, the fear turned to fury. He needed to lash out. She was the first one in line.

"Did you bring news of Evan?"

"No, Father, but —"

"Then get out," Declyn said.

Macie flinched. The finality in his voice cut all the way to her soul, but she ignored his demand.

"How are you feeling?" she asked, then picked up a hairbrush from the bed stand. "Would you like me to brush your hair?"

Declyn knocked the brush out of her hand and pointed toward the door.

"You and I have nothing to say to each other," he said, then frowned when Macie didn't budge. Her defiance was slightly surprising. He began to wonder if there was more of himself in his youngest child than he had realized.

Macie picked up the brush and laid it back on the stand, then sat down in a chair near the bed. Several seconds passed without either of them speaking.

Declyn glared.

Macie looked at him without comment.

Finally it was Declyn who broke the silence. "Well . . . spit it out. What do you have to say?"

"Yesterday I scattered Felicity's ashes in the ocean at La Jolla."

Declyn went from flushed to pale. Macie saw his jaw clench and his throat muscles spasm, as if he were fighting to gain control of his emotions. When he spoke, it was in anger.

"You had no right!" he said. "She was *my* daughter."

Macie's control snapped. "And she was *my* sister. What did you expect me to do? Leave her remains on a shelf in a mortuary and wait to see if you were going to live or die? She told me years ago that when she died, that's what she wanted. She said it was where she'd had some of her happiest times."

Declyn glared. This time, Macie glared back.

"You don't call the shots in my life anymore," she said.

"Just because your sister is gone, that doesn't mean you're going to get any of her inheritance."

Macie's breath caught in the back of her throat. For a few moments she was so stunned she couldn't find the words to speak. And then she shook her head and tried to laugh. It came out closer to a sob.

"You are pathetic. I never wanted your damned money . . . only your love. And now I'm not even sure I want anything more to do with that. You don't know how to love. All you know is how to control, and quite frankly, Father, you can yell and curse at me all you want, but it doesn't work anymore. Felicity is dead and Evan is missing, and all you want to do is yell at me? I don't know how you can face yourself in the mirror."

Declyn was so taken aback by her verbal attack that he was momentarily speechless. Before he could regain control of himself, the door to his room opened. Cold moved through him like a wave, chilling him from the tips of his toes all the way to his brain. He couldn't think of what to say, and at the same time he was afraid to open his mouth.

The man coming toward him was a ghost from the past, but the ghost didn't look like the young man he'd been fifteen years ago. There was a bitter twist to his mouth and a coldness to his countenance that hadn't been there before.

Declyn stared first at Jonah, then at Macie, and as he did, realized who was responsible for the return of the man who, even in his absence, had been his nemesis. Suddenly he felt sick to his stomach and wished to God he wasn't flat on his back in bed.

"What the hell is he doing here?"

"Trying to help us find his son," Macie said.

Declyn clenched his jaw even tighter. He'd never struck a woman, but the urge to do so now was stronger than it had ever been in his life.

"You had no right," he said.

"No, you sorry son of a bitch . . . you're the one who had no right," Jonah said.

Declyn went a whiter shade of pale.

"You said you weren't going to come in," Macie said.

Jonah looked her in the eye, daring her to deny him.

"I heard yelling," he said.

She started to comment, then thrust her hands into her hair and momentarily closed her eyes, as if willing herself to a calm she didn't feel.

Declyn stared, unable to believe what he was seeing. He was savvy enough to realize that something was going on between his youngest daughter and this man. He cursed beneath his breath, but it was loud enough that they heard.

"Would you like to repeat that loud enough for company, or are you too big a coward?" Jonah asked.

Declyn's anger spiked. "You couldn't have my oldest daughter, so you're working your way back into my life by fucking my youngest. And don't try to deny it. I'm not stupid."

Macie gasped, but Jonah only laughed.

"If you remember . . . I already had your oldest daughter. Evan was a result of that. I do not want into your life. And what's between Macie and me is none of your business. However, I'm going to have to disagree with your last remark, because I think you're not only stupid, you're pretty much an idiot. This lie . . . this perfect little lie that you persuaded Felicity to tell me, has put you and your entire family in jeopardy."

Declyn began to sputter. "Me? What are you talking about?"

"Has it ever occurred to you to wonder why there's been no request for ransom for Evan? Did Macie tell you that someone tried to kill her, too?"

Declyn's jaw dropped. He looked at Macie and saw the truth on her face.

"You didn't tell me. . . ."

"You don't care. Why bother?" she said shortly.

"If there's no ransom, then it's revenge," Declyn said. "I've made a few enemies in my time."

"Well, you do have a few brain cells after all," Jonah drawled. "Only the revenge isn't directed at you."

Declyn frowned. "What do you mean?"

Despite the fact that her father was bedridden, Macie could tell that it wasn't an issue that was going to slow either man from pursuing the fight. And while she understood

Jonah's fury, she still stepped between him and the bed where her father was lying before more than words started to fly.

"Jonah knows the man behind the attack," she said.

This time Declyn was taken completely off guard. He stared first at Macie, then at Jonah.

"Is this true?"

"Oh, it's true, all right," Jonah said. "Because of the lie Felicity told me, I believed there wasn't a person on this earth who cared if I lived or died. And because of that lie, I pursued a career that isn't healthy for a family man."

"What are you talking about?" Declyn asked. "What career?"

"Jonah works for the CIA. Undercover work," Macie said.

Suddenly all the defiance on Declyn's face disappeared. He wanted to look away, but Jonah held answers to questions that were driving him mad.

"What are you saying?"

"Felicity is dead because you lied to me. You were shot because of that lie, and my son — a son I didn't know I had — is now in the hands of one of the most ruthless drug lords ever to come out of South America."

"No," Declyn said, but it wasn't a denial as much as a plea for Jonah to stop talking.

"Yes," Jonah said.

"Are you sure?" Declyn asked.

"They're sure," Macie said.

"But why us . . . and why take Evan?" Declyn asked.

"I'm guessing, but I'd say that they killed Felicity because she's the mother of my son, and they shot you because you got in the way. They tried to kill Macie because she bears your name."

"But why did they kidnap Evan? Why didn't they just shoot him, too, like they did us?"

"Again, this is just a guess . . . but I think they want me to suffer like I made Miguel Calderone suffer."

Declyn didn't want to hear the answer, but at the same time, he had to know.

"What do you mean?"

"I killed his son. He saw it. He's the kind of man who believes in an eye for an eye. His son is dead, so he's going to kill mine. But he wants me to watch it happen. As long as they can't find me, Evan has a better chance of staying alive."

"Oh. God . . . I didn't know. . . . I didn't think . . ."

Jonah's cheeks flushed a dark, angry red.

"That's another lie. You might not have known about my lifestyle, but you did know what you did was wrong. You thought long and hard about it, then persuaded a weak, beautiful woman to go along with it so you could have your way. Now you need to pray, old man. You need to pray long and hard that we get a break in this case before it's too late . . . if it's not already."

Having said that, Jonah turned on one heel and strode out of the room.

Declyn looked at Macie. "I didn't know. If I had, I wouldn't —"

"He's right, Father. You're still lying." Then she turned toward the door.

"Wait! You've got to understand. I —"

"No. I don't have to do anything you say anymore." Then she took a deep, cleansing breath. "And don't you forget it."

Declyn was still talking as she walked out of the room, taking care to close the door firmly behind her.

The guard nodded at her as she came out. "How is your father, Miss Blaine?"

"His health is improving," she said. "Thank you for asking." Then she walked into Jonah's arms and buried her face against his chest.

To say Jonah was surprised was an understatement. He'd expected her to be angry that he'd confronted her father without her permission. He glanced up at Sugarman and Carter, who politely chose to look away, then he put his arm around Macie and led her toward a window at the end of the hall.

"I thought you'd be mad," he said.

Macie looked at him then, with the full

light of day shining on his face through the windows. He was a man who'd seen the dark side of life. It was there in his eyes. But he was also a man with a good heart and a tender soul. Standing this close to him was like being thirteen all over again. She was dumbstruck and in love, and so far out of her depth she was in danger of drowning.

"Macie . . . ?"

"What?"

"I'm sorry, but —"

She put her hand on his mouth, then shook her head.

"Don't apologize. I'm not mad at you. I'm just mad at myself. I used to want his approval so badly, and now it seems so unimportant. All I want now is Evan." *And you.*

But she couldn't bring herself to say aloud what was in her heart. As she moved her hand from his mouth, she curled her fingers into a fist in a futile gesture to retain the warmth of his lips.

Jonah nodded, but he was still smarting from a remark Declyn had made, and he wondered if it was bothering Macie as much as it was him.

"I need you to know something. When we made love . . . it wasn't because I was trying to get back at Declyn, or trying to regain something I'd lost with Felicity."

Macie flushed and then ducked her head. "I know. It's okay," she said quickly. "It happened because I asked."

He cupped her chin, then tilted it upward until she was forced to meet his gaze.

"No. It happened because I wanted to make love to you. I've wanted to ever since I saw you standing outside my apartment, but it's been hard for me to separate my anger at your sister and father from what I've been feeling for you."

Macie's heart skipped a beat. "Oh, Jonah, I —"

"Slade, we need to go," Sugarman said. "Ruger just called. He wants us to take you two back to the house. Now."

Jonah turned abruptly. "Is it Evan? Have they found him?"

Sugarman frowned. "I don't think so or he would have said. It's something else."

Jonah's hopes fell. There were only two other things serious enough to warrant an order this direct. Either he had intel that Macie's life was in danger again or Calderone's people were making a move.

"What's going on?" Macie asked as Jonah grabbed her hand and started with her toward the stairs, with the two Federal agents leading the way. "Why aren't we taking the elevator?"

"Too predictable."

"Oh, my God," Macie muttered as they started down the stairs.

"It's okay, Miss Blaine. This is just a precaution," Carter said.

"No, this is a nightmare," Macie said, then felt Jonah's hand on her shoulder.

"But you're not alone," he said softly. "Not anymore."

Evan sat on the side of his bed, staring at a spot on the opposite wall without really seeing it. Something was going on outside the room where he was being kept. The attitude of the guard who'd been begging him to eat had changed to one of disrespect. And while he hadn't expected any smiles or pats on the back that he'd begun to eat the food they were leaving, he could tell the mood of his captors was growing darker by the hour. It was frightening to think he might not live to see another day, although he'd been expecting to die ever since the day of his abduction.

He stared down at his hands, trying to curl his fingers into fists, then winced as pus oozed out from under one nail. He heard scratching in the corner of the room and turned just as the rat came out of the hole in the floor.

"Hey, Harold. How's it hangin'?"

The absurdity of what he'd just said suddenly hit him, and he started to grin. When the rat moved to the food tray on the floor near the door and began sniffing around an empty can of tuna, Evan chuckled.

"Sorry, Harold, nothing left. As you can

see, you're now rooming with a pig." Then he lifted an arm and smelled under his own armpit. "I even smell like a pig," he mumbled, then barked out a short laugh. "At least, I guess I smell like a pig. To tell you the truth, Harold, I've never smelled a pig. Have you?"

The whole conversation struck Evan as funny, and he started to laugh in earnest. Moments later, he fell back onto the bed in weary hysterics.

The rat sat up on its hind legs and stared at Evan, as if trying to figure out whether to stay or run.

Outside, the guard heard the sounds and came running. When he opened the door, he saw the boy lying on the bed and laughing like a crazy man.

"You! Shut up now!" the guard yelled.

The rat dove for cover.

Evan rolled over on his side, gasping for breath.

"Hey, smiley . . . what do you think?"

"About what?" the guard muttered.

"Do I smell like a pig? Harold thinks I do. What's your vote on the subject?"

The guard swerved, his gun aimed toward the bathroom.

"Who's this Harold?"

"I thought he was your brother. But if you don't know him, then I must have been mistaken."

The guard glared.

Evan collapsed into hysterics again. Every time he looked at the guard, he laughed even harder.

"This time tomorrow, you will not laugh," the guard yelled, then kicked the bed frame as he left the room, slamming the door hard behind him.

Evan's laughter ended on the next breath. Tomorrow. He said it would be tomorrow. Then he rolled over on his side in the bed and shoved the heels of his hands against his eyes, willing himself not to cry. He remembered reading a book once in which the hero said that tomorrow never comes. Obviously his captors had not read the same book.

The media that had been camped out a few blocks from the gate to the estate was noticeably absent.

"What the hell?" Sugarman muttered, as Carter sped past the place where they'd been gathered.

"I guess we're old news," Macie said. "Can't say I'm sorry."

Jonah frowned. There was no such thing as old news until something was over, and this was far from over. He figured Ruger had had them removed, but if so, then something bad was going down. He couldn't bring himself to think of the ramifications of the missing journalists, because if they'd left on their own, it could only be because the news regarding Evan Blaine's abduction had moved to a new location. But if that was so, then it would be because either he'd been found alive or his body had been recovered.

He said a quick prayer, making himself concentrate on the facts instead of the maybes. But as they pulled up to thc front of the house, his stomach rolled.

God, please don't let my son die.

12

Last night had been the first night in a week that the Snowman had been able to sleep without waking up in a cold sweat. It wasn't as if he'd never been threatened before. That came with the line of work he was in. But failing to satisfy Miguel Calderone was dangerous, especially when it involved revenge. He'd been toying with the idea of a new address and identity when he'd gotten the call from Calderone. If Slade hadn't been there, that might have been his only option. But Slade *had* been there. Where else would he have gone?

After letting Calderone's people know, the relief of having done what he'd been ordered to do put him in a very good mood. As he rolled through a yellow light, his stomach growled, reminding him that it had been a while since he'd had a good meal. His association with the Colombians had given him a taste for south-of-the-border cuisine, so he began cruising the area for a good place to eat.

Later, as he sat at his table in the Casa Paloma, waiting for his drink, he gave himself up to a brief moment of regret for the decisions he'd made in life. When he let himself think about it, which was rarely, he didn't relish living on both the just and the unjust sides of life. If he could choose and still have the money the criminal life was bringing him, he would of course choose to be righteous. But the Snowman was greedy, and he'd gotten too accustomed to the money accruing in his numbered Swiss account to stop now.

As he took his first sip of margarita, he had to admit that there was a part of him that empathized with Slade's situation. Truthfully, he had nothing against Jonah Slade. In fact, he admired the man. And he wouldn't wish Miguel Calderone's wrath on his worst enemy, but this was just a matter of business. Besides, Slade was a big boy. He knew what was at stake. Whatever happened after this was out of the Snowman's hands and off his conscience.

He smiled at the members of the passing Mariachi band and toasted their music with another sip of margarita. When the waitress finally brought his food, he leaned over the plate and inhaled slowly, savoring the spicy aromas wafting up his nose. Then he forked a bite of tamale on his plate, shoved it through the chili and then popped it into his mouth, groaning with satisfaction as the spicy Mexican food hit his palate. As he chewed, he glanced up at the night sky through the palm trees on the patio behind his table. The sky was clear, the night warm and balmy. Although he'd grown up in Michigan, he'd long ago become addicted to the warmer countries.

The pretty little waitress who'd brought him his food had already smiled at him much more than necessary. If he wanted, he knew he could go to bed with more than a full stomach tonight. He started to order a second margarita, then thought of the drive he had to make before getting to bed tonight. He finished his food, tossed a handful of bills onto the table, winked at the waitress and made his way to the door. Just as he stepped out onto the sidewalk, he was jostled by a man passing by.

"Hey, look out," he said sharply, then felt the bulge of an unfamiliar object that had suddenly appeared in his jacket.

He thrust his hand into the pocket, felt the outline of an envelope and a knife that hadn't been there before, and yanked his hand out as if he'd been burned. He looked around for the man, but he was nowhere in sight.

"Son of a bitch. This was supposed to be over," he muttered, then hurried to his car and got in, quickly locking the door before taking the envelope out of his pocket. The switchblade was symbolic of what Calderone would do if he did not adhere to the message. He opened the note with trepidation, wondering what was in store for him now.

The snake is on its way out. Be ready.

The meaning was clear. The note referred to the tattoo Calderone's people wore. The snake was Calderone. But he was in a Federal lockup in Lompoc. There was no such thing as a jail break at a Federal prison.

He leaned back in the seat, his stomach churning. The tamales he'd just eaten were threatening to come up.

"Son of a bitch. I want out of this game. Why can't the little bastard stay where he's put?"

Disgusted that Calderone was still calling the shots on his time and his life, he tossed the note out the window, put the knife in the glove box and headed out of East L.A.

Meanwhile, the "little bastard," as the Snowman had referred to Calderone, had no intention of staying put in Lompoc Federal Correctional Institution or, for that matter, in California. He dreamed of cutting out Evan Blaine's heart and laying it at Jonah Slade's feet, right before he cut out Slade's tongue. As soon as he had the satisfaction of watching Slade drown in his own blood, he was going back to the South American jungles. There were places there to hide that no white man had ever seen, and he knew every one of them.

But first, he had to die.

Calderone ran a hand through his hair, cursing the disheveled style and remembering the perfection of his appearance prior to being arrested. The lack of amenities in Lompoc was but another reason that kept his hate of Slade alive. He hadn't had a good night's sleep since Alejandro's death, and when he did sleep, he dreamed of revenge. He wanted to see Slade's face — wanted to hear his cries for mercy as he plunged the knife into the chest of Slade's son. He thought about it night and day — of the way the knife would feel as it sliced through bone and muscle. The boy would shriek and writhe, and Slade would beg and beg, but it wouldn't change a thing. He already had the boy. Within a matter of a day or so, he would have Slade, as well. Now all he had to do was get out from behind the walls of this prison.

The events that would help make this happen were already in motion. His woman, Elena, was coming again today, still masquerading as a nun. The prison doctor was going to play a key role in setting him free, although he'd had to do a little extra persuading, taking the doctor's wife to a nice hotel until the doctor had complied. Abraham Hollister was already in a conference room, awaiting Calderone's arrival. All Calderone had to do now was wait for a guard to come and get him.

He dug his hands through his hair, mussing it even more to give himself a harried appearance, then pinched himself on the face several times so that it would appear flushed. After a quick look through the bars to make sure he was still alone, he took his Bible from the shelf — the Bible that Elena had brought to him on a previous visit — then sat down on the edge of his bunk. Using his thumbnail, he picked at the inside cover flap until it started to come loose. When it did, he pulled, peeling it up all the way to the spine, and there, nestled within the folds of the spine, was a tiny plastic tube no larger in circumference than a piece of yarn. He lifted it out, taking care not to break it, then held it up to the light. The needle resting inside was thin and fine, hardly larger than the filament from a lightbulb. It looked innocent enough, but Calderone knew that even the smallest prick from that needle and he was going to be closer to hell than he'd ever wanted to be. However, it was his only chance to get out of this place.

Just then he heard the footsteps of approaching guards and slipped the minute tube into the pocket of his shirt. He shut the Bible, laid it back on the shelf beneath a small stack of paperback books and hurried to the sink. He splashed some water carefully about his face and neck and around the edges of his hair, making it appear as if he were perspiring, then sat back on the cot and slumped forward.

"Calderone, you have a visitor," one of the guards said.

Calderone stood, swaying slightly as he did.

"Step back," the guard ordered.

Again Calderone did as he was told, taking a step away from the door, then waiting for it to open.

As the cell door slid open, the other guard held out a pair of handcuffs.

"Step forward and hold out your hands."

Calderone pretended to stumble.

"What's wrong with you?" the guard asked, as he locked the cuffs around Calderone's wrists.

Calderone's heartbeat fluttered, but he remained outwardly calm. It wouldn't do to show any kind of emotion, although this would be the last time he would be fettered in such a demeaning way.

"Nothing is wrong," he said shortly, then pretended to wheeze slightly.

The guards looked at Calderone, then at each other, and shrugged.

"Walk," one of them said.

Calderone walked, and it was all he could do not to laugh. This time tomorrow, he would be free. After he'd dealt with Slade and his son, it would be back to his beloved Colombia.

Sitting still had never been one of Abraham Hollister's strong suits, but now was not the time to let his Adult Attention Deficit Disorder get the better of him. He needed to play it cool to make what was going to happen in the next few minutes look legitimate. He also knew that what he was doing was called aiding and abetting, and that he could do time if he was ever found out. However, once today's mess with Calderone was behind him, Hollister had made up his mind to retire. Three years earlier he had established a home and a new identity in Switzerland, in anticipation of just such an event. Working for Calderone had made him a rich man, but he had trouble sleeping at night. What good would the money be if he wasn't free to spend it?

Mindful of his part in what was about to happen, he took that morning's paper from his briefcase, opened it to the stock market section and started to read. He was frowning over an item on the NASDAQ when the door to the conference room opened. He folded up the paper and then stood. He'd been coached as to what to expect, and still he was shocked by Calderone's appearance as he entered the room. There was no acting involved as he expressed his dismay to the guards.

"What's wrong with this man? Why haven't you taken him to the infirmary?" Then he reached toward Calderone. "Mr. Calderone?"

Calderone took two staggering steps into

the room, grabbing his chest as he swayed. The tiny vial that had been so carefully removed from the bible broke beneath the impact of his fists. He clutched at the shirt fabric, accidentally ripping the pocket of his shirt as he cried out in agony. To the onlooker, it appeared that he was in the throes of great pain, when in reality he was making certain that the tiny wire in the capsule was piercing his flesh.

The impact was minuscule and brief. He barely felt the twinge of pain against his palm, but he knew it had happened, because the muscles in his body began to stiffen, and he imagined he could feel his vital organs shutting down one by one. Mentally he'd known what was going to happen, but experiencing it was something for which he could never have prepared. For the first time in his life, he knew terror. He was dying, and if his people failed him, then this was it.

"Help me," he groaned, gazing at Hollister with a look of disbelief on his face.

Hollister dropped to his knees by his client, cradling his head in his hands as he shouted to the guards, who were just starting to react.

"Get a doctor! Fast!" he shouted. "He has a bad heart."

Immediately one guard was on his two-way, while the other started toward them.

"Water!" Hollister yelled. "Get me some water."

The guard hurried to a small table in the corner of the room. While he was pouring water into a small plastic cup, Hollister wrapped up the bits of broken vial and the tiny, insignificant looking wire in his own handkerchief, then quickly put it in his pocket. He'd already been searched before coming in, and there was no reason for anyone to suspect he would be taking evidence out. He had to admit it was a marvelous plan. The only thing yet to be seen was if Calderone could be resurrected.

Moments later, a half-dozen guards appeared, carrying a stretcher, although, in Hollister's opinion, it was already too late. He watched as Calderone was loaded onto the stretcher and whisked out of sight.

"Where are you taking him?" Hollister asked.

"To the prison hospital."

"May I go with him?"

"No," the guard said. "Wait here."

Hollister blustered, asserting his presence as Calderone's lawyer, as they would have expected him to do.

"As his representative, I demand to —"

"Someone will let you know his condition," the guard said, then hurried from the room.

Once again, Hollister found himself alone in the conference room, only this time, the anxiety he'd been suffering from earlier was gone. Just a few more moves to be made and he would be gone. It was now up to the doctor Calderone had coerced. Whether Calderone succeeded or failed, Hollister was through with this rat race. His plane ticket was in his car, as was a small suitcase. It was time to put an end to this life and begin another.

Ralph Foster had been a doctor for more than twenty-seven years, and he'd been doctoring at Lompoc for nearly six. During that time, he'd seen just about everything one man could do to another. He considered himself immune to shock.

Still, he had not been prepared for the proposition put forth to him three days ago to help break a man out of Lompoc. He'd laughed in the woman's face and, of course, refused. Then, yesterday evening, his wife had not come home from the real estate office where she worked. Just as he was about to call the police, a knock had sounded on his door. Thinking it would be Patricia, who must have lost her key, he'd rushed to the door and found a strange man instead. He'd handed him a note and his wife's wallet, then walked away without uttering a word.

Foster opened the note and felt the room starting to spin. He'd never fainted in his entire life — not even as a med student during his first rotation in the morgue. But he felt like he needed to now.

Do what we tell you and your wife will be home tomorrow evening when you arrive. If you refuse or go to the police, there will not be enough left of her to identify.

Afterward, he'd thrown up on the doorstep. When he was finished, he'd hosed off the mess he'd made, then gone back inside. It was the longest night of his life as he waited for daylight. When he left for work the next day, he kept imagining the worst. What if he did help that man escape? He had no guarantee that they would keep their word and let Patricia go. But what if he didn't? Then it was certain that her death would be on his conscience. By the time he reached Lompoc, he'd made up his mind. He would do whatever it took to get her back alive. So when he got the call that they were bringing a man into the hospital, he knew what he had to do. When they wheeled the inmate into the emergency area, he hurried forward and helped them transfer the man from the stretcher to a bed.

"What happened to him?" Foster asked.

One of the guards looked nervous, as if afraid he would be blamed.

"We were taking him to see his lawyer when he grabbed his chest and then fell over. Is he dead? We didn't know he had a bad heart. No one told us."

"Get back," Foster said, as he put a stethoscope to Calderone's chest. The heartbeat was there, but so faint that if he hadn't known what to listen for, he would have missed it. He knew what he was dealing with. He'd already been briefed. Curare was rare in North America, but not where the man on the bed was from. Foster knew that a quick application of CPR would kick-start the man's heart within seconds. But that wasn't the plan. He had to appear to try to revive him, then quickly pronounce him dead.

A nurse hurried over, pushing a crash cart. Ordinarily that would have ended their charade before it began, but Ralph Foster was a careful man. He'd made sure that the defibrillator would be inoperable. It was against everything he believed in, but he loved his wife more than he cared about his honor. To make sure that she came home to him tonight, he was going to lie, and the lie would end in the release of a very dangerous man.

"Charge to two hundred," Foster ordered.

The nurse worked with the machine, fiddling with gauges, poking at buttons, but nothing would work. She looked up, her expression frantic.

"Dr. Foster! Something's wrong! It won't work!"

"Get on the phone! Get someone to bring the backup from the minor emergency area, and tell them to hurry!"

The nurse dashed out of the room. Foster

knew that by the time she returned, it was going to be too late. By now the guards were gone. He ordered a syringe of adrenaline to be administered intravenously, and when a second nurse went to get it, there was none to be found. He had a proper fit, as a doctor should have had on finding out that the ward was not stocked as he'd expected it to be, then sent the orderly and the nurse on a wild-goose chase for more.

By the time they all returned, he had pronounced the man dead. He looked up at the clock just as the nurse was returning.

"Time of death, 10:18 a.m."

Then he pulled a sheet over Calderone's face and told the orderly to get the inoperable defibrillator out of the room.

"I'm sorry, Dr. Foster," the nurse said. "Sometimes there's nothing we can do."

Foster frowned, giving them all an accusing glare as if the lack of medicines he'd needed had been their fault and not his.

"This was inexcusable, which makes losing him like this even more difficult to explain. Now, if you'll excuse me, I've got to notify the warden and then start the paperwork on the deceased."

One again masquerading as Sister Mary Theresa, Elena had already signed in as a visitor for Miguel Calderone. She'd been searched, told that his lawyer was with him and then sent into a waiting area. Conscious of the curiosity of the guards and other inmates, she lowered her head in an attitude of prayer, took out her rosary beads and began to pray.

"Hail Mary, full of grace . . ."

Moments later, she heard the sound of footsteps hurrying toward her and looked up, recognizing Miguel's lawyer on sight. She tensed. She could tell by the look on his face that all was going as planned. But she must maintain her demeanor until she'd been informed of Miguel's demise.

"Sister Mary Theresa?"

She nodded, then stood. "And you, sir, are . . . ?"

Abraham put a hand on her shoulder, aware that his every move was being watched.

"They told me you were here waiting to see Miguel. My name is Abraham Hollister. I'm his lawyer."

She smiled. "So you are through with your business now? I have come to pray with my brother."

Abraham squeezed her shoulder slightly, as if preparing her for the moment.

"I'm so sorry, but I'm afraid I have some bad news. Mr. Calderone suffered a heart attack only a short time ago and has passed away. They took him directly to the hospital here, but there was nothing they could do to revive him."

Elena gasped, then clutched her rosary beads to her chest.

"No! This can't be! Please, *señor.* Please tell me this isn't so."

"I'm so sorry, but it's true."

Elena dropped to her knees, then began to wail, rocking back and forth with the rosary beads pressed tightly against her forehead.

Within moments, another man entered, followed by a priest. They hurried to where the nun had fallen. The priest knelt beside her, speaking gently but calmly.

"Sister, I'm Father Michael. We are so sorry for your loss, but you know he is in a better place. Will you come to the chapel with me to pray? Maybe it will help calm your grief."

Elena let herself be helped to her feet. She accepted Hollister's handkerchief, blotted her eyes and then began gathering herself.

"I'm so sorry," she said softly. "It was just such a shock." She let a fresh set of tears roll silently down her face. "His heart . . . it was bad, you know. Still, one is never ready to lose a dear brother."

The man with the priest looked startled.

"Sister, I'm the warden here. My name is Thom Henry. Please know that I'm sorry for your loss. I didn't realize he was related to you. I thought you were here as a Sister, not as *his* sister."

Elena dropped her head, letting her eyelids flutter softly.

"There were once seven of us. Miguel and I were the only ones left." Then she choked on a sob. "Now I am alone."

Father Michael put his hand on her shoulder. "But, Sister, you are never alone."

"This is true," she said. "Forgive my selfishness. It comes from my grief." Then she lifted her head, glancing only briefly at Hollister before facing the two men. "It is now my duty to claim my brother's body. How is this to be done?"

The warden stepped forward. "I'm sorry, Sister, but first there will have to be an autopsy. If there's a number where you can be reached, I will have my secretary —"

Elena covered her mouth with both hands and took a step backward, as if in dismay.

"Oh, no, no!" she cried. "You cannot do this! His body must not be defiled in such a way!"

Henry frowned. Miguel Calderone was the kind of man who, in the time to come, would probably have been executed for the crimes he'd committed. It would have been a whole lot easier if he had waited to die that way. Damn the sorry son of a bitch for cheating justice. Then he sighed. He understood her feelings. It wasn't the first time a family member had objected to an autopsy, but protocol had to be followed.

"It's policy," he said.

"It is against Miguel's religion," she argued.

"He was not a Catholic, as I am. He followed the old ways of our people. It is one of the reasons I came so often to pray with him. I was hoping to lead him to God while there was still time to save his soul." She dropped her head, again as if in sorrow. "But as you can see, I was too late. However, I must insist that you do not cut or maim his earthly body. Surely you have rules for such things as this? Isn't there some kind of understanding for the practice of different religions?"

Warden Henry frowned. There were always exceptions, but he was a man who preferred routines and rules.

"Certainly, only I don't —"

It was time for Hollister to step in. "Warden Henry, if I may?"

Henry knew who Hollister was, and while he didn't have much regard for lawyers who twisted the laws of the land to the benefit of the criminals, he had to give the man his say.

"What is it?" Henry asked.

Hollister smiled. "Thank you, sir. You are being most kind. I understand the position you're in. However, surely we can release the body to Mr. Calderone's sister and allow it to be taken to the funeral home of her choice? They could delay the embalming for a day or so until you clear it with whomever you choose."

Henry frowned. Hollister was slick, but he

was also right. Not only could he do this, but he'd done it before in other instances. He glanced at the little nun, who stood white-faced and silent, awaiting his decision.

"Yes, all right," he finally said. "But only with the understanding that no embalming will begin until you hear from me."

"This I will do," she said. "But please, Warden Henry. Please tell your people how important this is to me."

"Yes, certainly," he said. "Again, I'm sorry for your loss."

Elena lifted her head and let her eyes fill with tears as she played the tragedy to the hilt.

"Is there a telephone I might use? I need to call a funeral home."

"There's a funeral home here in Lompoc that we've used numerous times," Father Michael offered.

Elena frowned. "Thank you, Father, but you don't understand. Because of my brother's beliefs, there are certain preparations that must be made to his body before he can be buried. Things that a regular funeral home might not know." Then she looked at Abraham Hollister. "Sir . . . as my brother's lawyer, may I trouble you to help me?"

Hollister glanced at the warden. "I'm sure Warden Henry has no objections. How may I be of service?"

"I will write down the name of a funeral home in East L.A. You will please call them for me and ask them to come get my brother's body. Also explain the warden's request about delaying preparations."

"Yes, certainly," he said.

Elena took a pen and paper that he offered, wrote the name quickly, then handed him the paper.

"I do not know the number," she said.

"No problem," Hollister said. "I can call information."

Satisfied that she'd done her part, she folded her hands demurely in front of her and turned to the warden.

"Would it be possible to see my brother? Even though he rejected my God, I would like to pray for him in my own way."

Henry stifled a sigh, then turned to the priest.

"Father Michael, if you would be so kind as to escort the Sister to the hospital?"

"Of course," the priest said, then glanced at Hollister. "We will be back shortly. You will be here for her?"

Hollister laid a hand on Elena's shoulder. "Of course. Say a prayer for me, too, Sister."

Elena nodded, then let herself be led away.

"Warden, is it all right to use my cell phone here?" Hollister asked.

"Yes, and if you need me, have someone ring my office. They'll know where to find me."

"Yes, thank you, Warden Henry. You've been of great comfort to Sister Mary Theresa."

"Yes, well . . ." Uncertain what else to say about a man his government had intended to try to execute, he left Hollister alone in the waiting area to make his calls.

Immediately, Hollister got on the phone. He didn't have to call information for a number. He'd memorized it days ago.

The call went out.

A man answered.

Hollister gave the order they'd been waiting for.

Exactly forty-five minutes later, a long black hearse that had been polished to perfection pulled up to the front gates of Lompoc Federal Correctional Institution.

After a thorough check of the vehicle and the two very well-dressed men inside, the guard directed them to the back entrance of the hospital. The men in dark suits got out. One opened the back of the hearse and took out a gurney, which they then wheeled toward the building. More guards awaited them, then led them to a small room and to the bed where Miguel Calderone's body still lay.

For a man as powerful as Calderone had been, he was a very unassuming presence beneath the government-owned sheet. The employees of the funeral home transferred the body to their gurney and were then escorted out the same way they'd come in.

It was a grander procession than Calderone might have expected. The guards watched without speaking as the body was loaded into the hearse. The gurney was locked in place, and the two men got into the car. Only after they'd passed through the main gates did they dare to look at each other. But the danger they had been in was far from over. The window of time was short for the *padrone* to be saved, and they didn't want to be the ones to fail him.

Fifteen minutes later, they pulled off onto a side street. A dark-haired woman wearing black slacks and a white tank top was standing beside an old gray van. It was a far cry from the nun's habit she'd been wearing earlier, but Elena Verdugo was a woman of many faces, and there was nothing she wouldn't do for Miguel.

When she saw the hearse, she grabbed a bag from the front seat and started running toward them. She jumped into the back, crawling on her hands and knees beside the gurney where Calderone was lying as one of the men slammed the door shut behind her.

"Go! Go!" she shouted, and yanked a portable defibrillator from the bag and fired it up.

Elena's hands were shaking, but this was no time to be weak. The curare in Calderone's system had rendered him virtually lifeless, but CPR should bring him back. At least that was what she'd been told. It was the *should* that had them all worried, that and the adverse effects that being "dead" might have had on his body.

However, now was not the time to wonder if the man they got back would still be the *padrone,* or if he would be some slobbering idiot who couldn't remember his name.

Elena yanked the sheet from the upper half of Calderone's body, plugged the portable unit into a battery pack set up in the back of the hearse and rocked back on her heels, watching a digital read-out until it clicked over to two hundred, then slammed the hand paddles to either side of his chest.

"Clear," she said, although there was no one but her and Calderone in the back.

She hit the triggers. Calderone's body bucked beneath the charge. She pulled back, waiting to see if a heartbeat would register.

Nothing happened.

She upped the voltage to three hundred, then waited for the digital read-out to register the change. Once it hit the mark, she triggered the paddles again, and again Calderone's body bucked.

"Madre de Dios . . . por favor," she muttered, as she stared at the screen, praying for a heartbeat to register.

Suddenly there was a blip on the screen,

and then the flat line began to change shape. Before her eyes, Miguel had returned from the dead. She tossed the paddles aside and took a small bottle of oxygen and a mask from the bag, adjusted the flow, then put the mask over Calderone's nose. For now, the worst of the danger had passed.

"Get us out of here," she shouted, and when the hearse took off, she laid her head against Calderone's shoulder and cried.

Jonah was sitting in the library, staring out the window.

Miguel Calderone dead? It had to be a mistake. Even while Ruger was assuring them that it was so, Jonah's gut was telling him different. Evil didn't die that easily. However, if what Ruger had just told them was true, then it would mean they'd lost their best chance to find Evan alive.

"Jonah . . ."

He looked up. Macie was standing by his chair, and he'd never even heard her approach.

"What is it?" he asked.

"Ruger wants to talk to both of us."

"What the hell else could he possibly have to say?" Jonah asked.

Still, he pushed himself up from the chair with the weariness of an old man. For the first time in his life, he wanted to give up.

She tugged at his hand. "I don't know, but

let's go find out, okay?"

Jonah wanted to cry. His son, his little boy — only not so little anymore — and he'd failed him.

Ruger was on the phone when they entered the makeshift command center. He motioned for them to come in, then held up one finger, indicating that they should give him one more minute while he finished the call.

Macie sat down. Jonah didn't. Instead he kept watching Ruger's facial expressions, trying to figure out if what he had to tell them would be good news or bad. Finally Ruger hung up.

"Sorry," he said.

"Tell me something good," Jonah said.

Ruger frowned. "It's true. Calderone died in Lompoc. His lawyer and a couple of guards witnessed it. He was pronounced in their hospital."

"Damn," Jonah muttered, then covered his face with his hands.

"His sister, a nun named Mary Theresa, claimed the body, but there's still some dispute about performing an autopsy. She said his religion forbade it."

Jonah's heart skipped a beat. Religion? The only god Miguel Calderone believed in was green and folded in his pocket. And a sister . . . ? Something rotten was going on here. He dropped his hands to his sides, and turned and looked at Ruger.

"I want to see his body."

Ruger's frown deepened. "The warden said they released the body to a funeral home in East L.A. I'll call him back and get the number."

"Do it now!" Jonah said.

Ruger turned around and pointed to a nearby agent. "Get the warden on the phone for me again."

"Yes, sir," the agent said, and made the call. A few moments later, he looked up. "He's on line one."

Ruger picked up the phone. "Warden Henry, this is Agent Ruger again. I have a request. We need the name and number of the funeral home that picked up Calderone's body."

"Just a minute," Henry said. "I have it here somewhere. They left a card with the release sheet. Oh, yes . . . here it is. Got a pen?"

"Yes, go ahead," Ruger said, writing quickly as the warden read off the name and number of the funeral home.

"Got it," Ruger said. "Thank you for your assistance."

"Glad to be of help," Henry said, then disconnected.

"Call them," Jonah said the moment Ruger hung up the phone.

"I'm calling, although I don't know how looking at Calderone's body is going to help us find your son."

"Damn it, Ruger . . . if you don't make the call, I will."

Ruger resisted the urge to roll his eyes and punched in the numbers. The phone rang once, then twice, then three times. Then a recorded message came on the line.

The number you have dialed is not in service.

"Hell," Ruger said, then hung up and dialed the number again. Again he got the same message. He handed the paper to his clerk. "I might have written the number down wrong. Call information and get the number for the La Paloma Funeral Home in East L.A."

"Yes, sir," the clerk said. A moment later, he looked up at Ruger. "Sorry, sir. There is no listing for a funeral home by that name."

Ruger was starting to sweat. He turned around and stared at Jonah.

"What the hell do you know that we don't?"

"You said they released his body to his sister. Miguel Calderone doesn't have a sister."

"How do you know that?"

"Because he used to brag about the virility of his *padre,* who'd fathered eight boys. Other than his mother and two daughters, the only females connected to Calderone were the ones he took to bed."

"Son of a bitch," Ruger said. "What the hell's going on here?"

Before Jonah could answer, Carl French came running into the room.

"What's going on?" Ruger asked.

"The agent who's been following the gardener just called. Something is going down. He thinks he's packing to leave."

"Calderone is dead," Ruger said.

"No. Calderone is gone," Jonah said. "He escaped."

Carl's mouth dropped. "He escaped from Lompoc? Impossible."

"Not for him," Jonah said. "They pronounced him dead, then hauled his sorry ass out in a hearse to a funeral home that doesn't exist. Figure it out for yourself."

Carl shook his head. "I can't believe this. Who claimed the body?"

"The sister he doesn't have," Jonah said.

"Oh, my God," Carl said, then looked at Jonah. "You know what this means?"

Jonah nodded. "Yeah. If Evan is still alive, it won't be for long." Then he started to pace. "I don't know how, but I would bet a year of my life that Calderone isn't dead and that he's just pulled off his own 'great escape.' "

Macie had remained silent until now, but she couldn't stay quiet any longer.

"People . . . I need some answers, and I need you to explain this to me in words I can understand."

Jonah cursed softly, then strode out of the room.

Macie turned to Carl. "Please. Tell me what's happening."

"If Calderone is out, and if he's alive, then he'll be heading for Evan. There's a little matter of revenge that he won't pass up. Not even if it means putting himself at risk to stay in the States long enough to do the job."

Macie felt sick to her stomach. She was afraid to ask another question for fear of the answer she would get. She needed to find Jonah. He would know what to do.

13

By the time Macie left the library in search of Jonah, he was already out of sight. Rosa came into the hall with a fresh bouquet of flowers for the table in the foyer as Macie was trying to decide which way to search.

"Rosa, did you see which way Jonah went?"

"*Sí,* Miss Macie. He went up the stairs."

"Thank you," she said, and hurried up the stairs, then down the hall to his room. The door was slightly ajar. She pushed it aside and walked in. Jonah was on his cell phone. She started to leave, but he motioned for her to wait.

Macie closed his door, then sat down on the edge of his bed. To her surprise, he circled the bed and sat down beside her, then put his arm around her as he continued to talk. Without thinking, she leaned into the comfort of his embrace and closed her eyes. Her heart hurt for Evan and for what he must be going through. She wouldn't allow herself to think that he was already dead. She couldn't think about that beautiful young boy on the verge of manhood never drawing another breath. The last time she'd talked to him had been less than two months ago, on his fifteenth birthday. His voice had been full of excitement as he'd talked about the time when he would be old enough to drive. If she didn't constantly fight the urge, she could so easily start screaming and never stop. The devastation that her family was suffering was true hell on earth. And then she began to focus on what Jonah was saying.

"Yes! That's the one. The new tracking prototype. Consider it a test run. Okay. Yes, sir. I appreciate it. And you'll get it back . . . one way or the other."

Jonah disconnected, tossed his cell phone aside and pulled Macie into his arms, holding her close, then burying his face in the tumble of her hair.

"You always smell so good," he said softly.

Macie's heart fluttered as she felt him shudder.

"Who were you talking to?"

"My boss."

"What's happening?"

"More news to back up my theory. Calderone didn't die. He gave himself some kind of jungle poison that mimicked death. The prison doctor was coerced into helping. They'd taken his wife and were holding her hostage until it was over."

"Oh, no," Macie said. "Is she all right? Did they let her go?"

"No. They found her dead in a motel on

Ventura Boulevard. The doctor killed himself after he heard the news, but he left a note explaining his part in Calderone's escape."

Macie shuddered. "He's crazy, isn't he?"

"Yes."

She looked up at him then, staring intently. "You're not telling me everything." She frowned. "You're planning something, aren't you?"

He hesitated briefly, then pulled back and looked at her. There was a steadiness in her gaze that gave him hope and a longing for more.

"I have no choice. We've run out of time."

Macie felt a weight settling in the pit of her stomach and knew that what he was about to tell her wasn't going to be good.

"But what can you do that hasn't already been done?"

"I know a way to get to Evan."

She frowned. "Then why have you waited?"

"Because I'm not sure if I can get him out alive."

"I don't understand," Macie said.

He sighed. "Basically, I give myself up to Calderone."

Macie froze. "You can't! Think of all the people he's already killed. You know what he'll do to you."

"No. I know what he *wants* to do to me. That doesn't mean I'll let it happen."

"This is crazy," Macie said, and grabbed

his arms, as if by holding on to him, she could keep him from getting away.

"So is the man who has my son," Jonah said.

Macie groaned. "Even if you do this . . . what guarantee do you have that you'll be able to get to Evan?"

"None, really, but I know Calderone. I know how he thinks. By now he's surely been told that I didn't know about Evan. It stands to reason that he will want me to bond with him just long enough to make watching him die that much harder."

"God almighty," Macie muttered. She pulled out of his embrace and stood abruptly. Her voice was full of anger, her eyes full of fear. "I don't want you to do this," she said. "What if Evan is already dead? Then all you'll have done is fall into Calderone's trap. He will have accomplished exactly what he set out to do. He'll have destroyed you and all you hold dear, and I'll be grieving for someone else who I loved and lost."

Suddenly Macie realized what she'd said and turned away, her heart pounding, her eyes filling with tears.

"Macie . . . honey, I —"

She felt Jonah's hand on her shoulder and twisted away, unable to bear his pity.

"Don't say it," she said.

He reached for her again, this time catching her, then holding her firmly against him.

"Don't say what?" Jonah asked, nuzzling the side of her neck. "Don't say that your smile makes me weak . . . or that the taste of your lips on my mouth drives me crazy? Don't tell you that making love to you was . . . is . . . the best thing that ever happened to me?"

She felt his sigh against her neck.

"I can't do that," Jonah said. "I won't. I'm falling in love with you, too, sweet Macie. The timing sucks, but such is life. No matter what happens tomorrow, I will be forever grateful that we had each other."

Macie turned within his embrace, then threw her arms around his neck.

"Jonah . . . oh, Jonah . . . my first instinct is to beg you with everything in my being not to go. But what you're going to do is only part of the reason I've always loved you. You put others above your own happiness and yourself in harm's way. Your heart is too big for your own good."

Jonah sighed, then lowered his head, crushing his mouth to her lips, then lifting her up and carrying her to his bed.

Before she could speak, he had locked the door and was taking off his clothes. By the time he reached the bedside, he was naked. When he grabbed the hem of her shirt and pulled it over her head, she moaned beneath her breath. And when her clothes were lying on the floor beside the bed and he was naked above her, she started to shake.

"Don't, baby," Jonah whispered. "I would never hurt you."

Macie pressed a finger against his mouth, as if to silence his words, then shook her head.

"Oh, Jonah, this isn't from fear. It's nothing but pure pain. I ache for you. Do what you have to do tomorrow, but for now, do what you must to me."

Jonah shuddered. There was no time for gentleness or foreplay. This was about the affirmation of the living and saying goodbye. It couldn't matter that it might be their last time together. If he let himself think about never seeing her again, he would go crazy. Instead, he didn't think at all.

She opened her legs for him, and he slid in. She was hot and wet, and he was hard and hurting — the perfect combination to go up in flames. Once inside, he paused for a moment, letting her body adjust to his size while he regained control of his lust. Then she said his name and started to cry. It was enough to break his heart.

"Ah, baby . . . don't cry. Not for me. I swear to God, if there is a way, I'll come back to you, and I'll bring Evan with me."

Nothing she'd experienced in life had prepared her for the past few days, yet the man in her arms knew nothing but danger and death. She didn't know what the next hours would bring, but she did know that if she lost Jonah, too, she would die.

"Make love to me, Jonah. Now."

He started to move, then groaned. "Damn, I forgot to get protection."

He started to reach toward the bedstand when she stopped him with a look.

"Don't," she whispered, and put her hands on the sides of his face.

His eyes went wide with shock. "Only once before have I ever been careless enough to make love without protection, and it got a woman pregnant."

"I won't ever lie to you, Jonah. Please, make love to me now . . . without caution or care. If you give me a child, then so be it. If you go through with your plan, it could be all of you I have left."

"Jesus," he said softly, then laid his forehead against hers and closed his eyes. He was shaking inside, both from the tenderness of her words and the thought of never holding her again.

"Please."

He groaned, then raised himself on his elbows and stared down at her face.

"It should have been you," he said quietly, then brushed the surface of her lips with a kiss. "If I'd known, I would have waited."

Macie sighed, touching his mouth, then his nose, mapping the feel and the shape of him into her mind forever.

"But then you wouldn't have had Evan, and he's so perfect. Go find him, Jonah, and bring him back. Just make love to me again before you go."

There was no more need for words.

The urge to move overcame whatever Jonah had been going to say. Macie arched to meet the thrust.

Time stopped, then started with the next beat of their hearts, and for a little while, there was nothing in their world but the heat and the joy.

After all his days in captivity, Evan had finally found a weapon, but his hands were so sore and swollen he wasn't sure he would be able to use it. And he'd found it because of the bugs on his mattress.

They often crawled on him while he slept. He'd felt them before, but couldn't bear the thought of looking to see what they were. He would always awaken just enough to brush them away and then let himself go back to sleep. It was there in his dreams that his world was still complete, and he hated to wake to the reality of his life.

But this time his sleep wasn't deep enough, and there were too many bugs. When they crawled on his face, he woke with a gasp and bailed out of bed, cursing as he pulled them out of his hair and flung them across the room.

He'd seen cockroaches before, but these were huge, some as long as four or five inches, and they were crawling up the walls and all over his bed. He kicked at the bed frame, taking some satisfaction in seeing them scurry.

"Son of a bitch!" he yelled, and kicked at the bed again, still shuddering as he ran shaky hands all over himself in an effort to rid himself of the feeling.

"What goes on in there?" the guard yelled.

"Bugs the size of Denver, you sorry bastard! That's what goes on in here!"

The guard laughed, then hit the door with a fist.

"You do not talk," he ordered.

"Then stop asking me stupid questions!" Evan yelled back.

There was a moment of silence, then nothing except the sound of fading footsteps.

"Good," Evan muttered. "Keep your stinkin' self as far away from me as possible."

Then he yanked the flat, filthy mattress from the frame and gave it a shake before stripping off his clothes, giving them a good shake, as well. The bugs were gone now, hiding as all cockroaches do when disturbed. Evan redressed himself, ignoring the stench of his body and his clothes. They were nothing compared to the pain in his hands.

It wasn't until he started to drag the mattress back onto the old metal cot that he saw it. Once it had probably been some sort of a brace for the springs, but it was now just a piece of thin, flat metal dangling from one bolt, almost dragging the floor. It was bent and red with rust, and almost twelve inches long, but it reminded him of a knife. It came loose without much effort, and the moment Evan had it in his hands, his hope was renewed.

He thrust upward, then downward, getting used to the feel of it in his hands. It hurt like hell to make a fist, but Evan bravely ignored the blood and pus oozing from his fingertips. After all they'd done to him, he knew he had the guts to plunge this into the soft flesh of his captor's neck. The only problem would be getting close enough to do it.

Excited, he slid it in the waistband of his pants, then groaned when it fell all the way through the pant leg and onto the floor. He'd known he'd lost weight, but not to this extent.

Frustrated, he picked up his weapon and was turning it over and over in his hands as he tried to figure out where to hide it when he heard footsteps outside his door again. His fingers tightened around the metal bar until they were throbbing. Finding a hiding place no longer mattered. He wanted to live, and to do that, he was going to have to kill.

As always, the guard entered carrying a tray of food in one hand and his gun in the other. When he saw the boy, not only out of the bed but near the door, he waved the gun in his face.

"Get away," he said sharply, and motioned with the tray to emphasize the order.

Evan moved, but it was forward, not back. He came at the guard, wielding the metal bar like a knife. It caught the guard's gun hand on the downswing, knocking the gun off to one side.

The guard grunted with surprise and tried to ward off the second blow with his other hand. In doing so, the tray of food he'd been carrying went flying, dumping part of the food on him and the rest on the floor.

Evan hit him in a flying leap, plunging downward with the bar as they collided. The broken end of it sliced through the guard's shirt, then dug into the flesh of his neck, drawing blood, but not deep enough to score a fatal blow.

The guard's roar of pain echoed within the small, airless room as he reached for the boy. Evan twisted swiftly, trying to get past the guard, but he was too slow. When he felt a hand suddenly grab his ankle and jerk, he kicked hard, trying to dislodge the grip. It was too little, too late.

The guard grabbed Evan's arm, wrenching the bar away, then throwing it out of the room. He staggered to his feet, dragging Evan upward with him and cursing with every step they took. He threw Evan against the wall, then caught him before he hit the floor, pummeling him over and over with his fists.

Suddenly another man was in the room, pulling him off of the boy and shoving him back against the wall.

"Stop, you crazy son of a bitch! If you kill that boy, Calderone will kill you."

The guard spun, instantly recognizing the man he knew as the Snowman.

"He tried to kill me," the guard said, and touched the side of his neck where blood still seeped.

The Snowman looked at the boy lying unconscious on the bed, then back at the guard and grinned.

"Looks like he's got a lot of his old man in him, after all . . . which is why I'm here. The *padrone* is out of Lompoc and out of patience. He will be here sometime tomorrow or, at the latest, the next day. Make sure the boy is still breathing, you hear me? The *padrone* intends to be the one to take his life."

The guard glared, then shrugged and nodded. "Yes, I hear." He looked back at Evan one last time, then kicked the side of the bed. Evan's body rocked from the impact, eliciting a slight moan, which was exactly what he intended.

"Little bastard. If not for the *padrone,* I would kill you now!" the guard yelled, then kicked the cans of food aside as he strode through the door.

The Snowman stood beside the bed, staring down at the boy. He'd been beaten badly. Calderone wasn't going to be happy, but at least the boy was still alive. He started to walk away and then, on impulse, leaned down and pressed two fingers against the pulse point on Evan's neck. Thc pulsc was rapid but steady.

"It's a shame about all this, kid. Looks like you would have made a damned good man." Then he chuckled. "Don't take any wooden nickels, although I guess it doesn't matter. You're not gonna live long enough to spend them."

Moments later, he was gone.

Evan heard the man's voice, but his eyes were too swollen to see. Rage came slowly, settling into his belly like food that had gone bad. Everyone kept telling him he was going to die. He never had liked being told what to do. And the smart-aleck tone of that other man's voice pissed him off, too. If his lips hadn't been so swollen, Evan would have told him not to get himself in a hurry about digging that hole to dump his body in. It wasn't over. Not by a long shot.

He shifted slightly, giving his aching ribs some ease, and exhaled slowly.

God . . . I don't know if you can hear me or not, but I sure do need help.

The rat came out of the hole, hesitating briefly as it crept up on the floor. When nothing and no one moved, it began confiscating the scattered bits of food from Evan's tray.

Now and then Evan would moan, and when he did, the rat would stop and look up, its little black eyes scanning the room for new signs of danger. Satisfied that all was well, it ate its fill while Evan struggled to draw breath against cracked and bruised ribs.

"*Corazón* . . . you have come back to me," Elena crooned, and laid her cheek against the stubble on Miguel Calderone's face.

Calderone heard the voice, but he couldn't concentrate enough to answer. His body felt weighted, his muscles aching as if he'd been beaten. He drew a slow breath, then exhaled on a moan.

Elena took the wet cloth from his forehead, dipped it back into a basin of water and wrung it partially dry before reapplying it to his forehead. The medicinal value of the wet cloth was nil, but it seemed proper and gave her something to do.

A man entered the room. She looked up, then smiled. It was Juan Carlos, Calderone's other son.

"Look!" she cried. "Your *padre* is waking up, just as he said he would do."

Juan Carlos nodded as he glanced at Elena. He had been waiting for three days at the northern California ranch. He liked it here and would have liked to stay. But thanks to his father's legacy, a normal life was not his to choose.

He moved closer to the bed, then laid his hand on Calderone's chest. Even though he could feel the heartbeat, it was hard for him to believe that it was so. He'd watched Elena administering the CPR. His father had been cold and lifeless; then he'd started to breathe. Juan Carlos tried to tell himself it was a miracle, but he was just superstitious enough to believe it was more likely the work of the devil. He started to step back when his father suddenly grabbed his hand.

He grunted in surprise. *"Padre?"*

Calderone took a slow breath, savoring the fill of air into his lungs. He tried to open his eyelids, but they had yet to respond to his mental commands.

"Mi hijo," he whispered.

Juan Carlos leaned over. "Yes, Papa, it is I, Juan Carlos."

"Stay."

Juan Carlos patted his father's cheek and then smoothed the hair from his forehead.

"Yes, Papa, I will stay. You are safe. Just rest and get well."

"Elena?"

She laid her hand on Miguel's other cheek.

"Yes, Miguel, I am here, and I, too, will stay. Sleep now. Sleep and grow stronger."

It was all Calderone needed to hear.

⋆ ⋆ ⋆

Jonah woke abruptly. For a few seconds he thought something had happened to Macie, but she was still there, asleep in his arms. But the notion that something terrible was happening was too strong to ignore. Confident that Macie was safe, he slid his arm out from beneath her neck, then got out of bed. After dressing quickly, he went downstairs in search of Ruger. There were things that needed to be said.

There were two agents in the conference room. One was stretched out on a sofa; the other was still sitting at a computer.

"Hey, guys. Anyone seen Ruger?"

"He left a little after seven," one of them said.

Jonah frowned. "Do you know when he'll be back?"

"He didn't say. Want me to call him?"

"That won't be necessary," Jonah said, and started to leave, then stopped and turned around. "On second thought, yes. I need to talk to him before morning."

The agent picked up a phone and punched in some numbers, then handed the phone to Jonah. Jonah counted the rings, frowning when he got nothing but voice mail.

"Ruger, it's me, Jonah. Call me at the estate as soon as you can."

Frowning, he hung up the phone. "Where're Sugarman and Carter?"

"Carter went home. His wife is having a baby. Sugarman is with Ruger, I think."

"What about my friend, Carl French?"

One agent looked at the other one, then shrugged.

"He left right after you did. Said he was going to get something to eat."

Frustrated, Jonah started to pace.

"In a couple of hours, a man will be bringing me a package. Let him in the house, then come get me."

"Will do," the agent said.

Jonah went back upstairs. Macie was still asleep, so he moved to the window, looking out onto the grounds below and letting his mind go free.

There was something he was missing here, but he couldn't quite figure it out. Who in hell did he know that was selling him down the river? He went over the list of things that had happened, trying to piece it all together.

Calderone had found out about Evan before Jonah did, which meant someone who knew both of them had told him. But few people knew anything about Jonah's background — especially before he joined the Company. Even more puzzling, who did he know who would have anything to gain by selling information about him to Calderone?

And then there were the attempts on Macie's life. There had been the bug planted on her at the hospital, the attempt to kill her on their way to La Jolla to scatter Felicity's ashes. Every time they'd left the house, it seemed as if someone had not only been waiting for them, but had also known their destination. The only way that could be happening was if someone on the inside was tipping off Calderone's people.

He wiped his hands across his face, then walked away from the window. It seemed impossible to believe, but it made more sense than anything else he could come up with. And, if that were true, what he was planning to do could blow up in his face.

Jonah sat down on the side of the bed and satisfied himself with just looking at Macie. She was so beautiful and caring, and he was falling so deeply in love. He closed his eyes in a brief but fervent prayer. He wanted his son alive and in his life, and he wanted Macie with him forever. It was a lot to ask, coming from a man who rarely prayed, let alone prayed for divine intervention, but the rest of his life was riding on the outcome. Too restless to stay with Macie, he pulled the covers up over her legs and then went back downstairs. He'd just decided a change of plans was in order when the house phone rang.

He picked it up without thinking.

"Blaine residence," he said.

"I'm Cecelia Bardley, a nurse here at Cedars-Sinai. May I speak to Mercedes Blaine?"

"She's asleep. May I give her a message?"

"Are you family?" she asked.

Jonah hesitated, but only for a moment. "Yes."

"I'm sorry to have to tell you this, but Mr. Blaine suffered a stroke a short while ago. We had hopes that it might be a temporary event, but the doctors are saying it was massive."

"Is he dead?" Jonah asked.

"No, sir, but he doesn't know anything or anyone and there's not much hope for his recovery."

Jonah sighed. "Okay. Thank you for letting us know. We'll be there as soon as we can."

"There's no need," the nurse said. "As I said before, he won't know you're here. The doctor just wanted to let you know."

"Yes. Well . . . thank you just the same."

He hung up the phone and then looked back up the stairs. Another burden to lay on Macie, and right when he could not be around to lighten the load.

14

Jonah went up the stairs, his steps a lot slower than when he'd come down. He walked into Macie's room and sat down on the side of the bed again. He hated like hell to wake her, but it had to be done. He wasn't leaving this news for someone else to give her.

"Macie . . . sweetheart."

She rolled over on her back, then reached for Jonah's hand and lifted it to her lips.

"Is it morning yet?" she asked.

He leaned down and kissed her, wishing he knew how to take away the pain of what he had to tell her.

"No, baby, it's still night. But I have something to tell you."

The tone of Jonah's voice soaked into her consciousness. Within seconds, she was awake and sitting up.

"What?"

"The hospital called. It's about Declyn. He's had a stroke."

Macie closed her eyes, then covered her face, too afraid to ask the inevitable question. Jonah anticipated her fear and took her in his arms.

"He's not dead. But the nurse said the stroke was massive, and that he doesn't know a thing."

Her voice started to shake. "It's my fault. I shouldn't have argued with —"

"Stop right there!" Jonah said. "You didn't do a damned thing to that old man that he hadn't already done to himself. It was probably a blood clot. It's common with gunshot wounds."

Macie listened, not sure if she believed Jonah, but wanting to — needing to — to be able to live with herself for the rest of her life.

"I hate that this happened to him," she said.

"I know, honey, but it did. Do you want to go to the hospital to see him?"

She was silent for a moment, and then she shook her head.

"Not now. I was there twice before when he was conscious, and all he did was yell at me. If by some strange chance he might know who I am, it could make him worse."

"It's your call. Maybe it's better this way . . . at least for now."

Macie took Jonah's hand, then threaded her fingers through his. His skin was warm, his grip firm but gentle, like the man himself. She kept trying to read what he was thinking, but he'd blocked off whatever emotions he was struggling with.

"Are you going through with it . . . giving yourself up to Calderone's man?"

"It's the only way."

Macie threw back the covers.

"What are you doing?" Jonah asked. "It's still night. Go back to bed."

"You expect me to sleep when I know what you're about to do? Don't be crazy, mister. I'm getting dressed, then I'll make us some breakfast."

"It's 3:00 a.m."

"Haven't you ever had an early breakfast before?"

He grinned.

"I've had all kinds of things, baby, but not with you."

"Then it's time you did," she said, and reached for her robe.

Macie was putting dirty dishes in the sink and Ruger was still gone when Collum McCallister arrived. It was a little after 4:00 a.m. Jonah took him straight up to his room, with only Macie as a witness to what was about to go down.

Collum McCallister had been a Company man for twenty-six years and figured he'd seen about everything there was to see in his career. He knew Jonah Slade — had worked with him more than once — and had been more than happy to deliver the goods that Slade had requested from the director. But he was not able to hide his shock when Jonah asked him to keep the operation a secret — at least for now.

"Damn, Slade, this doesn't feel right," Collum said. "What if something goes wrong? We won't have the backup in place to help you."

Panicked, Macie couldn't stay quiet.

"Jonah . . . maybe you shouldn't —" Then she saw the look on his face and stopped. "Sorry."

Jonah knew she was scared. So was he, but not of facing Calderone. What scared him most was the thought of finding his son alive and not being able to get him out and bring him home.

"I have to, honey. You know that as well as I do, and what Collum brought is going to make it happen."

"But why are you doing this without telling Ruger or Carl?"

He thought of Carl — his best friend for more years than he could remember.

"I'd tell Carl, but he's not here, and I don't know when he's coming back. I've left two messages on his voice mail, and he's not answering, so . . ."

Macie nodded. "I'm sorry for interfering. You're the expert in cases like this. I'm just worried."

"So am I," Jonah said. "But I'm more worried about Evan than ever now. Even though we have no proof that he's still alive, I know he is. I also know that's why Calderone wanted to get out of Lompoc."

Collum frowned. "Calderone's out, all right, but he's dead. How does that play into this?"

Jonah shook his head. "I'm betting my life — and Evan's — that Calderone isn't dead but is somewhere readying himself to finish what he started. And now that he's no longer behind bars, the time for waiting for the feds to find Evan is over. I've got to get to him before Calderone does."

"What if he's already there?" Collum asked.

Jonah wouldn't let that thought take root. "What if he's not?" he countered.

Collum grinned. "That's what I like about you," he said, and then pulled a small package out of the bag he'd brought with him. "This is what you wanted," he said, and began shaking the wrinkles out of an ordinary-looking shirt.

Macie frowned. "He brought you a shirt?"

Jonah grinned. "Not just any shirt, right, Collum?"

Collum arched an eyebrow. "Now why do I suddenly feel like Q in a James Bond movie?"

"I don't know," Jonah said. "Because I damn sure don't feel like 007."

"You're better looking," Macie offered.

Jonah chuckled. "I knew there was a reason I liked you."

Macie's smile turned into a smirk. "I thought there were other more obvious reasons than a compliment."

Collum grinned at Jonah. "I don't think I ever saw you blush before."

"You still didn't see it," Jonah muttered, as he pulled off his own shirt and then put on the one Collum handed him. "It fits," he said. "How does it work?"

"It's already working," Collum said, pointing to the small clear buttons on the front of the shirt. "These are state-of-the-art tracking units, but undetectable with any known debugging equipment. They activate the moment they're pushed through the buttonholes."

"How do you track me?" Jonah asked.

Collum pulled what looked like a small laptop computer from the bottom of his bag.

"With this," he said. "Let me boot it up and I'll show you what I mean."

Macie leaned over Collum's shoulder as the screen lit. With a few keystrokes, Collum had the program running.

"See that little blip?" Collum asked, pointing to the right of the screen.

Macie nodded.

"That's Jonah," Collum said. "There's just one drawback. I can only track you up to a distance of twenty-five miles. After that, you're off the scope."

"So don't lose me," Jonah said.

"Yeah, right," Collum said.

Still, Macie couldn't let go of her fears.

"What if you have car trouble? What if there's a traffic jam? You know how California traffic can be. Don't you think it would be better if you had a back-up car?"

"Not going to be in a car," Collum said. "I'm going airborne."

"Can you use that tracking system and still fly the chopper?" Jonah asked.

Collum nodded.

"Then that's good enough for me," Jonah said.

"But that doesn't make any sense," Macie said. "You'll be in the air. What if there's no place to land? How can you help Jonah if you're up in the air?"

Jonah slid a hand on the back of Macie's neck. "He's not going to be my rescuer, honey. He's going to be the one who calls in the dogs."

"What?"

"Once Collum sees where I've been taken, he'll notify Ruger. They'll take it from there."

"God," Macie muttered, and turned her back on the men. "This is crazy. You've got dozens of feds at your disposal, as well as at least one more Company man, and you're going to do this with only Collum as backup. How smart does that sound to you?"

"Just being careful," Jonah said.

"That's not careful, that's suicide," Macie argued.

"He thinks we have a mole," Collum said. "If he's right, the mole won't have time to alert Calderone that we're on to him."

Macie turned around, her expression blank with surprise.

"A mole . . . as in a traitor?"

Jonah nodded.

"Who?"

"If I knew that, I wouldn't be so concerned about keeping this a secret."

Macie sighed. "Okay. It doesn't make it any easier to face, but at least now I understand why."

"That's my girl," Jonah said; then he looked at Collum. "Let's get rolling. I want to get out of here before everyone comes back."

"Where to first?" Collum asked.

"I'm going to pay a visit to a gardener. I checked with the tail Ruger put on him. He's still there and he's my link to Calderone. After that, it may take a bit before things start moving."

"What do we tell the agents downstairs?"

"That we're going out for breakfast?"

"What about me?" Macie asked.

"You stay here," Jonah said.

"What if this mole, as you call him, figures out what's going on and comes after me?" she asked.

Jonah frowned. He'd thought of that, too, but their choices were limited.

"He can't take you out under force — not with all the Federal agents on the premises — so if you don't leave with anyone, you should be okay."

"Fine, but when everyone comes charging to the rescue, I'm not going to be the sweet little woman who stays behind and wrings her hands."

"You don't leave this house," Jonah said.

Macie's chin jutted. "I won't if you won't."

"I'm just going to step out in the hall while you two thrash this out," Collum said, and left the room, carefully closing the door behind him.

"Macie . . . please," Jonah said.

Macie threw her arms around Jonah's neck and kissed him soundly. His breath was soft on her cheek as they finally pulled back.

Jonah cupped her face, studying its curves and planes intently, as if he'd never seen it before.

"Macie."

"What?"

"You know I love you."

Tears welled. "I love you, too. Now go find Evan . . . and come back to me."

"I don't want to lose you," he said.

"I'm not going anywhere," Macie said.

"I know it's too soon to make plans for a future," Jonah said. "But I —"

Macie put her hand on Jonah's mouth, then shook her head.

"You don't need to make promises to me. We'll talk when this is over."

He raked a hard, angry kiss across her mouth one last time, then walked out of the room without looking back.

The gardener was getting used to answering to the name Felipe Sosa. He liked Sosa's job. He liked the little house he'd rented in Sosa's name. He especially liked his neighbor, Amelia Ramos. If it wasn't for the *padrone,* he would never go back to Bogotá. And yet, like all good things, the perfect little world he'd fallen into had to come to an end.

Felipe, as he called himself now, was in the small kitchen making coffee the Colombian way — thick and dark — when the knock sounded on his door. Not once in the weeks that he'd been here had anyone ever come calling. He thought about ignoring the sound, but when it came again, there was nothing to do but answer it.

The fact that it was a gringo surprised him; then Felipe realized he looked familiar. He leaned forward, eyeing the man's dark, short-clipped hair as well as his clothes. The plain cotton shirt was ordinary, as were his blue jeans and hiking boots.

"Aren't you going to ask me in?" Jonah said.

Felipe frowned. “I’m sorry, *señor,* but I do not know you.”

Jonah pushed his way inside the door and grabbed Felipe by the collar.

“Sure you do, you little bastard. My name is Jonah Slade. Calderone has my son, and I want him back.”

For a second Felipe’s heart stopped. He tried to pull away, but it was no use. The man was too big and his grip far too strong.

“Easy there, buddy. You’re not going anywhere,” Jonah said. “Let’s give the *padrone* a call and tell him you’ve found me, what do you say?”

Felipe felt sick. He peered past the man in the doorway, expecting to see at least two carloads of policemen come storming up the walk, but there was no one in sight.

“You surely have mistaken me for someone else,” he mumbled. “I do not know a Jonah Slade, or anyone named Miguel Calderone.”

Jonah shoved the man forward, quickly closing the door behind them.

“You don’t? Then what are you, psychic?” Jonah asked.

Felipe frowned. “I do not know what you mean.”

Jonah pulled the man a little closer, giving his anger free rein. “Don’t lie to me, you little bastard. If you don’t know Calderone, then you have to be psychic. Otherwise, how would you know his first name?”

Felipe's heart sank. *Madre de Dios.* He'd screwed up. "Please, *señor,* go away. I'm just a gardener. I know nothing of which you speak."

Jonah pointed to the tattoo on Sosa's arm. "All of the *padrone*'s men have one of those, so quit lying to me. We're running out of time."

Sosa didn't know what to do, but denial obviously wasn't working.

"Out of time? I don't understand," he said, still pretending ignorance.

"You work at the estate. You know Evan Blaine is missing. You know where he is."

Sosa took a step backward, reeling from shock. Now he remembered where he'd seen this man — in the company of Miss Macie Blaine, and again outside the toolshed. Still he blustered, refusing to admit any connection.

"I don't know any such thing," he argued. "I only mow grass and weed flower beds."

Jonah's patience snapped. He grabbed the man by the neck with one hand and shoved him against the wall.

"I'm tired of playing games with you. Get on the phone. Call your people. Tell them you found Jonah Slade. Trust me. They're going to thank you for the call."

Felipe's heart was pounding. He wanted his machete and all he had were his fists. Against this man, that meant nothing.

"All right, all right," he mumbled, aware

that he'd admitted his connection to Calderone by no longer denying it.

Felipe continued to hesitate, but only for a moment. Suddenly he was punching in numbers, then speaking rapidly in Spanish, unaware that Jonah could follow the conversation easily. Jonah stifled a snort when he heard Felipe saying he'd captured Jonah Slade. He didn't care what Sosa told them if it got him to Evan.

As he continued to listen, he realized that Felipe was having a hard time selling his story. Frustrated with the delay, Jonah grabbed the phone from Felipe's hand.

"This is Jonah Slade," he said. "Is my son still alive?"

There was a moment of silence on the other end of the line, and then a man spoke.

"You think we are stupid? We come to get you, we get ourselves arrested."

"You didn't answer my question. Is my son still alive?"

"Sí."

"Prove it to me," Jonah said. "Let me talk to him. If I can talk to him . . . if I know it's really him I'm talking to, then I'll give myself up to you."

"How do we know —"

"Look, you stupid son of a bitch. I want my son. Do you think I would do anything that would endanger his life even more?"

"Okay."

"Okay you'll let me talk to my son?"

"Stay there. You will get a phone call soon."

"If I haven't received the call in five minutes, I'm gone," Jonah warned. "Then it's on your head when the *padrone* finds out you let me go."

"No, no. You stay. The call will come," the man said.

Jonah disconnected without answering. The more nervous he could make them, the more likely it was that they would grant his request.

He grinned at Felipe and pointed toward an easy chair.

"Have a seat, Felipe . . . or whatever the hell your name is. We've got ourselves a little wait."

It hurt to draw breath, but Evan did it anyway. In a twisted sort of way, the pain was vindication. He'd fought his captors. The fact that he'd lost was immaterial. It was the first time since they'd taken him hostage that he didn't feel like a victim.

The food that had been on the tray the guard had dropped lay scattered all over the floor. Evan had confiscated a small can of pears, pulled off the pop-top lid and drunk the juice before eating the slices with his fingers. It had taken him longer to find the bottle of water, which had rolled under his bed, but after he found it, he took off his T-shirt, poured some of the water on the fabric and used it for a washcloth to clean his face.

Without a mirror, it was hard to tell what he looked like, but he knew it wasn't good. He'd only started shaving about a year ago, and then no more than two or three times a week. But he could feel the growth of his beard. It seemed fuller — even thicker. It was ironic that none of his family was there to witness another sign of maturity.

He ran his fingers carefully across his cheekbones, testing the length and depth of a gash just beneath his right eye, then down the side of his face to his mouth and chin. He didn't need to feel it to know his lower lip was at least twice its normal size, but he was surprised by the knot on his chin. There was a lot of the beating that he didn't remember, which was probably just as well.

He tossed the shirt across the end of the bed and then leaned over, pouring a bit more of the water onto the back of his neck as a means of rejuvenation.

The sensation immediately reminded him of his daily swims in the family pool and of his mother in her red bikini, lying in her favorite lounge chair with a stopwatch in her hand, cheering him on. Blinded by an unexpected gush of tears, Evan straightened, then took slow, steadying breaths. Now was not the time to let them see his weakness.

He glanced toward the window, trying to guess the time of day, but the slits were too narrow. All he could see were dust motes doing faint pirouettes within thin slices of sunlight.

He kicked at a package of crackers that Harold had been sampling, then toed it the rest of the way into the rat hole. Since the rat had already started eating it, Evan figured he should have the rest. He stumbled into the bathroom, holding his breath against the stench as he relieved himself, then hastened back out. The smell wasn't a lot better on the other side of the room, but enough that it was worth the effort to hurry.

Just as he was contemplating a bit of exercise, he heard footsteps, then frowned. The guard was coming back. He never came back this often. Something must be happening. The thought of another beating was almost more than he could bear. Fear spiked, leaving him weak and shaking. Was this it? Was this going to be the day he finally died?

The door swung inward. The guard had a gun in one hand and a cell phone in the other.

"You. Come here," the guard ordered.

Evan stood his ground.

"I said come!" the guard yelled. "You talk!"

Evan couldn't believe it. They were giving

him a phone? Except for his aunt Macie, there was no one alive who would possibly care about him. He moved quickly, then stopped abruptly when the guard swung the gun in his face.

"You do as I say or you die," the guard muttered.

Evan nodded, then held out his hand. The guard frowned but laid the phone in his palm and then took several steps back, still keeping the gun aimed at Evan's face.

After all this time, it felt strange to be holding something as ordinary as a phone, when before, he'd rarely been without one.

"Hello?" The word cracked coming up his throat and came out in a croak. He cleared his throat and tried it again. "Hello? Who is this?"

He heard the sound of a swiftly indrawn breath and then the deep rumble of an unfamiliar voice.

"Evan?"

"Yes. Who is this?"

"What's your mother's middle name?"

It was the last thing he had expected to hear, but somehow, he knew it was a test. Then he realized that whoever it was needed to know he was still alive.

"Felicity. Her first name was Laura."

"Well, hell," the man said.

"I answered your question, now you answer mine," Evan said.

"Ask."

"Who are you?"

"My name is Jonah Slade. Do you know it?"

Evan's knees went weak, but he wouldn't let the guard see the emotion he was feeling.

"Yes, I know the name . . . but not the man."

Jonah winced, but it was no more than he expected.

"You stay strong for me, Evan. I'm coming to get you."

"But —"

The guard yanked the phone from Evan's hand and then disconnected.

Evan moaned when the connection was broken, but he stood his ground, staring at the guard with a go-to-hell glare.

The guard glared back but didn't touch him. Instead, he slammed the door shut and walked away.

Evan dropped down to the side of the bed and then stared at the floor, trying to comprehend what had just happened. After a few moments, he started to grin, then winced as the motion shot pain through his jaws.

I'm coming to get you.

It was more than Evan had hoped for, yet everything he'd ever dreamed. Ever since he'd known of his father's existence, he'd wanted to see him. Slade was a strong-sounding name. Now he had a strong, steady voice to go with it. And if he could believe what he'd heard, soon he would see the man. It was almost more than he could hope for — but hope he did.

Jonah hung up the phone, then looked at Felipe.

"Now we wait."

Felipe wasn't all that keen on waiting, but no one had given him any choices. As he sat, the small clock on a nearby table chimed. It was only eight o'clock in the morning. How could so much have happened in such a short time when he had yet to eat his breakfast?

"Got any coffee around here?" Jonah asked.

Felipe jumped to his feet.

"I will get some."

"I'll go with you," Jonah said, and followed the little man into the back of the house.

Less than thirty minutes later, there was another knock on the door. Felipe's heart jumped again, this time with relief. Surely this would be the *padrone*'s men. The sooner they took this man away, the happier he would be. Of course, once he was gone, Felipe had no choice but to run. It was obvious that his cover was blown. When he saw the two men on the doorstep, he knew it was time, whether Calderone gave the order or not.

"Where is he?" one of them asked.

"I'm right here," Jonah said, sipping his

second cup of coffee. "Had your breakfast? Old Felipe here makes a pretty good cup of brew."

"Shut up," the man said, and knocked the cup from Jonah's hand, then pushed him face first against the wall. "Spread your legs," he said.

Jonah grinned. "Take it easy, guys. All you have to do is ask. I'd be happy to oblige."

The two newcomers looked at each other and frowned. This made no sense. The *padrone* was probably going to cut this man's *cojones* and fry them up to eat. He shouldn't be laughing. He also shouldn't be making this so easy. But they were ready for him.

"Esteban . . . test him."

Esteban took what looked like a thick black wand from his pocket and began running it up and down Jonah's body, just as if he was at an airport being checked with a metal detector. Only this time, it wasn't metal they were looking for, it was electronic bugs — tracking devices — anything that would alert them that the authorities would be trailing their every move.

But the wand didn't give off a signal, and the other guard could find no wires.

"He's clean, Raoul," Esteban said.

"Fresh as Irish Spring," Jonah quipped.

Esteban frowned. *"Que?"*

"Never mind," Jonah said. "It's an inside joke."

"I don't hear anybody laughing," Raoul said, then slapped Jonah across the face. "Now that was funny," he said, and began to laugh rudely as he tied up Jonah's wrists.

Jonah stifled the urge to kill him now, which he could. But it would solve nothing. Evan would still be missing, and he would have missed his chance to get to him.

"You through?" Jonah asked.

The guard seemed taken aback by Jonah's attitude.

"You shut up now," the guard muttered.

"You take me to my son," Jonah said.

"We'll take you where we choose," Raoul muttered, and pushed Jonah toward the door.

Jonah stopped in midstep, then turned around, facing both of them — unarmed, but deadly just the same.

"If, when we get to where we're going and my son is not there, I will kill both of you. Know that now."

Esteban looked at Raoul and tried to laugh, but the sound didn't quite make it past a grunt.

"You go now," Raoul said, and pushed Jonah toward the door.

The sun was already hot as Jonah walked outside. He eyed the van, then stopped at the door on the passenger side.

"I don't suppose there's any chance of riding in the front seat?"

"Shut your mouth," Raoul said, and shoved

Jonah inside the van, then crawled in and tied him up.

"There's really no need to do this," Jonah said. "I won't make any trouble for you — unless, of course, you've lied. You see, I've got a real problem with people who lie to me. In fact, that's what caused this whole mess. So you play straight with me, and I'll be straight with you."

Raoul glared, and then, to be on the safe side, after tying Jonah's feet together, he tied him to a railing in the back of the van.

"Didn't bother investing in seat belts, huh?" Jonah asked.

Raoul crawled out of the van, slammed the side door shut and hurried around to the driver's side to get in.

"What do I do now?" Felipe asked.

Esteban stopped, then turned around, eyeing the small, dark-skinned man.

"If you have to ask, then you don't belong to the *padrone*."

Felipe spun around and headed back inside the house to pack.

"Get in," Raoul said. "We've wasted enough time already."

When the van pulled out of the driveway, Jonah's muscles began to tense. Whatever happened now was out of his hands. All he could do was pray that they took him to Evan.

As they pulled out of the driveway, an undercover agent was up a telephone pole three houses down, pretending to be doing repairs. Ruger had told him to keep an eye on Felipe Sosa, which he'd been doing quite well for several days now. However, he hadn't expected to see Jonah Slade on Sosa's doorstep. And when two more men appeared later, then led Slade away, he knew something was amiss. He reached for his cell phone.

Ruger was dumping a packet of artificial sweetener in his coffee cup when Declyn Blaine's maid entered the conference room with a tray of sweet rolls.

"You like?" Rosa asked.

Ruger looked down at the fake sugar he'd just dumped in his coffee cup, then back at the tray of rolls, and grinned.

"Oh, I like them, all right."

Rosa smiled, then set the tray down on a table. "You ask me if you want more," she said, and hustled out of the room.

Ruger took a large cherry Danish from the tray and had just taken a bite when his cell phone rang.

"That figures," he muttered, trying to swallow as he answered the call.

"Ruger."

"Sir, this is Caldwell. Something's kinky here. Did you send Slade to Felipe Sosa?"

Ruger's heart skipped a beat. "Hell no."

"Well, he was here for almost an hour."

"What do you mean, *was?*"

"About ten minutes ago, a dark van pulled up at Sosa's house and two men went inside. A few minutes later, the two men who'd gone in came back out, and Slade was with them. I couldn't be sure from where I am, but it looked as if they tied him up in the van before they left. What do you want me to do?"

"Did you get the plate?"

"Yes, sir."

"Give it to me," Ruger ordered.

The agent rattled off the numbers.

"Okay, I've got them," Ruger said. "Now call in some help and pick up our gardener. I'll decide what to do with him later."

"Yes, sir," the agent said.

Ruger hung up, then tossed the Danish back on the tray as he headed out the door. He didn't know what the hell was going on, but he knew someone who might.

15

Macie was still in bed, unwilling to move and shatter the memories of last night and making love to Jonah. But the longer she lay there, the more panicked she became. By now he was already at the gardener's house in East L.A. Just thinking about what would happen to him after that made her sick to her stomach. The success of the mission teetered on one man's ability to track Jonah's whereabouts and Jonah's knowledge of what made Miguel Calderone tick. If anything — even the smallest of incidents — went wrong, it would be over before the FBI could intervene.

Twice she'd thought about getting up and telling Ruger everything. She wanted Jonah backed up with every man and gun available, but she hadn't said anything. She had to trust that he knew what he was doing, and that he had both his and Evan's best interests at heart.

She glanced at the clock. Almost nine o'clock. *Please, God, let them all be okay.*

Then she heard the sound of footsteps coming down the hall on the run. Her stomach lurched. No one ran in Declyn

Blaine's house unless something was wrong. Before the knock sounded on the door, she was out of bed and grabbing her robe.

"Miss Blaine? Miss Blaine, are you there?"

It was Ruger. She recognized his voice.

"Just a moment!" she called. "I'm coming."

She belted her robe and then hurried to the door.

The look on Ruger's face was frightening.

"What's wrong?" she asked.

"You tell me," he said.

Macie felt the blood draining from her face, but she stood her ground.

"I don't know what you mean."

"Where's Slade?" he asked.

Macie glanced toward his bedroom. "Isn't he in his room?"

Ruger shoved a hand through his thinning hair in disgust.

"This isn't the time for you to play dumb with me. I know he's been spending his nights with you, which is fine. In fact, it's completely immaterial to me what either of you do for the rest of your lives. But unless you tell me what you know about the stunt he just pulled, his life is probably going to be over."

Macie swayed on her feet.

"What are you talking about?"

Ruger flinched. It was the first time it dawned on him that she really might not know what was going on.

"Look, I'm sorry," he said. "But you two are so close, and I just assumed that you would know —"

"What the hell is going on up here?"

Ruger turned. It was Carl French.

"If all hell hadn't just broken loose, I might ask you where you've been, but I don't have time to play twenty questions. Besides, from the way this morning has started, I doubt I'd believe a damned thing you told me anyway."

Carl moved to Macie's side and put a hand on her shoulder.

"Miss Blaine . . . are you all right?"

She nodded.

Carl turned, fixing Ruger with a cool, steady glare.

"For now, I'm going to assume that you were overly excited and didn't really mean to scare the hell out of Miss Blaine."

Ruger glared back, tired of playing footsie with the Company during an FBI investigation.

"Excited? Oh, I don't think that's the word I would use to describe the fact that Jonah Slade was seen walking into Felipe Sosa's house just before eight o'clock this morning and later being taken out under guard by two other men and driven away in a van."

"Oh, God," Macie muttered, and turned around and staggered toward the bed.

Within the space of a heartbeat, the expression on Carl's face went from anger to shock.

"You're lying," he said, and then turned toward Macie. But the moment he saw her, he knew it was true. "What the hell is going on?" he asked.

Ruger snorted beneath his breath. "Sorry. I asked first."

Macie took a deep breath, gathering herself, then pushed herself up.

"I want both of you out of my room now. I need to get dressed."

"Listen here, Miss Blaine, you need to —"

Macie interrupted Ruger. "No. I don't *need* to do anything — however, I will tell you this. Jonah has his reasons for what he's doing, and he's not acting alone."

Carl's mouth dropped. "Why didn't he tell me? I'm his best friend, for God's sake. I would have —"

Macie shrugged. "He tried to call you. You weren't answering your phone."

Carl blanched. It was true. He'd turned it off on purpose. When he'd turned it back on, the battery had been down.

"God," he muttered. "He needed me, and I let him down."

"He's not alone," Macie repeated.

Ruger was livid. "I don't understand. Why pull this renegade stunt now?"

"Are you any closer to finding Evan today than you were yesterday?" Macie asked.

Ruger's chin jutted angrily. "No, but —"

"Jonah said time had run out for Evan. We all know that Calderone's 'body' never showed up at any funeral home. Whether the authorities are ready to admit it or not, they were duped."

"But —"

Macie interrupted. "I'm sorry, Agent Ruger, but there are no buts. The bottom line is that Jonah now believes that he was betrayed by someone he knew. He didn't know who to trust, and the investigation was going nowhere. All I'm going to tell you is that you will be hearing from another agent soon. Beyond that, I'm as much in the dark as you are."

It was the word "betrayed" that had ended all the anger. Ruger's eyes widened, his lips going slack. Carl French backed up to the doorway, then leaned against the wall as if he'd been sucker-punched.

"Betrayed? You can't be serious?" Carl said. "Why would he think that?"

"Because someone had to tell Calderone who Jonah really was, as well as about Evan's existence, and it certainly wasn't Jonah. The only people who knew anything about Jonah's past were within the security division of the Federal government."

Ruger's demeanor shifted. "Can you tell me anything more, Miss Blaine? Anything to shift this mess in our favor?"

Macie shrugged. "Just be ready to move. My suggestion would be to ready some choppers, as well as a ground force, although I don't suppose we can know for sure until the call comes."

"Jesus," Ruger said. "Can't you at least tell me who to expect the call from?"

Macie thought for a moment, then decided that the name of the agent wouldn't change what was already happening.

"Collum McAllister."

"Who's he?" Ruger asked.

Carl's expression was noticeably flat. "One of us," he said shortly, then pivoted angrily and stalked out of the room.

"Oh, great. Just what I need," Ruger muttered. "Another spook messing with my investigation."

"If you people would quit worrying about who's got jurisdiction and just find my nephew, we would all be a lot better off. Now, as I said before, please excuse me. I want to get dressed."

Ruger left, taking care not to slam the door behind him, although the urge to do so was strong. Spy? Traitor? Bull! That was what it was — a lot of bull. There were no traitors in his organization. He could not, however, speak for the Agency. What happened there was none of his business and out of his hands.

Collum McAllister was flying high, in more ways than one. It was a beautiful morning, almost devoid of smog. The blip on his computer was coming in loud and clear, and there was a second jelly doughnut still waiting to be eaten on the seat beside him.

He'd been nervous about pulling this off without telling the FBI first, but Slade had been adamant, and after learning that Slade really believed there was a traitor among them, he understood the need for secrecy. If it was true, it wouldn't be the first time an agent had turned bad, and it probably wouldn't be the last. But it was a sickening thing to believe that someone who was supposed to be on their side would sell out. He hoped to God it wasn't true.

He glanced at the blip as he reached for the doughnut. Wherever they were taking Jonah, they were still moving due south along the coast. He took a bite, considering the distance they had already gone from L.A., and got a little nervous, thinking about how far Ruger and his men would have to come before they would be of any assistance. Still, he had promised, and as far as he could tell, all was going according to plan.

Seconds later, he realized that the blip on the screen had stopped moving. Tossing aside the doughnut, he quickly wrote down the coordinates, then moved in for a closer look. He needed to see the area before calling it in so that Ruger would know what he was getting into.

Within a couple of minutes, he had the place in sight. It was a big clearing with a cluster of old Quonset-style huts. He counted five. Two vehicles were parked beside the largest, one of which was a dark van.

"Bingo," he said softly, then quickly banked toward the ocean and started out to sea. The last thing he wanted was for anyone to think he was spying. Now all he had to do was contact Ruger.

Collum was reaching for his cell phone when the engine began to sputter. Immediately his gaze went to the instrument panel. He was losing altitude fast. A second or two later, he realized that the pressure gauge was dropping, as well.

"Shit," he muttered, and tried without success to bring the craft under control. They must have made him, and someone must have gotten off a shot.

Now the chopper was losing altitude fast, dipping and swaying toward the surface of the water like a drunken dragonfly.

"Shit," Collum said again, then began to broadcast the alarm. "Mayday. Mayday. This is Tango Charlie niner niner seven. I'm experiencing engine trouble."

He gave out his coordinates as if in a dream, while thinking only three more years and he would have been able to retire. Then it hit him that Jonah was in even deeper trouble.

He reached for his cell phone and punched in the number Jonah had given him to call.

Ruger answered on the first ring.

"Hello. Ruger speaking."

"Don't talk, just listen," a man shouted in his ear. "One . . . half . . . South of La Jolla . . . five . . . War II . . . van . . ."

Immediately, Ruger knew this was the call they'd been waiting for, but the connection was so bad he could only hear parts of the conversation.

"Repeat! I say, repeat!" Ruger yelled. "You're breaking up."

"Water . . . coming up . . . not going to —"

Before Ruger could respond, there was the sound of rushing wind, then a horrible *whack* and *thump*. After that, nothing but silence.

He disconnected, talking to his men as he ran.

"Call the Coast Guard. Tell them that a plane or a chopper just went down off the coast somewhere south of La Jolla. And tell them to by God find him alive or this whole thing is a bust."

When the van stopped, Jonah's heart stopped with it. Either he was about to meet his son or his Maker, and the choice was out of his control. Suddenly the side door was yanked open. The same man who'd tied him up crawled in, cut the ropes binding his feet and dragged him out.

"You walk," he said, shoving a semiautomatic rifle in Jonah's back.

With one sweeping glance, Jonah realized that a rescue in this desolate place was going to be tough to pull off. There was nothing behind which to hide and nothing to conceal an approach, either by air or sea. But what was done was done, and he knew he could count on Collum.

The guard shoved the gun a little harder. Jonah started walking toward the largest building. As he did, it dawned on him where they were. Not that it any longer had a name, but he would have bet money that this had once been a World War II lookout post for Japanese submarines. The building toward which they were walking had probably been a hangar, although the landing strip, if there had ever been one, had either been destroyed or eroded through the years.

The wind off the Pacific was strong on the cliffs, buffeting both him and the buildings. As they entered, the shadows, coming after the heat of the sun, and the absence of wind provided welcome relief.

"There," the guard ordered, poking at Jonah's back again and directing him to the left.

A portion of the old hangar had been walled off into what he supposed had been offices.

God, please let Evan be here, and please let him be alive.

As they neared the area, another man suddenly appeared.

He was a tall, swarthy man with a Manchurian mustache and a pockmarked face. The derision on his face was evident as he laughed in Jonah's face.

"The *padrone* will be pleased," he said.

The other guards laughed, boasting in their native language about capturing the elusive Jonah Slade.

Jonah turned and looked at them, then startled them when he grinned.

Immediately their boasting turned to bluster.

"Lock him up with the pup," one of them said.

The pockmarked guard turned and unlocked the door behind him.

"In there," he ordered.

Jonah took a deep breath and moved forward. Almost immediately, he smelled urine and feces. Dread came over him in waves, fearing that next he would smell the sick-sweet stench of rotting human flesh. But he didn't.

He stumbled through the doorway, then stopped. The boy on the bed was a mass of dried blood and bruises. When he heard them talking, he stumbled from the bed and backed up to the boarded-up window, as if bracing himself for what was coming next.

Rage came swiftly as Jonah turned to the

men, looking for the one who'd hurt Evan. In one swift glance he saw the cuts and scrapes on the man's knuckles and knew it was him.

"You bastard. You slimy, egg-sucking bastard."

It was the last words the guard would ever hear on this earth. Before anyone saw it happen, Jonah swung his hands toward the man's neck. The sound of breaking bone, then the man's desperate gasps for air, stunned them all. They watched the guard die, drowning in his own blood.

"He shouldn't have hurt my son," Jonah said, then turned his back on the two guards as if they were nothing.

They stared at each other in disbelief, then took two quick steps backward, making sure they were out of his reach.

"The *padrone* will make you pay," one of them said.

"The *padrone* can kiss my ass," Jonah said. "Close the door behind you when you leave."

His unexpected defiance unnerved them, especially since they knew that using their guns on him would mean their death sentences. After quickly dragging the dead guard out of the doorway, they shut and locked the door, glad to put more than distance between them and the man who'd just avenged his own son.

With nothing but the sounds of his own heartbeat thundering in his ears, father stood before son; then he began to untie his hands with his teeth. A few moments later they were free. He tossed the thin rope aside and looked up.

"Evan?"

For a brief moment Evan Blaine thought he was dreaming. One second the man who'd beaten him had been laughing, and then he was dead. He stared at the man standing so quietly before him and then started to shake.

Jonah moved toward him. "I didn't know," he said. "I would never have —"

"Are you . . . are you Jonah Slade?"

Jonah nodded. "I told you I would come."

Evan shuddered. This was his father. He reached for him then, but his toe caught on a plank and he started to fall.

Jonah caught him, then pulled him close, feeling the bones beneath his skin and the heat of his flesh. The kid was burning up with fever.

Just the feel of Jonah's arms around him was enough to break what was left of Evan's defenses.

"Dad?"

Jonah's heartbeat surged. Never in his life had he imagined he would hear that word and know it was meant for him.

"Yes, son, I'm here, and I swear to God, when we get out of this, I will never leave you alone again."

Evan's fingers curled into fists as he

clutched at the fabric of Jonah's shirt.

"They killed Mother . . . and Grandfather. And they're going to kill me."

It was all Jonah could do to look at the wounds on Evan's face and not wail.

"I know about your mother," Jonah said. "And I'm as sorry as I can be. But your grandfather didn't die, although he's suffered a stroke."

"How . . . ?"

"Your aunt Macie," Jonah said. "She found me."

Evan wanted to be strong for this man who seemed impervious to harm, but thc tears were welling just the same. Even while he was wanting to hope, he was enveloped with hopelessness. His voice quivered.

"They're going to kill us."

"Not if I can help it," Jonah said.

It was the first time since hell had come to Evan's world that he believed he might truly live through it.

Elena was feeding Calderone soup, one spoonful at a time, taking care to blot any drips from his lips before they could fall.

"Eat well, my love," she crooned, then leaned forward and kissed his forehead. "Soon we will be home where we belong."

Calderone smiled and laid his hand on the crown of her head.

"You miss the *niña?*"

Elena's eyes teared. "*Sí*, although I know she is being cared for."

When she tried to feed him another spoonful of soup, he pushed it away.

"Enough. I will rest now. Tomorrow I will avenge Alejandro and then we will all go home."

"The man . . . Jonah Slade . . . he is with the boy now?" Elena asked.

Calderone nodded. "So I have been told."

A slight frown creased the middle of her forehead.

"It seems strange that he is captured so easily, don't you think?"

Calderone shrugged. "No man is as perfect as he seems . . . even me."

"No, Miguel, you are wrong. You are perfect in every way."

Calderone's gaze moved from Elena's lush mouth to the thrust of her breasts beneath her blouse.

"As are you, my love. Show me your perfection. I have need of you now."

Elena's heart quickened. Miguel Calderone was a lusty lover. Just the thought of him between her legs made her weak. Still, only yesterday he'd been lying near death. She laid her hand in the middle of his chest, assuring herself that the heartbeat was strong.

"Are you sure?"

Calderone grabbed her hand and moved it from his chest to the place between his legs.

"Feel this?"

Already his body was responding to her touch. She encircled him, then began to stroke, taking pride in the swell of flesh and muscle.

"Yes, my love, I feel you. Now feel me," she whispered, and replaccd her hands with her lips.

Calderone leaned back on the bed and closed his eyes, letting the pleasure of her mouth and hands shatter his control.

Collum came to, getting a brief glimpse of wreckage and the oil slick in which he was floating before a wave came crashing down onto his back. Once it had passed, he had time to ascertain his condition.

He was hanging on to a life vest. He had no memory of grabbing it, or of the impact of the plane, but he was alive, and for now that was all that could matter. He did remember calling the number Jonah had given him. But he wasn't sure it had done any good. He'd heard the FBI agent saying something about repeating the message, but by then the chopper had been on its way down.

Another wave came suddenly, shattering his concentration and making him scramble to hold on to the vest. Once his equilibrium was somewhat steady again, he thought of Jonah and groaned. His instincts had been right after all. He should have called Ruger earlier.

At least Jonah would have had a chance. This way, they were probably all going to die.

Something brushed against his leg beneath the water, and he froze. Earlier, the water that had washed over him had stung his back, so at the least, he had cuts, maybe worse. The fact that he was cut, meant blood in the water, which also meant sharks.

"Please, God, don't let me wind up in the belly of some fish."

He held his breath, waiting to see if there was any other contact, but thankfully felt nothing. As time passed, Collum began to realize that he was drifting away from the site of the wreckage. If there was a chance of rescue, he needed to stay close to where he'd gone down. He'd been flying below radar, so hoping that an air traffic controller would have seen the blip disappear was pointless. All he could do was hope that someone had heard his Mayday, or that Ruger had gotten more of his message than he'd thought.

But the longer he floated, the more certain he became that if he was to get out of this alive, he was going to have to save himself. Ignoring the shooting pains in his shoulder and his head, he moved the life vest out from under him and slipped it on. Once he'd secured it around him, he started swimming toward shore. It didn't take long for him to realize that he was caught in a current running parallel to the shore. No matter how hard he tried, he couldn't get any closer to land. Exhausted and weak from the pain of his injuries, he finally leaned back and felt himself being swept away.

Macie was bordering on the verge of hysteria. She'd heard just enough of the panic in Ruger's voice to know that Collum McAllister's chopper had crashed before he was able to give Jonah's location. It was her worst nightmare come to life, and there was nothing she could do about it. She'd gone to her room in complete dejection. As she was pacing the floor, a knock sounded at her door.

"Come in," she called.

Rosa entered.

"*Señora* . . . is there something I can do for you?"

The tenderness in the woman's voice was Macie's undoing. Her eyes welled.

"There's nothing anyone can do," she said.

Rosa touched Macie's arm, then shook her head.

"You are wrong," she said gently. "You can still pray."

She left, quietly closing the door behind her.

Macie stood within the silence of her room as the echo of Rosa's words played back in her head. She dropped to her knees and closed her eyes.

"God . . . please, God . . . don't let them die."

16

The Coast Guard found the crash site just after 5:00 p.m., but there was nothing to lead them to believe the pilot had survived. The largest piece of wreckage they pulled out of the water was part of a seat cushion. Bits and pieces of wreckage floated in an oil slick, but the body of the chopper was gone. Ruger was sick at heart as the chopper in which he was riding circled the area. He'd given up finding Evan Blaine alive. Now they were looking at having to recover Slade's body as well as the pilot of this ill-fated flight. The problem was that none of it should have happened. He'd let professional consideration for a fellow government agent override his good sense. He never should have let Slade in on what was going on or allowed Carl French to help with the investigation — for all the help he'd been. If French had turned up any new clues, he had yet to share them.

Ruger sighed. The press was going to have a field day with this. The fact that the grandson of one of the wealthiest men in the country had been kidnapped was bad enough, but trying to explain the involvement and death of two Company men in what should have been a Federal investigation was probably going to get him demoted, if not dismissed altogether. What was ironic was that he couldn't bring himself to care. He would quit the job himself if they could only find Slade and his son alive.

"What now, sir?" the pilot asked, as they circled the area one more time.

"Take it back," Ruger said. "But fly along the coast. There has to be something there that we're missing. The pilot was following Slade, so it stands to reason that he can't be far from where the chopper went down. Maybe we'll get lucky."

"What are we looking for?" the pilot asked.

"A miracle," Ruger muttered, then added, "That and a dark van."

It was ten minutes after 6:00 p.m. when Macie got the call from Ruger.

"Miss Blaine, Agent Ruger here. I'm afraid the news isn't good."

Macie's knees went weak. "Tell me," she said.

"We found the crash site, but there's no sign of the pilot, and without him, there's little hope of finding where Jonah was taken."

The floor tilted beneath Macie's feet. "No . . . that can't be right. There has to be something else you can do."

"We flew along the coast as we came back, but without knowing what we were looking for, it was impossible to make any kind of connection to what we saw. I'm sorry. We'll talk more when —"

Macie hung up the phone. She didn't need to hear any more platitudes, not when her heart was breaking. She leaned against the wall and then slid all the way to the floor. Her heart was pounding erratically; her skin felt cold and clammy. She was going into shock, but what she wanted to do was to die. She drew her knees up beneath her chin as she started to shake.

Time passed. She didn't know how much, but reason began to return, along with the sound of another person's voice. Someone was talking to her, trying to get her to stand up, but she didn't have the energy to tell them she was right where she needed to be. She wanted to die. They just needed to leave her alone long enough to let it happen.

Carl French had returned, but was he going to be in time? he wondered. He'd burst into the Blaine mansion with his briefcase in hand, expecting to see the place crawling with feds. Instead he'd found a couple of them manning the phones in the conference room, and they'd given him only vague answers to his questions. Otherwise, there were only the same security guards patrolling the outside grounds. Frustration had turned into temper as he'd demanded to be put in contact with Ruger and been ignored.

He hadn't told anyone where he'd been going, because he wasn't sure he could deliver the goods. But a desperate flight back to headquarters and some fast-talking with the director had yielded a second computer, set to track on the same wavelength as the onc that had gone down with McAllister. Now all he had to do was find Ruger and get it in the air.

But the FBI was no longer cooperating. He could only imagine what had happened in his absence. Then he thought of Macie. She would know what was going on.

He soon found her, but not where he'd expected. She was sitting on the floor in her room, with her back to the wall. The devastation on her face made him sick. He dropped to his knees beside her.

"Macie! It's me. Carl. You have to get up and tell me what's happening."

Macie buried her face in her hands. "It's all coming undone."

Carl cursed beneath his breath, then grabbed her by the shoulders and started to shake her.

"Stop it!" he yelled. "Pull yourself together and talk to me, damn it! I need to know what's happened."

Macie looked up, staring blindly at the man through a wall of tears.

"Happened? I'll tell you what happened.

Ruger called. They found where the chopper went down. There's no sign of the pilot, which means they can't find Jonah, which means now I've lost him, too."

"Maybe not," Carl said. "Get up and come with me. There may still be a chance."

Under Carl's guidance, Macie staggered to her feet, then let herself be led into the conference room.

"This is an emergency. Get Ruger on the phone right now," Carl ordered.

"He's already en route," the agent said.

"How long?" Carl asked.

"Thirty minutes, maybe less."

"Is he in the air?"

"Yes."

"Then tell him to refuel before he gets here and ask questions later."

"Yes, sir," the agent said, and reached for the phone.

"What are you going to do?" Macie asked.

Carl picked up the briefcase that he'd left there earlier and took out a small gray laptop.

"This is a duplicate of the one McAllister had when he went down. If we can get in the air with it, there's a chance we'll get lucky. But remember, we have to be within twenty-five miles of Jonah before we can pick up the signal."

Macie looked at the computer, then back up at Carl.

"Oh God . . . do you think —"

"I'm not promising anything," he said. "But it's damn sure worth a shot."

Macie threw her arms around Carl's neck. He was taken aback, but only for a moment. He grinned as he returned the hug, then gave her a friendly kiss on the forehead.

"It's a good thing Slade can't see me now. He's a little possessive about his things."

Macie laughed as he turned her loose. She wanted to shout — to weep for joy. But it was too soon for a celebration. Right now she was happy just to settle for a second chance.

The breakers were loud against the rocks as the sun began to set. Somewhere beyond where Collum was lying, he could hear the guttural grunts and barks of sea lions, and the occasional squawk of gulls as they squabbled over a bit of dead fish.

His body was shaking so hard his teeth were clacking. Either he was getting a fever or he'd gone into shock. Before he'd been so cold, but now, even with the sun beginning to set, he was too hot.

It had taken hours before he'd drifted out of the current and been able to swim to land. It was only then, when he'd tried to walk onto the tiny bit of beach, that he'd realized he must have broken his leg. It had buckled under him almost instantly, followed by a wave of mind-shattering pain. When the worst of the pain had passed, he started to crawl, making sure that he was high enough and far enough away from the beach so as not to be swept away by the rising tide. When he finally stopped and then rolled over on his back, limp from exhaustion, he realized that any planes would not be able to see him.

And he had seen the planes. He knew they were looking for him, because they'd been flying in search patterns for most of the afternoon. He'd tried to crawl out toward the water to wave for help, but he was too weak, and it was too far to the beach. All he could do was pray, as they flew out of sight, that with daylight they would return. He lay back, pillowing his head on the sand, and tried not to think of what was happening to Jonah.

Jonah stood at the window in the near-airless room, peering through the crack. He couldn't tell how late it was, but he knew it was nearing sunset. They should have been here by now, but they weren't, which meant something had gone wrong.

His gut knotted, but he refused to let on that he was in any way concerned. Maintaining a confident air for Evan was paramount, especially now, when their lives were hanging by a thread. He hunched his shoulders and then turned, eyeing the room in which they were locked. There had to be a way out of here. All he had to do was find it.

He glanced at the boy on the bed and was overwhelmed by the sudden surge of emotion. His son. God in heaven, that six-foot stretch of a boy was his son. There were so many things he wanted to know about him, but now was not the time. He began walking the planked floor, every now and then bouncing up and down on one board or another to test it for strength, but nothing seemed to give. He'd gotten out of bad situations before, but this time, time was not on their side.

Evan pretended to sleep, because he didn't know what to say to Jonah Slade, although he snuck a look every time Jonah's back was turned. It was as if he was trying to cram a lifetime of memories into what could be the last day of their lives. Even though Jonah kept saying it was going to be okay, Evan didn't believe it. However, it didn't seem so bad anymore. He wasn't alone. His father had cared enough to come looking for him, and he'd found him. It was the culmination of every dream he'd ever had.

Then he saw Jonah toeing the hole at the end of the room where Harold the rat always made his escape.

"That's where Harold lives," Evan said.

Jonah turned.

"Who's Harold?"

"A rat. When I was first brought here, he sort of saved me."

"Saved you how, son?"

Evan's heart skipped a beat. He'd waited all his life to hear this man call him son, and he had to concentrate to remember what it was Jonah had asked.

"Uh . . . it was the food. The first tray of food they brought was drugged. Harold got to it first. I saw him lying beside the partially eaten food and thought he was dead. I thought they were going to poison me. So I wouldn't eat. It made the guard pretty mad. There was even a woman who came once and tried to make me. I made *her* pretty mad, too. So mad that I think she would have killed me, but the guard stopped her."

"Damn him," Jonah muttered, thinking of Calderone. "Damn Miguel Calderone's sorry soul to hell."

Evan rolled over on the cot and started to get up, then winced when he put pressure on his hands.

It wasn't the first time Jonah had seen Evan cradling his hands beneath his arms, but he'd thought it was because of his ribs and the beating he'd taken. Now he wasn't so sure.

"Need some help?" he asked, and grabbed Evan's wrist.

The wince on Evan's face turned into a

shriek. The sound was horrifying, as was the pain on his face. Immediately he doubled over, rocking himself back and forth until the pain subsided.

Jonah was distraught. He didn't know what he'd done but was afraid to touch him to see.

"I'm sorry, I'm sorry," Jonah said. "What did I do?"

Evan shuddered, then shook his head, as if shaking off the shock.

"I didn't mean to . . . you didn't know that . . ." Then he sighed and held out his hands. "I think they're infected."

Jonah looked, then had to swallow before he could speak.

"What happened to them?"

Evan pointed toward the boarded-up windows. "The first day I was here, I kept trying to get out. Guess I tore them up pretty good."

"May I?" Jonah asked, and held out his hands, palms up.

Evan hesitated, then laid his own hands in his father's.

Jonah held them gently, trying not to show his concern, but it was no wonder the boy was feverish. The fingers were bad, as bad as he'd ever seen. They were swollen, and oozing blood and pus. And he could see the beginnings of some small red streaks running up his fingers.

God in heaven, the kid was bordering on blood poisoning.

He had to get him out. Another twenty-four hours, and if Calderone didn't kill him, this damn sure would.

"I'm so sorry," Jonah said, then urged Evan back to the cot.

They sat down together, and for a bit there was nothing but silence between them. Then Jonah took a deep breath and started to talk.

"Do you know why you're here?" he asked.

"Ransom?"

"No. It's because of me."

Evan frowned. "I don't understand."

Jonah glanced away, then made himself look back, studying the strength in his son's jaw and the intelligence in his eyes. It was obvious the kid was tough, but would he understand?

"Do you know what I do for a living?"

Evan shrugged. "Maybe. You work for the government, right?"

"I'm CIA, mostly undercover. About two weeks ago, I killed the son of a very powerful drug lord. Now he wants to kill mine."

Evan's heart skipped a beat. "Damn," he said softly. A minute passed without either of them speaking, and then Evan looked up. "So I guess ransom is out of the question, huh?"

The grin on Evan's face was the last thing Jonah expected to see. Pride, coupled with admiration, filled Jonah's heart, but he couldn't afford the sentimentality he was feeling. Too much concern and they would both fall apart. Instead, he grinned and laid his hand on Evan's knee.

"You're a tough nut, aren't you?"

Evan shrugged. "When Mother would get mad at me, she would always say I was acting just like my father."

Jonah straightened, closely eyeing Evan's expression.

"So how did that make you feel?"

Evan shrugged again. "I guess it made me feel good."

That hurt Jonah's heart even more. "For God's sake, why? You didn't know me. I was never in your life."

"But that wasn't your fault. Aunt Macie made sure I knew that."

"Still, it had to hurt that I didn't exist in your world."

"I guess." Then he looked away. "I guess I would rather have been associated with someone I didn't know than to be accused of being just like Grandfather. He uses people. I don't like to be used."

"Yeah, I know what you mean," Jonah said, then added, "still, you have every right to be mad about what's happened to you."

"Oh, I'm mad, all right," Evan said. "I'm mad at Grandfather for what he did to us, and mad doesn't cover what I feel about the people who killed Mom. But I'm not mad at you."

"I would understand if you were," Jonah said. "It wouldn't change how I feel about you."

Tears welled in Evan's eyes, but he wouldn't look up. He didn't want his father to see him cry, although he had to ask, "Uh . . . Dad?"

Jonah took a slow breath, trying to control his emotions. It still hurt like hell to hear that word and know he didn't deserve the title.

"Yeah?"

"Exactly how *do* you feel? About me, that is?"

Jonah slid a hand across Evan's shoulders and pulled him close beneath the shelter of his arm.

"I like knowing you're my son. I like being able to say, 'I have a son,' and right now, I'm pretty damned proud of you. When we get out of here, we're going to spend the rest of our lives making up for those lost fifteen years."

The tears welled and then spilled, sliding slowly down Evan's face.

"It's okay, kid," Jonah said, and pulled Evan that much closer. "You go ahead and cry. Cry all you want. God knows you've earned the right."

Evan shuddered; then his shoulders began

to shake. Even as he was trying to draw his next breath, it came up from his belly in a sob.

Jonah wrapped his arms around Evan and held on.

Carl French was running toward Ruger's chopper even before it had landed. Macie was right behind him. When it set down, Ruger jumped out.

"What's going on, and where the hell have you been?" he yelled.

"Inside!" Carl yelled, motioning for him to get back in the chopper. When Ruger complied, Macie began to follow.

"Wait a minute," Ruger said, as both Carl and Macie crawled into the back of the chopper. "You're not going anywhere," he said, pointing to Macie. "And I'm not so damned sure about him, either."

Carl motioned for Ruger to shut the door so they could talk above the sound of the spinning rotors. Ruger slammed it shut, then ordered the pilot to hold as he turned to face them.

"This has been a long day, and I'm not in the mood for any more games. So you better start talking and make sure I like it, or you're out on your ear."

"I flew to headquarters. I know how McAllister was tracking Jonah. I can't tell you where Jonah is right now, but get me up in the air and there's a chance we can find him before it's too late."

"What are you talking about?" Ruger asked.

Carl opened his briefcase and took out what looked to be a small laptop.

"State of the art. The only other one like it is probably at the bottom of the Pacific."

"Please," Macie begged. "I saw the other one and how it worked. If you can get within twenty-five miles of Jonah, it will pick him up."

"Those people aren't stupid," Ruger said. "If Slade was wearing a bug, Calderone's men have already found it and disposed of it, right along with him and the boy."

Macie slapped him. The shock was more startling than the pain.

"Damn you," Macie said. "Damn you for quitting on him. He wouldn't quit on you. If you're not going to help, say so now. You haven't discovered one serious clue to help with this investigation since I got here. Everything we know about this case is because of Jonah. If I have to, I'll get my own plane and leave you out of the loop. And do not refer to Jonah or my nephew in the past tense. Not in front of me, and not until you are looking at their bodies. Do you understand me?"

It didn't set well with Ruger to be told off by anyone, especially a woman. But he knew he'd overstepped himself by implying that

Slade and the kid were already dead.

"I'll take French," Ruger said. "But you're getting out right now. Civilians do not participate in Federal operations."

"Bull," Macie said. "You people use anyone you can, however you can, as long as it serves your purpose. Get this thing in the air, or I swear to God, you won't like the news coverage or my comments when this is over."

This time Ruger made no attempt to hide his rage.

"Are you threatening me?" he growled.

"Yes," Macie said, and buckled herself into the seat.

Ruger stifled a curse as he pointed at French.

"Keep her quiet, or I'll put both of you out."

Macie wouldn't even acknowledge Ruger's presence, which only made him that much angrier. He turned back to the pilot and gave a terse order beneath his breath that neither of them could hear, but moments later the helicopter was in the air.

Carl glanced at the woman beside him as the chopper lifted off. From the little Jonah had told him about the situation, she'd been ostracized by her family years earlier. But he wondered, as they flew into the night, if she knew how like her father she was at this moment — willing to do anything it took to get what she wanted. It was obvious that she wanted her family back. If it was humanly possible, he would see that it happened. If not, he didn't want to be anywhere near her when she came undone.

Soon they were flying south, enveloped by darkness and lit only from the lights on the instrument panel and the screen of the computer that Carl held in his lap.

Justin Blakely had the hots for Molly Dean. He'd been trying all summer to get into her pants. He'd tried every method of persuasion he knew, including some he wasn't too proud of, but she'd still held back. Now he didn't even know if he liked her anymore. It was just a matter of pride that he finish what he started.

And tonight he'd pulled out all the stops. He had his father's yacht, his father's crew and his father's stash of champagne. He had all Molly's favorite foods on board, as well as some of their favorite music. At the first course, they'd headed south, and now that dessert was but a chocolate memory on their tongues, they had dropped anchor near a tiny cove, barely visible in the moonlight.

"How about a midnight swim?" Justin asked.

Molly glanced at her watch. "It's almost three," she said.

Justin smiled, then leaned over and kissed her earlobe.

"Then how about an early-morning swim?"

Molly giggled.

"I didn't bring a suit."

"Neither did I," Justin said. "Although I'm sure there are some on board if you feel the need."

Then he stood up and started taking off his clothes.

Molly's heart began to pound. She wanted Justin Blakely more than she'd wanted any other man in her life. But she didn't want to be a one-night stand. She'd fallen in love and wanted to be his wife. She knew Justin's reputation, though, and holding out had been her only weapon.

But tonight seemed special. Maybe he'd brought her out here to propose. When he took off his shirt, he appeared like a young god in the moonlight, lean and bronzed, asking her for something she had yet to give.

As she watched, he shed the rest of his clothes, then turned and paused, giving her a full view of his body before he went over the side.

Her heart skittered. He'd been fully aroused. The sight made her ache between her legs. She glanced over her shoulder. The crew was nowhere in sight. Without giving herself time to reconsider, she slipped off her clothes and went over the side.

Justin stifled a grin as he watched her slim, pale body momentarily silhouetted in the moonlight, and then she was in the water beside him.

"Let's swim to the beach," Justin said, pointing toward the moonlit cove just past the shallow reef.

"What if there are sharks?" Molly asked.

Treading water, Justin cupped the back of her head and pulled her into a passionate kiss.

"The only shark in these waters is me," he teased, then started to swim toward shore.

Molly matched her pace to his, and before they knew it, they were walking through the surf to the lee side of a large outcropping of rock.

Justin had fucking on his mind, but it ended when they saw the body clinging to a small spit of stone.

Molly screamed. Justin froze. He couldn't believe what he was seeing. Of all the stupid, mind-blowing luck. The beach he'd chosen had washed up a stiff.

Then the stiff moaned and moved, and everything changed.

"He's alive!" Molly screamed. "Go get help . . . and bring me my clothes."

Justin sighed. The night was obviously over. He headed back to the yacht to get help and, of course, Molly Dean's clothes.

Collum thought he was dead. The angels standing over him were beautiful, which he'd expected angels in heaven to be. But he was a tiny bit surprised by their nudity, until he realized that in heaven, shame would not be an issue.

However, he hadn't expected to still be feeling such pain, nor had he expected to ever meet a girl angel named Molly. So, ever the good agent that he was, he decided to hedge his bets. Just in case he wasn't in heaven, he thought he should notify the FBI. He kept trying to grab Molly's hand, to tell her to call a Federal Agent named Ruger, but he wasn't sure she understood, or if he'd even been talking. Maybe it was all in his head. Maybe this wasn't really happening after all.

17

Calderone woke abruptly, covered in sweat. Elena's arm was draped across his chest, and one of her legs was over the lower half of his body.

Ah, he thought, that was why he'd felt so heavy. For a moment he had believed himself to still be immobile from the poison of the curare. That in itself had been a hell on earth, and if it had not been for Elena, the ruse might not have worked. Despite the enormous amount of money he'd paid that prison doctor, Calderone believed he would have backed out on the scam if she had not been there.

Now that he knew he had only been dreaming, he took a deep, cleansing breath, then shoved her aside without ceremony. She rolled without waking, snuggling her nose deeper into the pillow. He eyed her voluptuous curves and thick, dark hair, and thought for a moment about waking her, then changed his mind. Instead he rolled to the side of the bed, but when his feet touched the floor, he was filled with a sudden anxiety.

Ever cautious, he picked up his gun, then

strode through the ranch house, searching the moonlit grounds outside for signs of intruders. All was silent. Even the mongrel dog on the veranda was motionless in sleep.

Satisfied that all was well, his mood shifted to what lay ahead. He knew himself well enough to know that what he was feeling had its roots in the past. He was well, he was free, but his beautiful Alejandro was still dead.

His thoughts jumped to the coast and to the hangar where Evan Blaine was being kept. They'd used the old buildings, as well as the ruined landing strip, morc than once to bring in cocaine. And when the timing was right, that would be the rendezvous point during the time of the assassination. Just because his original plan to kill the president had been delayed, that didn't mean he'd given it up. The arrest of the other partners at his *hacienda* had been a source of embarrassment to him. His reputation had been damaged. It would be difficult to persuade other dissidents against the American government to join up with him again. But Calderone hadn't gotten where he was by believing himself defeated. Not now. Not ever. When the time was right, he would find others who believed as he believed.

For now, he had to be satisfied with exacting revenge, and using something that belonged to the United States government for illicit purposes was a huge source of satisfaction. Still, as he stood in the dark, his instincts kept telling him something was amiss. When the phone began to ring, he was not surprised. He glanced at a digital clock, then frowned as he went to answer the call.

"Sí?"

"*Padrone* . . . Carlos Padillo . . . he is dead."

Calderone's hand tightened on the receiver. Padillo was the boy's guard. If the guard was dead, then where was the boy?

"What happened?"

There was a moment of hesitation, as if the man knew what he said was going to make Calderone mad.

"The man . . . Jonah Slade. His hands were bound and yet he . . . it happened so fast."

Calderone felt the ground falling out from beneath his feet. "Are you telling me that Slade killed one of my men — with his hands still tied — and you stood there and let him?"

The lack of emotion in Calderone's voice made the guard sick to his stomach, but it had to be said.

"But, *Padrone* . . . you have given orders not to touch either him or his son, and that the honor of avenging Alejandro's death is to be yours. What were we to do?"

Calderone was so angry he had started to shake.

"And you would be right, but I also assumed you had enough *cojones* to keep one man and one boy subdued without incident."

"They are safely locked up, *Padrone* . . . waiting for your arrival."

"*Bueno,* but until I get there, you stay away from that man."

"We will, *Padrone*. It was Padillo's fault, anyway. You told us not to touch Evan Blaine, and he had beaten the boy very badly."

"That," Calderone said, "is nothing to what I am going to do to him . . . and to his father. I will be there soon. Try not to disappoint me again."

"*Sí, Padrone*. All will be as you wish upon your arrival."

Calderone disconnected, then threw the phone across the room. It shattered against the wall in a splinter of wire and plastic. He had underestimated Jonah Slade, but it wouldn't happen again.

"Get up!" he shouted, and started going through the house and turning on lights. "Get up! Get up!" By now the household was in an uproar. People came running with guns drawn, expecting that they were being raided, only to find Calderone issuing orders. "Get dressed. We leave now for the south."

One of his men, a simple man named Jaime Avila, thought Calderone was still weak, possibly hallucinating from the drug he'd taken, and tried to get him back to bed.

"Please, *Padrone* . . . you should rest."

Calderone lifted the gun he was carrying and shot him, point-blank, in the chest. The stunned assembly gasped en masse, then froze as Avila fell to the floor.

"Do what I say!" Calderone shouted. "I need to be at the hangar by daybreak or it will be too late." Then he pointed at the man on the floor. "Get rid of him. I don't want to be reminded of people who doubt me."

They scattered like quail, running to do the *padrone*'s bidding, because to argue was to suffer the fate of poor Jaime.

Before the hour had passed, Calderone was in the air. He glanced down at his watch. It was ten minutes to five. It would be daylight by the time they arrived, which was perfect. He could not wait to see the look of horror on Jonah Slade's face when he ripped the heart from his young son's chest.

They'd been in the air for almost two hours without getting a hit on the tracking device. Ruger was thin-lipped and silent. A thin film of sweat had beaded across Carl French's forehead as they'd flown mile after mile without anything showing up on the monitor.

But none of this seemed relevant to Macie. It only deepened her resolve. To her way of thinking, they'd been given a reprieve. She wouldn't let herself believe that God would do this to her twice — to wipe everyone she loved from the face of the earth. And then they got a call from Agent Sugarman that reaffirmed her beliefs.

"He's alive? Where did they find him? Can he talk? Good man," Ruger said, then grabbed a pen and began scribbling down some directions. "Great! Got it! Scramble the other choppers and get them on the move ASAP. I have no idea how much backup we're going to need, but this is one time I'm calling out all the dogs."

Macie grabbed the shoulder of Ruger's jacket.

"What is it?"

The news had put Ruger in such a good mood that he actually smiled at her.

"They found McAllister."

"Alive?" Carl asked.

"Yes. He was a little out of his head, but he kept repeating the same set of numbers over and over. Sugarman checked an aeronautical map. It matches an abandoned airport on the coast."

Macie's fingers curled into the fabric. "How far are we from there?"

Ruger looked to the pilot who checked his bearings, then looked at Carl puzzled that they'd missed the location.

"We've been too far inland. It's about

thirty minutes north," Carl said.

Ruger nodded, satisfied with Carl's explanation. Thirty minutes. Macie could only imagine what could happen in that space of time.

"Please," she said. "Please hurry."

Ruger understood her panic. "Yes, ma'am."

With that, the chopper banked to the right, then veered closer to the coast and began to retrace their flight path.

Footsteps sounded outside the room; then a thin sliver of light appeared beneath the door. Jonah sat at the foot of the small cot, placing himself between Evan and whoever was coming in.

A lock turned; then both of the men who'd brought Jonah here were standing in the doorway with rifles drawn. They looked startled to see him so near and took a defensive step back.

"You, get back!" one of them ordered.

Jonah stood up. "Not as long as you've got those guns aimed at my son."

They looked at each other. It wasn't going any better than they'd expected. Still, the *padrone* was coming, and they had to make sure there would be no surprises from this man when he walked into the room.

The bed squeaked behind Jonah. Evan was awake.

"What's going on?" Evan asked.

Jonah held out his hand. "Get behind me."

Seconds later Evan's hand was on his back, letting him know he was there. Together, they moved to the right, giving the two guards room to come in.

"The place is a little crowded," Jonah said. "And someone needs to let the landlord know the plumbing is backed up. Otherwise, the accommodations are just fine."

Ignoring his sarcasm, the guards tore the mattress off the small bed, then turned the bedframe upside down. Once they had decided that there were no concealed weapons there, they glanced toward the small bathroom.

One guard waved his gun toward the room. "You look. *I* will keep them covered."

The other guard snorted. "No, you look. I will keep them covered."

Jonah laughed. "Come on, guys. No guts, no glory."

They shuffled nervously, uneasy with a man who could laugh in the face of his own death.

"We go now," they both said, then quickly left the room.

Jonah heard the lock turn, then the sound of receding footsteps.

"What was that all about?" Evan asked.

"I don't know, but let's put the bed back together, what do you say? You can get some more rest."

Together they reassembled the cot; then Jonah shoved it into a different corner of the room.

"Why did you do that?" Evan asked.

Jonah grinned. "The room is out of balance. I think the bed looks better against this wall. Now all we need is a table and a lamp, maybe a stack of good books and a cooler of Cokes, and we're good to go. You know that Feng Shui stuff really works. I think those guys would be a lot easier to get along with if they'd just rearrange a little furniture."

Evan laughed as he eased down on the side of the mattress, unconsciously cradling his hands as he sat.

Jonah noticed but didn't comment. For now, there was nothing he could do to help ease his son's pain, but the time was coming. He wouldn't let himself believe that they'd come this far for it to end badly.

"Feel like talking?" Jonah asked.

"Yeah, sure. About what?"

Jonah sat down beside him, then leaned forward, resting his elbows on his knees.

"We'll catch up on your favorite music and food later. For now, what can you tell me about the people who brought you here?"

A slight frown knitted its way across Evan's forehead.

"Not much. There was the guard you . . . uh . . ."

"Killed. Say it, Evan. And know this. For

what he did to you, I would do it again, only slower."

A muscle jerked at the side of Evan's jaw. "I don't think I said thank you, did I?"

Caught off guard, Jonah didn't know quite what to say. He'd expected Evan to be horrified, even disgusted, by what he'd seen him do, but it had been a knee-jerk reaction to everything that Evan had already been forced to endure, and as he'd just said, he would do it again.

"It's not something a kid like you should have seen," Jonah said.

Evan was silent for a moment, then mumbled, almost beneath his breath, "I'm not a kid anymore."

Jonah sighed, then laid his hand on top of Evan's head.

"Yeah, I know. I'm still sorry, just the same."

"It's okay," Evan said. "As I was saying, there was the guard . . . oh yeah . . . and the woman who came to try to make me eat. There was another man with her, but I think he was sort of like her bodyguard or something. They were the only faces I saw."

Jonah thought of the woman he'd known in Colombia who'd never been far from Calderone's side and guessed it was her.

"Probably the same one who posed as the nun," Jonah said, more to himself than to Evan.

"What nun?"

"Never mind," Jonah said. "She wasn't really a nun, and she helped Calderone escape."

"Who's Calderone?" Evan asked. "The one whose son you killed? What did he do?"

Jonah frowned. "He's a very powerful drug lord from Colombia. Besides running drugs all over the U.S., we've suspected him of being involved in a plot to assassinate the president."

"Wow," Evan said, eyeing Jonah with new respect. "And you helped capture him."

"Yes, but you and your family paid a very high price for what I did."

"Dad, Aunt Macie told me something once that I never forgot. She told me that I can't be responsible for other people's mistakes, so neither can you. It's not your fault you didn't know about me, and it's not your fault that man, Calderone, is evil."

Jonah didn't bother to hide the pride he was feeling.

"You're quite a man, aren't you, son?"

Evan met Jonah's gaze. "I don't know, Dad. Am I?"

"Hell, yes," Jonah said gruffly, and then gave him a quick hug. "Now, back to the nun who wasn't a nun. Is there anything else you can remember."

Evan frowned. "Well . . . the woman I saw sure didn't act like a nun," Evan said. "She was yelling and screaming at me, and pretty much having a fit. Finally she left." Then he added. "Oh, yeah . . . there was someone else who was here a couple of times, but I only heard his voice. He was American, though."

Jonah's stomach knotted. Was he the link he'd been trying to find? The traitor who'd given up Jonah's real name and family to Calderone?

"How do you know he was American?" Jonah asked.

Evan shrugged. "He didn't speak Spanish to them. Besides, I could tell by his voice."

"Would you know it again if you heard it?" Jonah asked.

Evan frowned. "Yeah, maybe."

"Did he say anything distinctive? Maybe he had an accent you would recognize?"

"No accent. The only thing I heard him say was when he was leaving. Something about not taking any wooden nickels."

"That's a pretty common phrase," Jonah said.

"Yeah, I know."

"That's okay," Jonah said. "Just keep his voice in your mind. If you ever hear it again, I don't want you to let on."

Evan nodded, then asked, "Okay, but then how will you know?"

"How about a code word?" Jonah asked.

Evan's eyes widened. Jonah could tell he

liked the idea of being secretive.

"What word should we use?" Evan asked.

Jonah thought a moment. "You remember what I asked you on the phone . . . when I needed to know it was really you I was talking to?"

"Yeah, you asked me what Mom's middle name was."

"Right. So how about if we use the word Laura — for her first name?"

"Good choice, Dad!"

"Right."

"It's a deal," Evan said.

He was still smiling when Jonah heard something that brought him upright.

"What is it?" Evan asked.

"Sssh," Jonah said, then ran to the boarded-up window and pressed his ear to the crack. "Listen."

Evan cocked his head sideways. For a few seconds he heard nothing but the sound of distant waves crashing against the shore. Then he, too, began to hear it. The familiar popping sound that only the rotors of an approaching helicopter can make.

"Someone's coming!" he cried.

Jonah turned abruptly and looked toward the door.

"Yes, someone's coming," he said.

It was less than ten minutes to daybreak when Carl picked up a blip on the screen.

"I've got him!" he yelled. "By God, I've got him!"

Ruger gave them a thumbs up, then leaned over and said something to the pilot as Macie grabbed Carl's wrist.

"Can you tell if they're okay?" she asked.

Carl wouldn't tell her that the screen would register the same whether Jonah was lying dead somewhere or still standing.

"I wasn't as briefed on this as McAllister was. All I know is if Jonah is still wearing the shirt, it will give us his whereabouts, right down to an inch of where he's standing."

"I can't bear this," Macie said, and covered her face with her hands.

"Don't quit on him now," Carl said. "Not when you've come this far."

Macie shook off the panic as she looked out the window toward the horizon and the faint crease of light to the east.

"It's almost dawn," she said.

"A brand-new day," Carl said. "So think positive."

She nodded, but her stomach was in knots.

Ruger turned around. "Miss Blaine, when we set down, I'm going to ask you to do something for me."

"Anything," Macie said.

"Stay in the chopper with the pilot."

"Yes, of course. I'm not foolish enough to think I should go charging in on the kidnappers, but as soon as you can, you've got to let me know if . . . you must promise to —"

"Don't worry about it," Ruger said.

Macie leaned back in the seat and closed her eyes.

Ruger figured she was praying. God knew they could use all the help they could get, and the tremor in her voice had pushed him beyond his anger at her to understanding. The past few days had been hard on everyone, but especially for her. This was her family that had been decimated. Of course she was desperate to know if they were alive.

He keyed the radio in the cockpit, checking the ETAs of the backup choppers. One was less than ten minutes away, the other less than five. That was good. They were going to converge on the old airstrip at almost the same time.

The repetitive thump of the helicopter blades was like a pulse. Calderone imagined it beating in rhythm with his own as he stroked the blade of the knife in his hands. He held it firmly, yet lovingly — as lovingly as he made love to Elena. The metal was warm, the edge honed to perfection. He shuddered, anticipating the give of flesh and bone as it yielded to the finest steel. His nostrils flared, and his eyelids fluttered shut as his heartbeat began to pulse against his eardrums. Killing was orgasmic to Calderone. For him, the thrust of his penis into a woman's body was like thrusting a knife into her womb. He craved the sensations, knowing he held the power of creating life or taking it. He felt Elena's hand on his thigh, then the whisper of her breath against his cheek as she spoke against his ear.

"My love, we are almost there."

Calderone took a deep breath and then opened his eyes. Sunrise was imminent. Already the depths of night were giving way to the day, the light now casting shadows where there had been only darkness.

"There! See? On the horizon are the rooftops of the buildings."

Calderone's gaze remained motionless. Suddenly he turned, grabbed Elena by the back of the hair and yanked her forward, raking his mouth across her lips. The pain was sudden and vicious, and she reveled in knowing that she could give her Miguel what no other woman could bear. Like him, it was pain that made her come. She shivered with longing, imagining the fierceness of their lovemaking once his revenge had been slaked.

He turned her loose as suddenly as he'd taken her. When the chopper began to descend, he smiled.

"Who is it? Who's coming?" Evan asked.

Jonah wouldn't lie. Their lives depended on Evan being able to react.

"I don't know for sure," Jonah said. "But

either way, you've got to promise me something. When I tell you to run, you will run. And you won't look back."

The hope in Evan's eyes went blank.

"Evan?"

"I heard you," Evan said.

Jonah took him by the shoulders, feeling the gangly length of him and yet knowing that a fierce heart beat within his chest.

"Can you do that for me?"

"Yes."

"If it's not the right people, you head for the beach. It can't be far. Better to die in the water than by their hands. Promise me, Evan."

Suddenly Evan threw his arms around Jonah's neck. He wanted to cry but instead just held on.

"I promise," he mumbled. "I won't let you down."

Jonah's arms tightened as, for a few seconds, he allowed himself the luxury of the embrace.

"Maybe it's the authorities," Evan whispered.

Jonah felt sick. "Yeah, maybe so," he said softly, and silently cursed whatever Fates had caused their plans to go awry.

Evan pulled back abruptly, then looked at Jonah. It was obvious that he was struggling with something. Then he blurted it out.

"Uh . . . I need to say something," Evan said.

"Okay."

"I'm really proud that you're my dad."

Jonah groaned inwardly. "Thank you, son. More than you will ever know, but know this. I'm the one who's got bragging rights. You're one hell of a man, Evan Blaine."

Then footsteps sounded outside their door. Jonah shoved Evan behind him as they turned toward the sound.

18

Miguel Calderone was swaggering as he walked through the old hangar, his footsteps echoing with every step he took. The way he looked at it, he had a right to swagger. He had tricked the United States government — the strongest power on the face of the earth — and was free to tell the tale. The armed guard in front of him stopped and then pointed to a door.

"In here, *Padrone*."

"Open it," Calderone ordered.

The guard took out a ring of keys and inserted one of them into the lock. Seconds later, the door swung inward and Calderone found himself once again face to face with the man who'd killed his son.

"So . . . we meet again," Calderone said.

Knowing that Calderone enjoyed a verbal battle as much as a physical one, Jonah chose to say nothing.

Calderone's eyes narrowed. He had expected a response, not a cold, emotionless stare.

He marched forward — then drew back his hand and slapped Jonah's face.

"Have you no anger?" he demanded.

Jonah blinked, his cheek stinging from the force of the blow. For a few seconds he said nothing, and then he smiled.

It was the last thing Calderone expected to see. In that moment, he knew that once again he might have underestimated his opponent. He pulled his knife, brandishing it in the air like a little boy wielding a pretend sword.

"Take the boy!" Calderone yelled. "We'll see if he still smiles."

Jonah's muscles bunched. Behind him, he could hear the frightened gasp of Evan's breath as the two guards started toward them.

"Evan?"

"I remember," he said.

"For me, son," Jonah said, then yelled, "get down!"

Evan dropped to the floor as Jonah erupted in a motion almost too swift to see. One moment one of the guards was standing, and the next thing Evan knew, Jonah was in the air. He thought the heel of his father's boot caught the man on the chin, but he couldn't be sure. All he knew was that there was one less man standing than there had been a second before.

Calderone gasped and took a quick step backward. Before he could get out of harm's way, the man he'd sworn to kill had his arm around his neck, with his own knife held to his throat.

"Kill him!" Calderone screamed. "Shoot him now!"

"You move and your *padrone*'s tongue is going to fall out of the hole I put in his neck," Jonah warned.

The men were motionless, uncertain what to do next.

Calderone kept screaming out his orders, but no one would move. Then he remembered the boy.

"Shoot the boy! Shoot the boy!" he shouted, as he struggled to free himself from Jonah's grasp.

Jonah shoved the blade of Calderone's knife into his throat. Not enough to kill, but enough to hurt. Blood spurted, then flowed down the front of his shirt.

"Aaiiee!"

Calderone's shriek was a combination of shock, rage and pain. This wasn't the way it was supposed to happen.

Suddenly there was movement at the door and Elena was there. She was looking at Jonah, but her gun was aimed at Evan's chest.

"Turn him loose," she ordered. "Turn him loose or I will kill the boy."

Before they could react, the sound of more approaching helicopters could be heard. The shock on her face told Jonah all he needed to know. If they weren't expecting backup, then it had to be Ruger. She glanced over her shoulder, her features contorted in anger and disbelief. It was then that Jonah made his move.

With one smooth motion, he pulled the knife across Calderone's throat, then shoved him forward. He was already in the act of throwing the knife when Elena turned. She saw Calderone's body slumping to the floor and raised her gun, screaming out her grief as she aimed.

She didn't see the knife until it was imbedded in her chest. Even as she was trying to pull the trigger, her fingers were going numb. The gun fell from her hand to the floor. She looked down at the knife protruding from her chest and grabbed it with both hands.

One of the guards bolted; the other stood, caught in the trap of Jonah's stare.

"Now, Evan! Now!" Jonah said. "Run and don't look back."

"But the other choppers . . ."

"They're ours," Jonah yelled, and jumped the last guard. They wrestled each other to the floor as Evan bolted.

He ran past death on shaky legs, looking toward the open end of the hangar, only to find himself blinded by the morning light. Staggered by the brightness, he almost fell. Before he could regain his momentum, someone was calling his name. He saw the silhouettes of men running toward him, yelling at him — calling his name, telling him to get down — and they were speaking in English.

Someone grabbed him by the arm.

"It's okay, son. You're safe now. Come with me."

Relief hit him hard as he dropped to his knees. They were saved.

"My dad," he said, and pointed behind him.

"We'll get him, too," the man said. "Can you stand?"

"My hands," Evan said. "Don't touch my hands."

The agent looked down, his stomach turning as he saw their condition.

"Don't worry, son. We've got a medic standing by."

The guard was desperate. The moment he'd found himself on the floor beneath Jonah Slade, he knew he'd made the wrong choice. He should have left with Julio. At least then he would have had a chance. This man was like a madman — destroying everyone who'd had a hand in what had happened to his son.

"Mercy! Mercy!" he yelled, and suddenly threw his hands up over his head.

Jonah doubled up his fist and coldcocked the man, then took off the man's belt and bound his hands behind his back. It would last long enough for Ruger's men to handcuff him.

Finally he straightened, then turned and looked at Calderone. To his surprise, Calderone was still alive and watching him with hate in his eyes. Jonah walked toward him, then stopped just outside the pooling blood.

Calderone made a fist and shook it at Jonah.

Jonah's lips curled. "Did you think that I would stand by and let you destroy my son?"

Calderone clutched his own shirt above his heart, trying to indicate his own grief.

"Yeah, I know your son is dead," Jonah said. "If you hadn't raised the back-shooting little son of a bitch the way you had, he'd still be alive. Go to hell with that thought in your head."

Calderone's eyes bulged. Blood frothed at his lips as he clutched at the slit in his throat while helplessly drowning in his own blood.

Jonah stood for a moment, watching, almost reading Calderone's mind.

"I didn't kill you, you know. You already died in Lompoc. In the eyes of my country, you're already dead."

With that, he walked out of the room, past the guard whose neck he'd snapped, then past the woman who'd tried twice to kill Evan. As he moved toward the front of the hangar, he threw back his head and inhaled deeply, breathing in the fresh air, leaving the death and the stench of that room behind him.

Men in army fatigues were swarming through the buildings. Jonah walked past them, his gaze on the big Huey and the soldiers spilling out of its belly.

"Way to go, Ruger," Jonah muttered, and then he saw someone climbing out of a smaller chopper and froze in his tracks.

"Macie?"

Suddenly he was moving toward her, first lengthening his stride, then jogging until he was in an all-out run. He caught her in midair, inhaling the sweetness of her and the joy of feeling her body against him.

Alive. He was still alive.

"I thought I'd lost you," she said, and then buried her face against his neck.

His arms tightened. Tears swelled at the back of his throat.

"Never," he said hoarsely; then he put her down. "Evan? Where's Evan?"

"In the chopper," she said. Then she started to cry. "Oh, Jonah . . . you did it. You saved him. Thank you, thank you."

"He's a hell of a kid," Jonah said. "I'm thinking as the story comes out, we're going to find out he went a long way toward saving himself."

"Like father, like son," Macie said.

Jonah grinned. "And don't you forget it."

"Hey, good buddy, long time no see."

Jonah put Macie down as he turned around. When he saw Carl, his grin widened.

"Carl, you sorry so and so, where in blazes have you been?"

Macie grabbed Jonah's arm. "You wouldn't believe what hell we've been through. McAllister's chopper went down before he could tell us where you were and —"

The smile died on Jonah's facc. "Oh, no. Please tell me he's all right."

Carl grinned. "Well, yes. You can't keep a good Company man down. They rescued him about an hour ago. He was pretty much out of his head, but he kept repeating the coordinates where we could find you."

"Thank God," Jonah said. "I owe him big time."

"You owe Carl, too," Macie said. "He flew back to CIA headquarters and got the only other computer system that could track you. We were already in the air when we learned Collum had been rescued."

A long look passed between Jonah and Carl, and then Carl shrugged and grinned.

"Yes, I am a hero, and I expect a letter of recommendation in my file."

Jonah clapped him on the back as he put his arm around Macie.

"Shut up, you fool, and come with us. I want to introduce you to my son."

Carl fell into step beside them as they hurried to the chopper. Immediately, Jonah crawled in, then knelt at Evan's side. The medics already had him hooked up to an IV and were pumping electrolytes and antibiotics into his system as fast as they dared.

"How is he?" Jonah asked.

The medic turned. "Pretty good, sir, considering. He's a bit dehydrated, and I don't like the look of his hands, but we're taking care of both."

"Don't leave without me," Jonah said.

"Right. We won't be airborne until we get the go ahead from Agent Ruger."

"Where are you taking him?" Jonah asked.

"I asked them to take him to Cedars-Sinai," Macie said.

Jonah nodded, then glanced down at Evan.

"You did good, son. I told you it was going to be okay."

Evan tried to smile, but they had given him something that was making him very sleepy. All he could manage was a nod.

"Evan . . . I want you to meet Carl French. He's not only my best friend, but he's a pretty good agent, as well."

Carl leaned into the chopper and tugged gently on Evan's foot.

"Hey, kid . . . glad to meet you. We'll talk later when you're feeling better, okay?"

Evan looked at him a minute, then tried to sit up.

"Easy boy," Carl said. "I think you've had enough excitement to last you a lifetime. You let these people take care of you now, and we'll get better acquainted later, okay?"

Evan continued to struggle as Carl backed out of the cockpit.

"Take care, kid, and don't take any wooden nickels, okay?"

Jonah almost missed what Carl said until Evan grabbed his wrist. It was then that he remembered. He looked down, staring at the grip Evan had on his wrist. The boy's knuckles were white, and as Jonah watched, they started to bleed from beneath the nails, yet he didn't make a sound. There was only one thing Jonah could think of that would prompt his son to withstand so much pain. He didn't want to accept it, and even as he was looking at his son and seeing him mouth the word "Laura" he already knew.

"Okay, son, okay. I got the message. You're sure?"

Evan nodded as his eyes filled with tears.

Jonah laid his other hand on Evan's chest. As he did, the boy began to relax and let go.

"I'll take care of it. I promise."

Then he backed out of the chopper. When he turned to Macie, he was smiling.

"Honey, there are some things I need to finish up here with Ruger. Why don't you go with Evan to the hospital now? He's in too much pain to have to wait another minute on me. As soon as we're through here, I'll catch a ride in one of the other birds and meet you."

"Are you sure?" she asked.

Jonah wanted to throw his arms around her and weep upon her breast. There was so much pain inside him that it felt like he would burst. But this was something he had to finish on his own.

"Yes, I'm sure. Evan needs immediate care, so climb in and buckle up. I'll wave you off as soon as I clear it with Ruger."

Macie climbed inside, still smiling as Jonah shut the doors to the cockpit.

Ruger was only a short distance away. She watched as Carl and Jonah walked toward him, then breathed a sigh of relief as Jonah turned to the pilot and waved him on with a thumbs-up. Seconds later, they were in the air.

Jonah stood until the chopper was gone; then he looked at Carl.

"Walk with me, will you?"

Carl slid an arm around Jonah's shoulder as they walked back toward the shade of the hangar. Soldiers were still swarming the area, carrying out bodies and confiscating everything that looked to have been part of Calderone's drug trade.

Once inside the mouth of the hangar, Jonah turned.

"How long have you been on the take?"

Carl looked as if he'd been sucker-punched.

"What the hell are you talking about?"

Jonah was so angry his whole body was

shaking. "Don't fuck with me, Carl. I need to understand how you could betray me before I break your damned neck."

All the color washed from Carl's face, and then he took a step backward. Suddenly he reached in his jacket and pulled out a handgun.

"Don't be foolish," Jonah said. "The feds are everywhere. You pull that trigger and you're a dead man."

"I'm already dead, so what does it matter?" Carl said.

The words tasted bitter in his mouth, but Jonah said them just the same. "Damn you, Frenchy . . . damn you to hell. Tell me why you did this. Make me understand."

Carl stared for a moment, then shrugged. "I like the finer things in life."

Jonah stared at him, hearing the words but unable to believe what he'd heard. Had he ever known Carl French? Suddenly he didn't think so. Finally he spat out the words.

"I don't believe you."

Carl shoved his glasses to a more comfortable spot on his nose and then pursed his mouth.

"Really? Ever hear of the Snowman?"

"You know I have, but what's a hit man got to do with —"

Jonah stopped, not bothering to finish his own question. "Jesus Christ!"

Carl grinned. The smile was so familiar

that it hurt Jonah's heart.

"You! You're the Snowman?"

Carl's grin widened. "Ain't that a kick in the pants?"

"How did it happen? What was it that made you turn?"

"Money." Then he laughed aloud. "It was so damned easy. We were already trained to kill. All I did was point the gun and collect the money."

"How did you find out about Evan?"

"Oh, that was easy," Carl said. "Remember a couple of years ago when we were in Thailand and you got that fever?"

Jonah nodded.

"You were out of your head for three days, and we were alone in the jungle. I listened, that's all. And when we got back to the States, I did a little digging. I found out about the kid then and started to tell you, but I changed my mind. In my line of work, I never knew when I'd need a little insurance."

"You son of a bitch," Jonah said softly.

Carl shrugged. "Well, yes, but I'm a rich son of a bitch."

"You're never going to live to spend it."

"I've been in tight spots before and escaped," Carl said. "In fact, that's why I told Calderone about Evan. He was pretty pissed that I hadn't warned him earlier about the raid. It brought great shame on his name that he'd let two of the most important Yakuza and two big shots from the Russian Mafia get caught. But when you killed Alejandro, you gave me no choice. It was you or me, and frankly, my friend, I'm just selfish enough to choose my butt over yours."

Jonah was sick to his stomach. It hurt to say it, but he'd been a man who could always face the truth. Now was no exception.

"I'm not your friend," Jonah said. "I don't even know who the hell you are."

"I'm the Snowman," Carl said, and twirled the gun on his finger like an old-time gunslinger.

"And I'm leaving," Jonah said, then turned and strode out into the sunlight, well aware that Carl's gun was aimed at his back.

Carl was stunned. He hadn't expected that. Then he started to chuckle. He should have. Jonah Slade never did what was expected of him.

He put the gun back in his jacket and headed for Calderone's chopper only a short distance away. Jonah might be mad, but he wouldn't stop him from getting away. Of that he was certain.

As he neared the chopper, he lengthened his stride. The rotors were still turning. It wouldn't take but a few seconds to rev the engine and lift off. He would be up and gone before Ruger knew what was happening. Then all he had to do was head south and get lost in the South American jungles long enough to get some new papers. From there, he could begin a new life. Maybe in Tahiti, maybe New Delhi. He liked Indian food. He liked the Indian women with their jewel-colored saris and their dark, secretive eyes. Living was cheap there. He could spend the rest of his life there and live like a king. He kept on walking and didn't look back.

Jonah's mind was blank except for the knowledge that he couldn't let Carl go. He stopped the first soldier he came to and ripped the rifle from his hands.

The soldier recognized Jonah and didn't argue. Then he saw Jonah turn and aim the gun toward Carl French. That was when he reacted.

"Sir! You can't —"

Jonah shoved him aside and took aim. The moment he had Carl in his sights, he yelled out, "Carl French! Stop and drop your weapon! Now!"

Carl's heart lurched in his chest. God! Less than fifteen feet from the chopper, and he wasn't going to make it after all.

He thought about giving himself up, then realized he wouldn't last a week in the pen. Once the inmates realized they had a dirty spook on their hands, his life would be over. His only hope was that Jonah might miss. He started to run.

"Damn you, Carl, don't make me do this," Jonah muttered, then yelled out again, "Don't be a fool, Carl! You won't get away!"

Carl vaulted toward the cockpit, then spun around and fired two rapid shots in Jonah's direction, hoping that would make everyone take cover and give him time to lift off.

He was wrong.

Jonah never moved from where he was standing. Instead he took aim and, reluctantly, pulled the trigger.

Carl's foot was on the runner as the first bullet caught him square in the back. It didn't really hurt. It was more like he'd just lost his breath. Then the second one caught him in the shoulder and spun him around. Scrambling, he managed to make it into the cockpit, but when he tried to inhale, he felt something bubbling inside his chest.

He turned then, staring blankly at Jonah from across the distance. Like Calderone, he'd underestimated this man, a man he'd thought was his friend. He thought of the boy who'd gotten caught up in the midst of a madman's revenge. There was a lesson he'd just learned, although it was probably going to be too late to apply it to the rest of his life. Blood really was thicker than — Then the words left his mind. His back was starting to hurt, and Jonah's image was wavering, as if he were standing on the back side of a mirage. Suddenly Carl lifted his hand and waved at Jonah, then slid into the pilot's seat, unaware that the entire front of his shirt was rapidly staining with blood.

At the sound of the first two shots, Ruger spun abruptly. Everyone was running for cover. Except Slade.

"What the hell?" he muttered, then saw Slade taking aim at French.

The first shot hit French in the back, the second in his shoulder.

"Don't let him get off the ground!" Ruger yelled, but Jonah waved them all away.

"Let him go!" Jonah shouted. "Let him go!" Then he said, more to himself than the others, "He can't go far."

Unaware of the drama beyond the cockpit, French had hit the juice to the engine. The rotors began picking up speed, sending a huge cloud of sand and gravel into the air.

"I can do this . . . I can do this," Carl said, even as his feet were going numb.

Jonah handed the gun back to the soldier just as Ruger grabbed him by the arm.

"What in the name of God just happened?" he yelled.

"Killed the traitor," Jonah said.

"What traitor? I thought that man was your friend."

Jonah watched as the chopper began to ascend in a wobbly motion.

"Yes, so did I."

It wasn't until the helicopter began to blur

that Jonah realized he was crying.

"He's getting away," Ruger said, and started to send up another chopper, but Jonah grabbed his arm.

"No, he's not going far. He can't."

Ruger looked at Jonah, then back toward the ocean. No one moved. No one spoke. Silence enveloped the area as everyone watched the inevitable horror unfold.

A few seconds passed, and then suddenly the chopper lurched. When it began to spiral downward toward the ocean, Jonah flinched; then he turned his back, unwilling to watch the impact. When it hit, it burst into flames before sinking to the bottom of the Pacific in a ball of fire and steam.

"How did you know?" Ruger asked.

Jonah needed to throw up, but he wouldn't let himself feel the pain.

"Evan recognized his voice. When I confronted Carl, he admitted it."

"But why?" Ruger asked.

Jonah turned around then, searching the horizon and seeing only a spiral of steam coming up out of the water. He stared, remembering the life and the laughter he'd shared with a man he'd never really known. Then he looked away, meeting Ruger's gaze without blinking.

"Money."

"I'm sorry," Ruger said. "That's got to be tough, losing a friend like that."

"He was no friend of mine," Jonah said, then turned his back and walked away.

They'd flown to Cedars-Sinai with Evan. As soon as they reached the emergency area, they rolled him away, leaving Macie alone in the waiting area. Police were everywhere, keeping the media out and making sure that no one from Calderone's organization took the opportunity to finish what their *padrone* had started.

She knew it would be a while before she could see him again, but that was okay. He was alive. He was safe. But there was something else she had to attend to before the circle of her life was complete.

She asked the nurse at the desk if they'd moved Declyn Blaine to a different room after he'd had his stroke.

The nurse checked the computer. "No, Miss Blaine, he's still in 407."

"Thank you," Macie said, and headed for an elevator.

The guard was still on the door. He recognized Macie on sight.

"Miss Blaine! Are you here alone?"

Macie nodded. "It's all right," she said. "I think the worst is over."

"Really? I hadn't heard."

She smiled, but it felt as if her heart was breaking into a thousand pieces.

"You will. There's enough press outside the

emergency room door that soon everyone will know." Then she pointed to the door. "I'm going to see my father."

He nodded. "I'm real sorry about his condition."

Macie sighed. "Yes, so am I."

The room was quiet as she walked inside. The shades had been drawn against the bright light of day, but the smell of dying was in the room. She looked at the ceiling, then the walls, and even the curtains over the windows, before she could bring herself to look at the man on the bed.

When she finally turned her gaze to Declyn's face, her heart came up in her throat. His features were contorted on one side of his face and completely slack on the other. His eyes, normally dark and fierce, were staring fixedly at a point somewhere over the television set mounted on the wall. It was all she could do to move closer, but it had to be done.

"Dad?" She touched his arm. He didn't move. He didn't blink. "Dad, it's me, Macie." The monitor continued to register a monotonous beep without recognition.

Macie's eyes filled with tears. She slid to the side of the bed, then leaned over.

"I thought you'd like to know that Jonah found Evan. He's alive, and he's safe. We just brought him to this very hospital. He was injured some, but not severely. When he feels better, he'll come and see you, okay?"

There was no acknowledgment of the information in any way.

"Oh, Daddy," Macie said. Then ever so gently, she laid her head against his chest and pretended that in a moment she would feel his arms enfolding her into one of the infrequent hugs she'd known as a child.

"I'm so sorry," she said softly. "But it didn't have to be like this."

Macie was in Evan's room when Jonah arrived. As soon as she saw his face, she knew something had happened. She put a finger to her lips to indicate Evan was sleeping, then walked with him out into the hall.

"Tell me," she said.

"Tell you what?"

"Jonah, a woman knows when something is wrong with those she loves." Then she touched the side of his face. "And I love you so very much . . . so talk."

It hurt to say the words, but they had to be said.

"Carl is dead."

Macie gasped. "What? Oh my God . . . sweetheart, I am so sorry. What happened?"

"Evan didn't tell you?"

"Tell me what?" Macie asked.

Jonah took her by the hand, then led her toward the empty waiting room at the end of the hall. Once inside, he sat down, then pulled her close.

"Jonah, you're scaring me," Macie said. "Please talk to me."

"Carl was the traitor. He's been on the take for years, hiring himself out as a hit man between assignments. He'd been tight with Calderone and then got into trouble with him when the raid went down. He gave me up to save his own hide. Told Calderone about Evan to get Calderone off his back. He knew where Evan was all along."

Macie gasped. "No. Oh, no. I can't believe it! He seemed so sincere . . . even going all the way to CIA headquarters to get that second computer. We were in the air for hours searching for you."

"He knew where I was. I'd lay odds he didn't even have the tracking software on. If you had flown anywhere along the coast after you passed La Jolla, it would have picked me up."

"This is so awful." Then it dawned on her that he'd said Carl was dead. "You said Carl was dead? How did it happen?"

"I shot him," Jonah said, then got up. "I want to see Evan. What did the doctor say about his hands?"

Macie stood up with him, but she wouldn't let him leave. Not yet. "Jonah?"

He was moving toward the door.

"Jonah . . . look at me."

He stopped, but he wouldn't turn around. Right now, it was hard to face himself.

Looking at Macie would be next to impossible. What would she think about someone who could do what he'd done?

"I'm waiting," she said.

He sighed, then turned around. "What?"

"I'm sorry you had to go through that, but right now I'm so proud of you, I don't know what to say."

He couldn't hide his shock. "Proud? I killed four people today."

"From where I'm standing, you rescued your son, saved your own life and brought a traitor to justice."

"You aren't disgusted by what I did?"

Macie shook her head. "I think they should give you a medal," she said, and then opened her arms.

He walked into her embrace, and when her arms closed around him, he knew he'd come home.

"I don't want a medal. I'd rather have you and Evan."

She smiled. "Well, then, that's easy, because we're already yours, heart and soul." She kissed him quickly, but leaving him with no misunderstandings as to how she would have liked to continue. "Now, let's go say hello to your son. He's been waiting anxiously for you. At least now I know why."

Hand in hand, they retraced their steps to Evan's room. They were almost there when Jonah remembered Declyn.

"How's your father?" he asked. "Have you seen him?"

"I saw him," she said, shaking her head.

Jonah didn't ask anything more. When she was ready, she would talk. For now, Evan was uppermost in their minds.

They entered quietly, thinking Evan would still be asleep. Instead, they found him wide-eyed and watching the door. When he saw Jonah's face, his expression shifted from fear to relief.

"Dad?"

"It's all right," Jonah said. "Everything's been taken care of."

"What about —"

"It's over. All of it," Jonah said. "Just close your eyes and rest, and know that I'm here for you always."

Evan sighed and closed his eyes; then, despite his heavily bandaged hands, he reached for Jonah.

Jonah laid his hand on Evan's forehead, then pulled up a chair beside his son's bed.

"I'm here, Evan, and when I leave, you're coming with me."

Evan's eyelids fluttered. "And Aunt Macie?"

"You two aren't getting away without me," Macie said.

This time Evan managed a smile before the drugs pulled him under.

"What will he think about us . . . together, I mean?" Jonah asked.

"That I have good taste and that he's a very lucky young man?"

Jonah sighed, then leaned back in the chair.

"God . . . I feel like I could sleep for a week."

Just in case Evan wasn't really asleep, Macie leaned over and whispered in his ear, "Not without me, you don't."

Jonah grinned. "Honey, if I'm in bed with you, rest is the last thing I'll be getting."

Macie blushed and glanced nervously at Evan.

"Sssh. What if he's still awake?" she hissed.

"Then he'll learn what good taste his father has."

Epilogue

Key Largo, Florida

"Dad! Look at this!" Evan yelled.

Jonah turned to look at his son, who was standing at the end of the boat dock, holding a fish in one hand, and a rod and reel in the other. Jonah gave him a big thumbs-up, then watched as Evan dropped the fish back into the bay. Even though it had been ten months since the kidnapping had come to an end, he still woke up each morning thanking God they'd all survived.

He tossed the last coil of rope onto his boat, then jumped out onto the dock. The *Second Time Around* was his first charter boat, but plans to expand were already in his head. He knew just how he was going to swing it. Today was a slow day, though, and he was glad. It was giving him time to spend at home, which was his favorite place to be. He had started toward the end of the dock, where Evan was still fishing, when he heard Macie calling.

"Jonah! Telephone!"

He turned around, saw her waving at him from the patio of their beachfront house and started toward her at a jog. She was seven months pregnant and blooming. It was the only way he could describe how she looked to him. They were all counting the days until the baby's arrival, especially Evan. The name was already picked out and the nursery was almost finished. When Carrie Blaine Slade made her arrival, she would be welcomed into a very happy family and sleep in a haven of pink fluff.

"Who is it?" Jonah mouthed as he reached the back door.

Macie shrugged and handed him the phone.

"Hello?"

"Slade, is that you?"

Jonah frowned, trying to remember where he'd heard that voice.

"Yes. Who's speaking?"

"Darryl Ruger. I've got some vacation coming, and I'm anxious to try some deep sea fishing. Someone told me you run a pretty good charter service. Think you can hook me up?"

Jonah grinned. "If this is the same Ruger who all but told my wife to kiss his ass, then I expect I can."

Ruger snorted rudely into the mouthpiece. "I never said an off-color word to your wife and we both know it."

"That doesn't mean you didn't want to, though, does it?"

Ruger chuckled. "She's pretty tough when she has to be."

Macie was standing nearby when she heard what Jonah said. She turned around, a look of surprise on her face. Jonah blew her a kiss.

"Who are you talking to?" she asked.

"My wife wants to know who I'm talking to," Jonah said.

Ruger sighed. "Are you going to refuse me the charter if she nixes the deal?"

Jonah grinned at Macie and then winked. "Hell no. Business is business. You just say the word, and I'm yours for as long as you want."

Macie frowned. This didn't sound good. She hadn't asked him to quit the Company, but she'd been heartily glad when he had. Now, with the baby coming and Declyn in a nursing home nearby, it was all she could do to get through a day. And only recently she'd given her assistant at Blaine Import-Export a raise and a promotion. Now she stayed connected to them by Internet and phone. If Jonah went back on active duty, life wasn't going to be hard, it was going to be impossible.

"How about the first five days of next week?" Ruger asked.

"Let me check the book, but I think that's okay," Jonah said.

He hurried inside to the desk, opened the booking log, then checked through the dates.

"Yes, that will work out just fine," he said.

"My next charter isn't until the week after."

"Great. See you then," Ruger said.

"Hey, wait," Jonah said. "Don't you want to know how to get here?"

Ruger laughed. "I'm a fed, remember? I can find you, no matter where you are."

"Yeah, right," Jonah said, and hung up the phone.

"Jonah?"

"Yes?"

"Who was that?"

"Ruger. He booked a charter for next week." Then he ran a hand through his hair in pretend frustration. "God. Five days with that man just might put me in the nuthouse."

"Thank goodness," she said. "For a minute I thought it might be someone from the Company."

The smile slid off Jonah's face. "Oh, baby . . . come here."

Macie walked into his arms, never tiring of the feel of his embrace.

"I'm through with that," Jonah said. "The day I got Evan back alive was the end of my old life and the beginning of a new one. A better one, okay?"

"Okay."

"So don't ever think — not even for a moment — that I miss that life or that I might ever go back. Even before I knew about Evan . . . even before I found you again . . ."

"I found you, remember?" Macie said.

He laughed. "Yeah, right. Even before you found me again, I had already made up my mind that it was time to pack it in."

"Really?"

"Yes, really."

"So this is a good thing we're doing, right?"

Jonah knew what she meant. They'd turned their backs on all the Blaine money while making sure that it was put in trust for Evan. Declyn Blaine had paid dearly for the lie he'd perpetrated. He'd lost his children; then he'd lost his mind. The fact that his heart was still beating was almost ironic. He was alive, but unable to live beyond his room at the nursing home. His food was poured through a tube in his belly. When he drooled, it hung on the edge of his chin until someone came along and wiped it off. There wasn't an indignity that he had not already suffered. The only blessing was that they were pretty sure he didn't know it.

Jonah smiled, touching her hair, then her cheek, with the back of his hand.

"Yes. As long as you're happy, it's a good thing."

"I want you to be happy, too," Macie said.

Jonah closed his eyes. When he opened them, he was looking at her through a blur.

"God, woman, if I got any happier, I'd be a blubbering fool. I go to bed at night knowing I'm blessed and wake up the same way every morning. I have you and Evan and our baby on the way. What more could a sane man want?"

"I don't know. Sometimes I just worry," Macie said.

"Then don't. As far as I'm concerned, I'm living heaven on earth."

"Hey, Dad!"

Jonah kissed Macie's nose, then turned toward the doorway as Evan came running into the house. When he saw his father's face, he rolled his eyes and groaned.

"Are you guys kissing again?"

Jonah grinned. "How do you think your little sister got started?"

Macie gasped and then hit Jonah on the arm. "Really," she muttered, then glared at both men and walked out of the room.

"She's ticked off at you," Evan said.

"Nah, she loves me . . . and you, too," Jonah said, then grabbed Evan by the neck as they wrestled themselves onto the floor.

Macie heard the thump and then the bumps as they both hit. She rubbed her belly and smiled.

"Hang in there with me, baby girl. I hope you can handle the men in your life."

About that time, the baby kicked. Macie winced.

"Oh, well, excuse me," she said. "Of course you'll be able to handle them. All you'll have to do is smile."

About the Author

Dinah McCall finally realized that the daydreams she'd been having all her life were a gift, a talent she could no longer ignore. "It hit me that I was destined to be a storyteller." Dinah made the decision to write tales of substance. These stories have captured the hearts of many readers and have earned bestseller placements. Dinah lives in her native Oklahoma, where she also writes as Sharon Sala.

The employees of Thorndike Press hope you have enjoyed this Large Print book. All our Thorndike and Wheeler Large Print titles are designed for easy reading, and all our books are made to last. Other Thorndike Press Large Print books are available at your library, through selected bookstores, or directly from us.

For information about titles, please call:

(800) 223-1244

or visit our Web site at:

www.gale.com/thorndike
www.gale.com/wheeler

To share your comments, please write:

Publisher
Thorndike Press
295 Kennedy Memorial Drive
Waterville, ME 04901